# Trouble is Brewing

**Kensington Books by Vicki Delany**

The Tea by the Sea mystery series

*Tea & Treachery*

*Murder in a Teacup*

*Murder Spills the Tea*

*Steeped in Malice*

*Trouble Is Brewing*

# Trouble is Brewing

# VICKI DELANY

Kensington Publishing Corp.
www.kensingtonbooks.com

KENSINGTON BOOKS are published by

Kensington Publishing Corp.
900 Third Ave.
New York, NY 10022

All Kensington titles, imprints, and distributed lines are available at special quantity discounts for bulk purchases for sales promotion, premiums, fund-raising, educational, or institutional use. Special book excerpts or customized printings can also be created to fit specific needs. For details, write or phone the office of the Kensington Special Sales Manager: Attn. Special Sales Department, Kensington Publishing Corp., 900 Third Ave., New York, NY 10022 Phone: 1-800-221-2647.

Library of Congress Control Number: 2024934885

KENSINGTON and the KENSINGTON COZIES teapot logo Reg. U.S. Pat. & TM Off.

ISBN: 978-1-4967-4727-3

First Kensington Hardcover Edition: August 2024

ISBN: 978-1-4967-4729-7 (ebook)

10 9 8 7 6 5 4 3 2 1

Printed in the United States of America

To Alex, teatime companion

# Chapter 1

I love my job. Like any job, like life, it has its ups and downs. It has its difficulties and problems, crises and disasters. Some days, I've been overwhelmed and wanted nothing more than to throw in the dish towel and walk away from Tea by the Sea, my tearoom.

But I never do. I take a deep breath, center myself, and ask what I should bake next.

Then there are days like this when everything comes smoothly together, and I do what I do best: make people happy.

And that makes me happy.

"When I get married, if ever I do," Bernadette Murphy said to me, as she dumped a tray-load of used dishes onto the counter next to the dishwasher, "you're going to cater it, Lily, and I'm going to have the reception here."

"You're going to have your wedding in my kitchen?" I grinned and looked around the small space. The Tea by the Sea kitchen is crowded when I'm the only one in it.

Today I was not the only one in it: as well as my two regular assistants, the mother-daughter duo of Cheryl and Marybeth, my friend Bernie had pitched in to help.

Bernie didn't bother to reply.

"I hope," I said, "I'll be outside at your wedding, drinking tea and nibbling on scones, wearing a gorgeous dress and a fabulous hat, making polite conversation with interesting people, not stuck in here, working." I leaned back against the butcher block in the center of the room, rotating my shoulders to give them a long, luxurious, welcome stretch.

"I might let you have a few minutes off," Bernie said, "as long as you don't take advantage."

"Anything in particular making you think of your own wedding, Bernie?" Marybeth reached around my friend to get at the row of tea canisters on a top shelf, and Bernie ducked.

"Don't we all think of weddings when we see other people being happy at theirs?" she said. "I don't," Marybeth said. "I think, sometimes, I might have been too hasty rushing to the altar, never mind having the kids so soon."

"Marybeth—" I said.

"Oops." She let out a choked laugh. "Did I say that out loud? Don't let my mom hear; she'll launch into a round of I told you so's."

"Don't let me hear what, and why am I going to say, 'I told you so'?" Cheryl asked. She also carried a tray piled high with used dishes and empty teapots.

"Nothing!" Marybeth said.

"While you're getting the tea, honey, can I have another pot of Darjeeling, please?"

"What's happening out there?" I asked. "Are they almost finished?"

"They are. The food's mostly gone, for now. Several tables have asked for another round of tea and some want top-ups of the wine. The bride's about to open her gifts, and her mother sent me in to ask if you'd be so kind as to come out so she can thank you."

"Me?"

"Yes, you, Lily. Simon's already taken his bows as the provider of the floral arrangements, and he's showing some of the guests around the gardens."

"What about me?" Bernie said. "Do they want to thank me for putting the scones and sandwiches on the stands in such an organized fashion?"

"No," Cheryl said with a grin.

Bernie laughed.

I untied my apron, pulled off my hairnet, and adjusted my ponytail. I never tire of being thanked. It doesn't happen often enough in the restaurant business.

My name is Lily Roberts, and I am the proud owner and head baker of Tea by the Sea, a traditional afternoon tearoom located in the Outer Cape region of Cape Cod. I'm a culinary-school trained pastry chef, and I worked for many years in some of the best bakeries and restaurants in Manhattan before taking a deep breath and making the plunge to open my own place. This is our first summer and so far the venture has been a roaring success. My restaurant serves afternoon tea only, and I have some worries if that's going to be enough to see us through the long winter when the gardens are bare and the tourists scarce. But I can adjust on the fly, and I'll make additions to the menu, or even branch out into catering, if I have to.

Never mind that: today was all about enjoying the day and helping a young bride enjoy hers. Tea by the Sea had been taken over for a wedding shower. Twenty women were gathered on the patio to enjoy the best of my offerings and to celebrate love. In case of rain, the group booked the interior of the restaurant as well. Fortunately, the indoor refuge proved unnecessary.

They'd paid handsomely for the privilege of taking over my place, and I'd gone all out with the food and table settings. Our gardener, Simon, spared no effort in assembling individual floral arrangements for the tables and ensuring the plants in the pots scattered around the low stone walls and the flagstone paths were in their best shape.

Cheryl and I left the kitchen, followed by Bernie and Marybeth. The main room of the restaurant was empty, lights turned low, tables laid for tomorrow.

"Was it the bride's mother who asked for me?" I said to Cheryl, "or the groom's?"

"I don't know. I didn't catch any names. Early sixties, silver pantsuit, tons of jewelry?"

"Sounds like Mrs. Reynolds. She's the groom's mother. She's the one who paid for it all. The bride's mother was part of the Zoom call when we made the arrangements, but she didn't have much input." In fact, she had pretty much no input at all. Every time she hesitantly tried to get a word in edgewise, Mrs. Reynolds laughed lightly and carried on talking.

"The guests are a mismatched lot," Marybeth whispered behind me.

I knew what she meant. I'd been outside when the mothers arrived, wanting to greet them and ensure everything was in order. Sophia Reynolds, mother of the groom, pretty much screamed money, with her Boston Brahmin accent, slightest hint of Chanel No. 5, silver designer suit sized in the low single digits, rows of pearls, Jimmy Choo stilettos, perfectly cut and dyed blond hair, equally perfect make-up and manicure. Whereas Jenny Hill, mother of the bride, wore a perfectly nice off-the-rack pink dress with a black belt cinched too tightly around her ample middle, pantyhose that bunched around her ankles, and solid black flats with laces. She, or someone else, had made an attempt with her makeup, but her eyebrows were overgrown, her lips cracked and dry. Her brittle brown hair, streaked with gray, was pulled behind her head and fastened into a tortoiseshell clip.

The smile Jenny gave me was warm and genuine, whereas Sophia Reynolds peered down her long nose at me and the edges of her lips turned up, ever so slightly.

"Thank you so much, Lily." Jenny twisted her hands in front of her. "Everything's been marvelous and Hannah is thrilled."

"It's all been perfectly satisfactory," Sophia said. "Dear Jenny wasn't sure about having a tea for this precious day, but I told her it would be absolutely perfect. Didn't I, dear?"

Jenny let out a slightly embarrassed giggle. "And you were right, Sophia. As you usually are. I've never had high tea before, and I didn't know what to expect."

"Afternoon tea, dear," Sophia said. "Not high tea. I told you, they're totally different, isn't that so, Lily?"

Jenny flushed. Behind me, I heard Bernie, never one to fail to express her opinion, mutter, "How kind of you to point that out."

I spoke quickly. "My customers use the words interchangeably as do many Americans these days. Although, yes, afternoon tea is the correct term."

Sophia waved her left hand. The diamond caught the sunlight. If the International Space Station had been passing at that moment, the astronauts might have seen the resulting beam.

"People are *soooo* uncultured here in the colonies." Bernie stepped forward. "Bernadette Murphy. Of the Lower East Side Murphys. So pleased to meet you." She shoved out her right hand. "I don't actually work here. I'm a novelist by profession, but I offer Lily a hand now and again when she needs it."

Sophia blinked and cautiously accepted Bernie's hand. Bernie shook it as though she were trying to get a ball out of a dog's mouth.

I stifled a groan. Bernie was not only not from the

Lower East Side, she wasn't a novelist. Not yet anyway, having not completed her first book. But Bernie, always one to make instant judgments, had instantly decided she didn't like Sophia Reynolds.

I didn't like her much, either, but she was paying me a lot to entertain her guests, and after years spent in the restaurant business I know being nice to the customers is part of the price.

Bernie, before taking time off to write her book, had been a forensic accountant at a major Manhattan criminal law firm. Being nice to the clients had never been in her job description.

"That lady's waving her glass at us, Bernie," I said, indicating a woman in her early eighties, overdressed, over-hatted, over-jeweled. "Why don't you get her a refill?" Marybeth and Cheryl were busy refreshing teacups and clearing tables.

"Okay." Bernie sauntered off.

I turned to the mothers and caught the tightness in Sophia's lips and the shadow behind her eyes. She blinked and focused on me again. "That lady is Mrs. Regina Reynolds. My mother-in-law. She does enjoy a tipple in the afternoon now and again."

Jenny raised her eyebrows at me but said nothing.

It was a spectacular Cape Cod summer's day, warm but not too hot; a handful of fluffy white clouds slowly crossing the brilliant blue sky. All the tables on the patio were taken and the air was full of the scent of fresh baking, salt from the sea, and the lush English-style country garden beyond the low stone wall. Mismatched and cracked teacups hanging from the branches of the massive oak tree in the center of the patio tinkled cheerily in the soft breeze coming off Cape Cod Bay. Women cradled their fine china teacups or flutes of sparkling wine, leaned back in their chairs and chatted. A few of the guests had gone for a stroll in the gardens or down to the bluffs to admire the view over the bay. The first round of food, scones with butter, jam, and clotted cream; and delicate tea sandwiches, had been consumed. In contrast to the usual way of presenting afternoon tea, I'd been asked to bring the desserts out later, after the bride opened her presents. As well as an assortment of teas, we served guests prosecco. Bottles of excellent champagne were cooling in the fridge, to accompany the sweets course and to toast the happy couple.

At Sophia's request, we'd dragged a wingback chair out of my grandmother's drawing room to serve as the bride's throne, and Bernie and Marybeth had draped the chair with yards of shimmering white and gold cloth. Jenny had brought an enormous bunch of cheerful balloons in primary colors and tied it to the back of the chair. The table beside the chair was buried in gaily wrapped presents.

The tea guests were all women. The groom and some other men would join us later for desserts and champagne toasts. They wouldn't have far to come. The groom's family and his best man were staying at Victoria-on-Sea, my grandmother's B & B. Tea by the Sea sits at the end of the long B & B driveway, close to the road.

"I don't believe you've met my daughter," Jenny said to me. "Our guest of honor. Hannah!"

I didn't need to have the bride pointed out to me. As she walked from table to table, chatting to her guests, exchanging some air kisses and some genuine hugs, she simply glowed. So much so I thought she might also be able to be seen from space. Hannah Hill wasn't a beautiful woman, but she was lovely, in the way all young, healthy, happy women are. She was on the short side, as was her mother, at about five foot four; not overweight and not too thin. Her hair was almost jet black and fell in gentle waves to the center of her back. Most of the hair was held back by two pins glistening in the sunlight, but a few soft tendrils framed her lightly tanned face. She heard her mother's call and turned to us with a sparkle in her warm dark eyes.

Jenny's own eyes glowed with adoration as she watched her daughter cross the patio toward us. I glanced at Sophia and saw something very different there. Her face was tight and her jaw set. Her eyes narrowed with what might have been anger.

Then the young woman reached us, and Sophia wrapped an arm around her shoulders. "My son's bride, Hannah. I suggested the ladies dress formally for afternoon tea, but dear Hannah always prefers to go her own way, don't you, my darling."

"It's a summer afternoon in Cape Cod, Sophia," Hannah said with a smile, as she shrugged the arm off. "I don't have a suitable tea dress."

In my opinion, Hannah was dressed perfectly for the day in a simple yellow sundress with a thin black belt and low-heeled black sandals. Gold studs were in her ears, a plain gold chain around her neck. The diamond in the ring on the third finger of her left hand was small and discreet, but the ring was beautifully designed.

"My congratulations," I said. "I'm Lily, the cook here, and I hope you enjoyed everything."

"It truly was marvelous, thank you. You couldn't possibly have arranged a better day, weather-wise. Can you make sure we have the same on Saturday?"

"Lily's a miracle worker." Assigned task complete, Bernie rejoined us. "But even she can't do everything. Congratulations."

"Thank you," Hannah said.

"I'll try my best," I said. "But I suspect you don't need any luck from me. You're having your reception at the yacht club, I hear. It's a beautiful setting, and they know how to accommodate whatever weather comes their way."

"It is lovely there. I'd never even been to Cape Cod until

I met Greg. His family loves it so much, Sophia persuaded us to have our wedding here."

"My family had a vacation home not far from Provincetown for many years," Sophia said. "A long time ago. To my intense disappointment, my parents sold the property shortly before my own marriage. They said they didn't get enough use out of it. Ralph and I have often discussed buying a similar place for our family, but the time never seemed right. I don't suppose it will ever come. Not now the children are grown and with the constant pressure of the family business. You know how it is."

"I so do," Bernie said. "My own real estate ambitions are being held back until I can get that leaky roof fixed."

Sophia threw Bernie a look, suspecting she was being insulted. Which she was.

Another young woman joined us. She was about the same age as Hannah, with the same gym-toned body and flawless skin of Sophia. She'd dressed for afternoon tea in a calf-length beige dress with three-quarter-length sleeves trimmed with white lace. A fascinator in the same shade as her dress, topped with three blue feathers, was arranged in her sleek golden hair. She was the same height as Hannah and her mother, but today she towered over them in her four-inch heels. "Are we ever going to get this show on the road, Mom? Jack keeps texting me to ask if I'm finished yet."

"Well pardon me if Jack's getting inpatient," Sophia snapped. "I told you you could invite him to join us when Greg and the rest do."

"Well pardon me if Jack doesn't want to hang around with this lot any more than necessary." Her tone and accent were exactly the same as Sophia's, and it was obvious they were closely related. "Tea and gardens aren't exactly his thing."

Hannah raised her eyebrows at her own mother and Jenny shrugged.

"Not exactly mine, either," the newcomer muttered.

Sophia clapped her hands lightly. "As rudely as McKenzie might have put it, it is time we got on with the party. I told Greg and his father to be here at five, and we never want to keep the gentlemen waiting now, do we?"

"Good heavens no," Bernie exclaimed. "That would never do."

I threw her a furious glare. Bernie mouthed, "Sorry."

Sophia issued instructions. "Jenny, dear, you may escort Hannah to the bride's chair. McKenzie and the other bridesmaid, whatever is her name again? Never mind, they can hand Hannah her presents and clear up the wrapping and other trash. Do remember to keep the cards with the gifts. Hannah will have to send thank-you notes and she needs to keep them straight." Without waiting for anyone to reply, she clapped her hands, loudly this time. "Ladies, ladies. Your attention, please. Darling Hannah, our blushing bride, would like to open her gifts now."

"Diane isn't here!" Sophia's mother-in-law yelled.

"That is not my problem, is it?" Sophia muttered under her breath.

"Bernie," I said. "Would you go and round up the guests who're visiting the gardens, please. I noticed a few heading to the back of the house to see the view."

Bernie had donned a knee-length black skirt and plain white blouse as her waitress uniform. She picked up the hems of her skirt in both hands and gave me a little curtsey. "Yes, m'lady."

"Might I have read anything your friend has written?" Sophia said as Bernie scurried away on her errand, and Hannah, Jenny, and a scowling McKenzie headed for the bride's chair. "I'm on the library board of our town, where my husband's family has always been generous patrons."

"Bernadette Murphy," I said. "Remember the name. You will be hearing it someday." *If she ever gets the blasted book finished.*

"I hope she's not writing any of that genre stuff. I mean fantasy and murder mysteries and the like. So common." Sophia sniffed and followed her future daughter-in-law.

# Chapter 2

I'd prepared pistachio and hazelnut macarons, raspberry tarts, maple pecan squares, and miniature coconut cupcakes for the sweets course, doubling the quantity as the "gentlemen" would be joining us. Everything was ready and laid out in the kitchen to be served when Sophia gave me the nod. As Hannah opened her gifts, and her family and friends cheered and laughed, Marybeth and Cheryl continued moving between the tables, offering to refresh teapots or refill glasses of iced tea or prosecco. Bernie returned from her errand, herding excited women before her. She joined me to stand next to the gate on which a sign had been hung saying: CLOSED TODAY FOR A PRIVATE EVENT. HOPE TO SEE YOU AGAIN SOON.

I spoke to her in a low voice. "You don't need to be so out-and-out rude to Sophia Reynolds."

"She won't even notice. That sort are so wrapped up in themselves it would never cross their minds someone isn't basking in their glow."

"She may or may not notice, but I certainly have. You might not like her—"

"That's putting it mildly. I've run into more than a few

of her sort in my day. Male as well as female. Come to think of it, my firm put more than a few of them behind bars. Because it never crossed their minds to think some eagle-eyed young lawyer was not asking all those questions in order to bask in the glow of their cleverness." She gave me a mischievous grin.

"Bernie, you're working here today as a favor to me, and I said I'd pay you for your time. But Marybeth and Cheryl need more than that. They rely on their tips and this is the only group we've had in today. You can insult the person paying for it all you want, on your own time, but not here where it could potentially threaten those tips."

The smile died. "I wouldn't want anyone to lose out."

"Not to mention it would be nice if Sophia recommends this place to all her friends. She looks to be well-heeled enough, no doubt she mixes with the ladies-who-lunch and country club sets, and I gather they live near Boston. Plenty of Boston-area people vacation on the Cape."

Bernie looked genuinely contrite. "I am sorry, Lily. I guess I never thought."

"As you so often don't."

She broke into a grin and dug an elbow into my side. "Which is why you love me, right?"

I didn't say, "Right." But she *was* right. Bernie and I had been friends for a long time, and I sometimes thought we were so close because we were so different. I think things through carefully before acting—sometimes too much. She doesn't think things through and rushes in where angels fear to tread—sometimes too hastily. She encourages me to take the leap, and I advise her to hold back. Generally, it all works out.

"I couldn't help but notice more than a small amount of tension between the mothers," Bernie said. "Probably natural enough in situations where they both want to be in charge but one's a lot pushier than the other. Judging by appearances, it looks like there's a big financial gap between the families, too. Which can't help."

"Financial gap between their invited guests," I said. "Clearly they're from opposite sides of the tracks."

"The stuff of which romance novels are made. Hey, that might be an idea. Tessa falls in love with Rose's brother and—"

"No," I said. Tessa and Rose (named for my grandmother) were the opposite-side-of-the tracks friends in Bernie's novel. Bernie was having trouble keeping her attention focused on her main plot, thus my worries that the book would never get finished.

A blushing and beaming Hannah had been seated on the big chair. McKenzie soon dropped out of her bridesmaid's duties and found a chair at the far reaches of the patio, leaving another young woman to sort through the gifts prior to presenting the packages to Hannah. Sophia and Jenny stood on either side of the bride, smiling broadly. Jenny's smile seemed genuine, and she gazed down at her daughter with pride and love. Sophia looked as though she was making the effort and not doing a particularly good job of it.

Some of the women seated at the edges of the patio had moved their chairs forward and others stood up to get a better view. It was, I thought, easy to tell who was with the groom's side and who the bride's. Half of the guests were in perfectly put together designer clothes, either flowing cocktail dresses or pale linen trousers and shirts, many with big sun hats or tiny fascinators. Michael Kors and Kate Spade handbags were tossed over the backs of chairs or resting on tables and Jimmy Choo shoes were under those tables. Diamond tennis bracelets wrapped around thin wrists, and gold earrings glimmered from ears.

The other half wore mostly nice dresses or white pants

with sensible shoes or sandals; a couple of them were in jeans and T-shirts. The accessories didn't have designer names, the hair wasn't as expensively cut and colored, the makeup not as perfect, and few had had recent manicures.

But all the women, with the notable exception of Sophia and McKenzie Reynolds, had one thing in common—they were enjoying themselves enormously and happy to be part of Hannah's celebration. McKenzie had pulled out her phone and was scrolling idly through it. Her legs were crossed and one shoe dangled from a foot. She had an air of total boredom around her, but I got the feeling she was holding in some barely concealed tension. Afraid, perhaps, her mother would do something to insult Hannah or Jenny. Or even Sophia's own mother-in-law, who I assumed was McKenzie's grandmother. The older Mrs. Reynolds was watching the events with a neutral smile on her face and a glass of wine at hand. Contrary to what Sophia had implied, I hadn't seen her having more to drink than anyone else, and less than some.

I was in no hurry to get back inside, and was enjoying the warmth of the sun on my head and the fresh salty air on my face. I saw Simon, our gardener, heading our way and gave him a wave.

"Nice affair," he said in a low voice. "You should consider doing more of this sort of thing, Lily. Private parties I mean. Might be an idea to add a garden tour as part of the event. Several women were interested in having a chat with me about what I do here."

"I bet they were." Bernie threw me a wink, and I smothered a laugh at the confused expression on Simon's face. He was six feet tall, his face and arms heavily tanned and well-muscled, his fair hair sun-streaked, the result of a job that involves working outside all day. He was not only young and handsome, but he had an English accent that made some American women swoon.

Which, I have to confess, made me swoon as well.

"Here come the rest of them now," Bernie said.

A group of men stepped off the veranda of Victoria-on-Sea, my grandmother's B & B, and headed our way. "Who are they?" Simon asked.

"The groom and his party. His family's staying here. I don't know where the bride and her side are being put up."

"Looks like they've invited a special guest," Bernie said.

My grandmother, Rose Campbell, had her arm linked through that of a smiling young man. She'd dressed for a garden party in a riot of color. Wide-legged black pants with a pattern of huge yellow sunflowers, shockingly purple blouse, green and yellow paisley scarf tied loosely at the neck. Her short steel-gray hair was carefully arranged into spikes and her makeup, as usual, heavily applied. Her pink cane hung loosely from her left arm.

Several other men accompanied them, all dressed nicely in open-necked shirts, ironed pants, and good shoes. They ranged in age from late twenties to late seventies. The family resemblance between several of them was strong.

At the gifts table, Hannah was alternately weeping and laughing as she opened her presents, then jumping to her feet to hug the gift giver and express her appreciation. The gifts weren't as expensive or over-the-top as I might have expected, but practical, sometimes whimsical, things.

"Okay," Bernie said. "The future mother-in-law might be a horror, but the bride's really nice. They all look so happy. Makes me happy just watching."

"What's wrong with the mother-in-law?" Simon asked. "She admired my plants earlier. I thought she was grand."

"I'm sure she was perfectly polite to *you*," Bernie said. "But it's obvious she isn't too fond of her son's bride and equally obvious the girl's mother knows that, although

Hannah herself does not. Or, if she does know, it doesn't bother her."

"That's not obvious at all, Bernie," I said. "The feeling I get from Sophia is that she's more than a bit of a control freak and she's worried about losing control. The detail she went to in planning this shower was incredible, and you have to admit it turned out exceptionally well."

"It would have turned out exceptionally well if she'd done nothing but pay, Lily. You know how to make things perfect without anyone's help."

"Shush," Simon said. "They're almost here."

I plastered on my best professional smile, as Simon swung open the gate. "Welcome," I said. "I'm Lily Roberts. Please make yourselves comfortable."

"We're early, I know," the man who'd escorted Rose said, "but I couldn't wait any longer. I mean, Mrs. Campbell, your house is nice and all, but—"

"But, when a young man's thoughts turn to love," Rose said, "all else is forgotten."

He blushed. "I'm Greg Reynolds. This is my dad, Ralph, my brother Ivan, and Dave, who's going to be my best man at my wedding. The rest of this motley crew don't need to be introduced."

"Greg!" Hannah ran across the patio toward us. Her intended let go of Rose's arm and swept her up. The couple laughed and kissed. Everyone either smiled indulgently or looked away, embarrassed.

Everyone except Ralph Reynolds, who threw a look at the bride that was so cold, it had me sucking in a breath.

Sophia and Jenny, mothers of the couple, joined us. "Glad you could make it, Ralph," Jenny said. "I hope you didn't have to cut your golf game short."

The words were friendly enough, but there was a bite to her tone.

"For you, Jenny,"—the smile he gave her didn't reach his eyes—"I'd—"

Fortunately we didn't have to hear what he'd do as Sophia interrupted. "None of that now. Lily, Hannah only has a couple more gifts to open and then we'll be ready to enjoy our desserts."

"We'll start bringing them out," I said.

"Can't wait," Greg said.

Hannah grabbed his arm and pulled him, laughing, across the patio. Cheers and applause rang out. A beaming Jenny followed. Sophia and Ralph exchanged a look before they forced their faces into smiles and joined the party.

I headed back to my kitchen, followed by Bernie and Simon. "Okay," I said. "You were right. The families hate each other. I'm glad that's none of our business."

"I'm getting Montague and Capulet vibes here," Bernie said.

"Never took you for a Shakespearean scholar, Bernie," Simon said.

"Don't have to be an expert to know the basic plot of *Romeo and Juliet*, and 'never a story of more woe.'"

"What do you want me to do, Lily?" Simon said.

"We've got this. You go back outside and charm the ladies. Rose will want to show you off. Talk gardening to anyone who wants to."

"I'm show-offable?" he said with a boyish grin. "That's nice to hear."

While Hannah opened her gifts, Marybeth had been busy in the kitchen laying the desserts on serving platters and washing the crystal flutes, while Cheryl set the tables with fresh linen napkins and clean dishes and cutlery.

I gave the display a quick glance, to make sure it all looked perfect. And it did. The little tarts and macarons glowed like precious jewels, the cupcakes were perfectly iced, the shortbread lightly browned to perfection. Marybeth and Cheryl got the chilled champagne bottles out of the fridge.

"Let's go, women," I said. "After you."

Bernie and Marybeth carried out dessert platters. Cheryl brought a tray of champagne flutes, and I carried an armful of chilled bottles. We arranged everything on the serving counter and waited until the present opening finished and people resumed their seats.

Greg had taken his mother's place next to Hannah. The table in front of them was piled high with an assortment of small gifts, and a snowstorm of colored wrapping paper and bright ribbons covered the ground. Only one present remained to be opened. A box about two feet square, wrapped in pale sliver paper, tied with an enormous silver bow, sparkling in the sunshine.

Most of the guests had gathered around Hannah. Even McKenzie put her phone away, scrubbed off the oh-so-bored expression, and turned her attention to the bride and groom.

"We saved the biggest until last," Hannah said, her smile radiant. "Before we open it, we want to thank you all for your thoughtfulness and kindness, and for remembering that Greg and I asked for small gifts."

Greg poked the top of the box. "Small in monetary value, not small in sentiment or, it would appear, in size."

Everyone laughed.

Ralph Reynolds noticed the drinks had come out and started to head in our direction. His wife shot out a hand and jerked him back to his place next to her.

Rose had taken a seat beside Sophia's mother-in-law. Regina said something to my grandmother and Rose pointed toward me. I gave her a wave in return.

Hannah leaned over and fumbled through the bow at the top of the package, searching for the card. "It doesn't seem to be here. Mom, is there a loose tag somewhere?"

Jenny swept her eyes across the table. "Don't see it."

"Okay," Greg said, " 'fess up. Who's this from?"

Everyone shrugged.

"A secret admirer," Ivan, Greg's brother, called. He was a couple of years older than Greg, not as handsome and not, today at least, as happy.

"Get on with it," a woman called. "The champagne's getting warm."

Laughing, Greg and Hannah pulled off the ribbon and tore at the wrapping paper. Together they lifted the top of the box and peered in.

Hannah pulled sharply back but, failing to notice her reaction, Greg reached into the box, a puzzled look on his face. He lifted out what I first thought was a ball. All around us the laughter began to die. Someone said, "What the—"

Greg was holding a head by the hair, staring at it in shock and disbelief. Round blue eyes, dots of color on cloth cheeks, a wide smile, masses of curly red hair.

Hannah leapt to her feet, screaming. She kicked wildly at the box and it toppled over. The rest of the doll tumbled out. Headless.

# Chapter 3

Greg threw the head aside in shock. It bounced on the flagstone floor, rolled twice, and came to a stop face up, staring into the sky. The woman at the chair next to it screamed and tripped in her haste to get away. She clutched at the tablecloth and, to my horror, my lovely dishes began to slide toward the edge of the table. Disaster would have struck had not her quick-witted table companion wrenched the tablecloth out of her hands and stopped its descent.

All over the patio, chairs were pushed back and people leapt to their feet with cries of "What's happening?" and "What's that?"

McKenzie pushed her way through the crowd to get a closer look.

My first instinct was to check on Rose. I looked across the patio to see that she'd placed a hand lightly on Greg's grandmother's arm. She saw me watching and gave me a nod, saying all was okay there.

While I was visually checking on my own grandmother, Bernie and Simon darted past me. Bernie whipped off her apron as she moved and used it to scoop up the doll's head and fold it into a bundle. Simon grabbed the body and shoved it back into its box. Bernie threw the head in after it, and Simon closed the flaps.

It had been, I realized, a traditional-looking Raggedy Ann doll.

Jenny, her face pale with shock, was leading a weeping Hannah away. Greg recovered his senses and hurried after them. The bridesmaid was frozen in place, her eyes darting everywhere in confusion. The noise was deafening as everyone began to speak at once. Marybeth and Cheryl stood by the serving counter, unsure of what to do. I held a hand up, palm out, telling them to remain where they were.

Ralph Reynolds pushed himself through the crowd of onlookers. "What's gotten into that girl? What's going on here?"

"A joke. A silly practical joke," Sophia said. "Everyone, please, resume your seats and let us continue with the celebration. Ms. Roberts, we'd like our desserts now, if you please."

"Never mind the desserts," Ralph said. "People need a drink. Let's get those bottles of champagne open, why don't we?"

Slowly, nervously, people began to sit back down. They talked in low, anxious voices among themselves, but no one relaxed or resumed light conversation. Sophia might say this was a practical joke gone bad, but it was obvious Hannah was not taking it that way. A few people gathered around the box, staring at it, but no one made an attempt to open it.

"Looked like a doll to me," a man said. "Don't know why someone would give an about-to-be-married couple a doll. Do you think that was a hint?"

"I think you need to be quiet," his wife snapped.

Simon picked up the box. I could tell by the way he balanced it easily in his arms the doll was the only thing in it.

"I'll find a place to put this out of the way for now. Garden shed?"

"Good idea," I said.

Marybeth ran up to me. "That present. I found it."

"What do you mean, you found it?"

"We were getting the patio ready, and I spotted it. It was sitting near the driveway, on the other side of the gate, about half an hour before the guests were due to get here. I assumed it was a shower gift, so I put it on the table, where the bride's mother had indicated the presents would go. Maybe I shouldn't have done that?"

"If saw it, I would have also assumed it was intended for Hannah. No other reason anyone would drop off a wrapped present here today."

"Whoever brought it didn't want to be seen," Bernie said.

"Did you notice if a card accompanied it, Marybeth?"

"No. But I didn't look for one. We were busy, so I just brought it in and forgot about it. Until now."

"You do your calm, everything's-under-control restaurant owner act, Lily," Bernie said. "Go check on Hannah. We've got this. Come on, Marybeth. Put that smile on." They joined Cheryl at the serving counter. Bernie picked up a dish towel and wrapped the top of a champagne bottle in it prior to popping the cork.

Hannah and Jenny were standing on the far side of the gate, the shaking bride enveloped in her mother's comforting arms. Greg and the bridesmaid hovered next to them, not sure of what to do.

I slipped through the gate. "You're understandably upset, Hannah. You need some time to yourself. If you don't want to continue with the party, why don't we go up to the house? You can have a seat in the drawing room, and I'll bring you a cup of tea. If you haven't had enough tea already, that is."

"Thank you," Jenny said. "That's very kind."

"What on earth is going on?" Sophia marched through the gate, followed by her daughter, McKenzie. "Greg, Hannah, you have guests. People need to be assured you're fine."

"Leave it, Mother," Greg said. "Please."

"Leave what? I don't see why you're making such a deal over a silly practical joke. It might not even have been a joke. The head came off when the box was moved. I'll admit it was shocking, at the time, but the fuss is over now. Not helped one bit by that woman who acted as though something was crawling out of its grave after her."

McKenzie laughed. No one else joined in.

"That someone," Jenny snapped, "is my cousin, Alice. As you well know, Sophia. If you'd been sitting where she was, I'm sure you'd have acted the same."

"Unlikely," McKenzie said. "My mom doesn't do drama."

Sophia ignored them both. "Hannah, dry those tears and let's return to the party. People are concerned."

"I. *Really*. Do. Not. Care"—Jenny tightened her arm around her daughter and threw daggers at the other woman—"whether or not you and your self-obsessed, stuck-up relatives are concerned. Which, by the way, I don't believe they are. All they're after is fodder for the gossip mill at the country club."

"I wouldn't say we're stuck-up," McKenzie said. "But self-obsessed, yeah, we can be that."

It wasn't easy but I managed to keep my face impassive. *What was with these people?* All this squabbling was bad enough, but to do it in front of a total stranger.

"You're not helping," Greg said to his sister.

"Not trying to help. I thought it was fun. Added some drama to a *boooring* afternoon."

"That comment was way out of line, Jenny." Ralph

Reynolds joined us. He'd been first in line at the makeshift bar, and carried a glass of champagne in his right hand. "Apologize to Sophia."

The look on Jenny's face indicated she would do nothing of the sort.

"Oh, goodie," McKenzie said. "Champagne's being served. At last." She slipped away, chuckling at her own wit.

"It's all right, darling," Sophia said to her husband. "Hannah's upset. Let her be upset. All that fuss and bother about nothing. They can do what they want." She slipped her arm through her husband's. "People are watching us. We need to join our guests. Come along, Greg, darling. You can make Hannah's apologies."

He hesitated. Hannah lifted a tear-streaked face to look at her intended.

"Time's come, my boy," Jenny said in a low voice. "Time for you to decide, once and for all."

Greg hesitated, for a fraction of a second, then he stretched his neck, pulled his shoulders back, and straightened his spine. I didn't know him at all, but to me, standing quietly on the sidelines as the family drama played out, it was obvious he'd come to a decision. "It's okay, Dad, Mom. You take care of our guests. I'll see Hannah and Jenny get up to the house okay."

Ralph's face tightened. Sophia sighed and gave her son a stiff smile. "Of course, dear. And so you should. Come along, Ralph. Try not to drink *all* the champagne before our guests can enjoy some, will you."

They walked away. Jenny let out a long breath. Greg put his arm around Hannah, and her mother stepped away. "You okay, babe?" he asked.

Hannah wiped at her eyes. "I will be. If you stay with me."

"Always," he said. Holding each other close, they walked slowly down the driveway toward Victoria-on-Sea.

"Glad to hear it," Jenny muttered. She might have intended to speak only to herself, but I heard. She gave me a rueful grin. "In-laws. Always drama. Greg's a good boy, and he loves my daughter to pieces. As he should. But, sometimes, he doesn't stand up to his parents as much as a soon-to-be married son should. I'm sorry you had to witness that, Lily."

I could say nothing in response to that, so I didn't.

"Jenny." The bridesmaid came out of the patio. "Is Hannah okay? Do you need anything?"

"She's going to sit down for a few minutes, and I'm going to follow. You're welcome to join us if you'd like, Samantha."

"Thanks, I will. Sophia's doing a good enough job of pretending everything's okay. What happened there? Everyone asked me, but I didn't know what to say."

Jenny just shook her head and hurried after the young couple. Samantha threw me a questioning glance and then went after her.

I turned to have a quick look at the patio before following. Bernie was moving between the tables, pouring champagne, while Marybeth made the rounds with the teapots, and Cheryl laid out the dessert platters. There wasn't much laughing going on, and voices sounded pinched and tense. Sophia plunged into the party, attempting to calm everyone, chatting cheerfully, laughing lightly, once again the consummate hostess. Ralph stopped Bernie and held out his glass for a refill.

McKenzie came through the gate once again. She had a glass of wine, bubbles dancing cheerfully, in each hand. She saw me watching, but said nothing. She rounded the low stone wall enclosing the tearoom patio and headed in the general direction of the shed, where Simon had taken the unwanted gift.

I'd earlier noticed McKenzie attempting to flirt with Simon, while he pretended not to notice and paid her no more attention than he did to any of the other ladies who wanted to talk gardening with him.

Simon, I figured, could handle himself, and my staff (and Bernie) clearly had everything under control. I broke into a run to reach the house at the same time as my guests.

# Chapter 4

I showed Hannah and the others into the drawing room. "Tea?" I asked.

"A glass of water would be fine," Hannah said. "If you don't mind?"

"Of course I don't mind. Anyone else?"

"Water'd be good, thanks," Greg said.

"Nothing for me," Samantha, the bridesmaid, said. She was not far off Bernie's height of almost six feet, and very thin, with long gangly arms and legs. Her hair was died a deep black and cut perfectly straight at the line of her chin, with thick bangs covering her eyebrows. The skin on her heart-shaped face was pale, except for a patch of red on her pert nose where she hadn't applied enough sunscreen.

Hannah dropped onto the couch with a sigh. Greg sat next to her and took her hand. I slipped out.

Everything had happened so fast, I hadn't had time to think about it. But as I went down the hall to the kitchen, got out a tray and glasses, and filled a pitcher with ice and water, I thought.

That had been no practical joke, and the doll's head hadn't fallen off in the box as Sophia suggested. Dolls' heads don't become detached with a bit of shaking. It hadn't been an ordinary doll, either, something bought last week at a toy store. These days Raggedy Ann dolls are collector's items or, if newly made, often purchased for sentimental reasons.

I could understand how shocked and upset Hannah had been, but there was more to it, I thought. She hadn't laughed the incident off, or even gotten mad at whoever'd done such a thing. I remembered the look on her face when she first saw it. She'd been genuinely horrified.

Back in the drawing room, Hannah and Greg sat close together on the couch, gripping hands. Jenny stood at the window, looking out over the wide veranda to the gardens. The bridesmaid ran to help me when I came in with the tray and glasses. "This is a gorgeous house. Is it yours?"

"My grandmother's," I said.

"Oh, gosh, I'm sorry," Greg said. "Your grandmother. I forgot about her and left her at the party."

"She's fine," I said. "She's far fitter than she sometimes pretends to be. But thank you for thinking of her." Samantha poured water, and I handed around glasses.

Hannah lifted her head and gave me a weak smile as she accepted a glass. "Thank you. I'm sorry to cause such a fuss."

"No bother at all. I'm sorry your shower ended that way. You're welcome to remain here as long as you like, if you don't feel like going back to the party. Greg and his family are staying here. Are you and your mom at a hotel?"

"We're at the Pierside Hotel," Jenny said, referring to one of the nicest hotels in North Augusta, located next to the pier that marked the center of town. "Hannah and I."

"The peasantry, meaning Jenny's friends and the rest of her family, are at the misnamed Oceanview," the bridesmaid said. "It might have a view of the ocean if you go onto the roof and climb a very long ladder. It's not as bad as it first appeared. Sorry, we haven't met. I'm Samantha Dowling, commonly called Sam or, as Greg's mother says, 'Who are you, again, dear?' "

"Lily Roberts."

"I'm sorry I spoiled your party, Mom," Hannah said.

Jenny snorted. "You didn't spoil anything. Whoever gave you that doll spoiled it. And it wasn't my party anyway, as we all know, but Sophia's. She graciously allowed me to think I had some input and to invite a couple of my own friends. Sorry, Greg, but that's how it was."

"How it always is, with my mom." He stroked Hannah's pale hand. "She learned that skill very quickly from the master herself—my grandmother. Do you . . . want to talk about it, babe?"

"I'll leave you now," I said. "Make yourselves at home and, as I said, stay as long as you need."

"Stay, please," Hannah said. "You and your staff were so kind and did such a wonderful job making everything perfect for me. I feel I owe you an explanation."

"You do not," I said.

But, I have to admit, I was curious.

She sipped her water. The drawing room at Victoria-on-Sea is used as a common room for B & B guests. It's a big, comfortable room with plenty of chairs and sofas, a table for playing cards in rainy weather, and a big desk in case someone wants to write a letter or get work done while looking out over the gardens. Old board games and well-thumbed paperback books fill the shelves.

Hannah nodded toward one of those games. "Clue. We used to play Clue for hours, when Dad was alive. Do you remember, Mom?"

"I certainly do," Jenny said. "Your father loved that game."

"One of the things, one of the many things, I'm loving about being back in your life, Jenny, other than Hannah of course, is playing games," Greg said. "Board games, cards. We never had much of that in my family. My mom plays tennis, of course. Gotta keep up with the country club set, don'cha know. She never had any interest in teaching me to play. My mom never had a lot of interest in teaching me anything . . ." His voice trailed off.

I'd taken a seat, thinking as I'd been invited to stay, it would be polite to make light conversation for a few minutes and then go back to work. This conversation had gotten uncomfortably intimate very quickly.

"That doll," Samantha said at last. "The head was cut off deliberately. It must have been. You know that, Hannah."

"Yeah. I figured."

"I don't want to talk about it," Jenny said.

"We have to," Hannah replied.

"I've never had one," Samantha said, "but I recognized it as a Raggedy Ann doll. Hugely popular in the early twentieth century, I believe. If you don't mind my asking, does a doll like that mean something to you, Hannah? Something in particular? Aside from the damage, I mean."

"I don't—" Jenny began.

"It's okay, Mom," Hannah said. Some of the color was returning to her cheeks and her breathing was settling into a regular pattern. "I kinda overreacted, I guess."

"You did not," Greg said. "I remember when we were in a toy store a couple of months ago, getting a present for your friend's new baby. You saw a doll like that and told me you had a similar one when you were young, right? You kept it on your bed for years."

Hannah nodded.

"I remember." Jenny's voice was low and tinged with sadness. "You so loved that doll."

Greg turned to me. "Perhaps I should explain some of

the drama surrounding our families. Hannah's late father, Max, worked for my dad for years, at the company my family owns. More than just that he worked there, he and my dad were close friends. They had a falling-out, I never really found out why. It happened before Hannah or I was even born."

Jenny shifted uncomfortably in her chair but said nothing.

"We live in a small town not far from Boston, where the company's offices are located," Greg said. "Small towns, everyone knows everyone else, right? It's hard to avoid people you'd prefer not to see."

"Max and I ran into Sophia and Ralph on occasion," Jenny said. "They were always icily polite to us, but nothing more. Max left the company shortly after he and Ralph . . . fell out, as Greg puts it."

"Hannah's dad died when she was . . . how old were you, honey?" Greg asked.

"Ten," Hannah said.

"They moved away not long after that. And then, about a year ago, Hannah and I ran into each other at a mutual friend's party in Boston." He smiled. "We got to chatting and realized we remembered each other from school and . . ." He took her hand. "Here we are today."

"That doll, the one in the box, was downright creepy," Samantha said. "A mean trick. We couldn't find a card to go with the box, so whoever sent it doesn't intend to claim responsibility. My money"—she looked directly at Greg— "is on McKenzie."

"No," Greg said. "That would be way too subtle for her. My dear sister thinks she's so clever, and she likes to make a big splash."

"I'd say whoever sent that doll made a big splash," Samantha said.

"Who else then?" Jenny said. "Who would have done something like that? Did anyone see who brought it?"

"One of my staff found it by the gate and brought it in," I said. "She didn't see anyone with it."

The room fell silent. Greg and Jenny looked at each other for a long time.

I shifted in my seat and was about to stand, when Greg spoke again. "It's no secret my parents aren't wild about Hannah and me getting married, but they wouldn't do anything like that. Not this late in the game. I mean, the wedding's the day after tomorrow. The guests are gathering, the venue and catering have been paid for."

"There's got to be more behind this," Samantha said. "I mean, a headless doll is mighty creepy, but it wasn't just a doll to you, was it, Han?"

Hannah shuddered. She glanced at her mother, sitting stiff and tight-lipped at the chair by the big bay window. Past her, I could see a few cars pulling out of the parking area, and people saying their good-byes by the patio gate prior to heading for their own cars. Greg's brother and another young man, along with two women, walked up the steps to the veranda. Ivan carried an ice bucket containing a bottle of champagne. They dropped into chairs and stretched out their legs.

"Not long before he died," Hannah said, "my dad gave me a Raggedy Ann doll. A real old-fashioned-looking one, with a round, soft face, and curly red hair made out of yarn, and big black feet. I loved that doll. Do you remember, Mom?"

Jenny nodded mutely. She swallowed. "Dear Max. I miss him every day. He was a good man. An honest man." A sad smile touched the edges of her mouth.

"I treasured that doll for a long time," Hannah said. "Then, well, I grew up. I went to college; started work. I moved out of Mom's house and packed away my childhood things. I haven't seen the doll for a long time. Do you know where it is, Mom?"

"I assume it's in a closet somewhere," Jenny said. "I haven't thrown it out. I haven't thrown any of your things out. Silly sentiment, I suppose."

"Obviously, with my wedding fast approaching and finally getting married to"—Hannah smiled at Greg—"the love of my life, I've been thinking about Dad. A lot. I hope he'd be happy for me."

"Happy, and so proud of the woman you've become," Jenny said.

Hannah leapt to her feet and enveloped her mom in a hug.

I stood up. This was getting way too emotional and personal for me to be witness to. Greg watched his fiancée with a smile on his face. He did love her, I thought. *How lucky they are.*

Jenny and Hannah rocked back and forth for a few minutes before Hannah broke away. She wiped fresh tears from her eyes. "Seeing that doll, such a powerful reminder of my father . . . like that . . . at such an emotional time. It was awful. I guess I overreacted."

"You reacted," Greg said, "as anyone would. If I find out who did it . . ." He glanced out the window, to where his brother and his friends, laughing and drinking, were continuing with the party, and his eyes narrowed.

I let out a breath, and wiped my hands on my pants. "I have to get back. Stay as long as you like."

"Thank you," Hannah said, "but I'd like to go to the hotel and lie down for a bit. We have nothing on tonight, do we, Mom?"

"Nothing until the rehearsal dinner tomorrow evening," Jenny said.

"Do you mind if I don't return to the party? I don't want to talk to anyone right now."

"Of course I don't mind, dear. It's not as though it's our

party anyway, is it?" She looked at me. "Greg's parents sorta took over."

"Nor is it going to be the wedding we wanted," Greg said. "But . . . my mom is a force of nature, and she loves a big party. It's not likely McKenzie will be getting married anytime soon."

"I hope not," Hannah said. "Imagine having Jack as a brother-in-law."

Samantha held up her phone. "Jenny, it's Alice, wondering what's going on. She said everyone's leaving and asks if she should grab a cab."

"Tell her we're ready," Hannah said. "Thank you, Lily, for giving us a place of refuge. And such a lovely tea. I'm sorry if it didn't end as we might have hoped."

"You are more than welcome. It was a pleasure having you."

"Sophia will be settling the bill," Jenny said. "If the tip she leaves for your staff is . . . inadequate, let me know."

"What would you like us to do with the doll?" I asked.

Hannah shuddered. "Burn it. I don't want to ever see it again."

# Chapter 5

"That was an unexpected development," Rose said.

The party was over, the guests long gone, and we were gathered in the kitchen of Tea by the Sea. I'd be open for regular business tomorrow and had work to do tonight to get food prepared. Marybeth was taking dishes out of the dishwasher and putting them away while Cheryl put the patio to rights. Bernie was pretending to help me bake while catching up on the gossip of the afternoon, and my grandmother wasn't even pretending to help.

"Downright creepy," Marybeth said. "Like something straight out of a horror movie. Who would do that?"

"The whole thing was weird." Bernie stopped cutting scones and waved the cutter in the air. "Like a gathering of the Hatfields and the McCoys. Each group kept strictly to themselves, trying to pretend the others weren't there."

"You're full of literary references today, Bernie," I said. "Earlier it was Romeo and Juliet."

"Them too," Bernie said. "Feuding families."

"Except for the bride and groom," Marybeth said. "I thought they were both lovely. And so clearly in love, it was nice to see. I saw some of the guests sitting on the veranda at the house after. Are they staying with you, Rose?"

"The groom's family is, yes. They've taken five rooms until Tuesday."

"It was a strange bunch," I said. "The two groups are so different, but the families are intertwined in a way none of them like."

"Except Greg and Hannah," Marybeth said.

"Young love," Rose said. "I remember young love. Vaguely."

I smiled at her. No one ever had any doubt my grandparents had loved each other until the day my granddad died.

"Anyone at home?" a voice called from the restaurant.

"Speaking of young love," Rose said in a whisper, with a glance at me from under her mascaraed lashes.

"We're in here," I replied, trying not to blush too much.

Simon came through the swinging door. "I knew that. Didn't want to interrupt if you were talking about me."

"Now why would we do that?" I asked.

He kissed the top of my head.

"Earlier I saw McKenzie heading your way with an extra glass of champagne. Did she find you?" I tried to keep my tone neutral but I fear a touch of jealousy might have crept in.

"That one. Yeah, she found me. She's had a lifelong interest in gardening, she said. I asked her what was her favorite annual and she said roses."

Bernie laughed. "A trick question. Clever you. Did she then suggest you offer her private lessons in gardening?"

"She might have, but I told her I had to go and turn the compost, so she suddenly remembered her boyfriend was waiting for her in town." He kissed me again, and said, "Need a hand?"

"As Bernie seems to have forgotten what she's been

asked to do, can you finish the scones please? Cut them out and lay them on that baking sheet. Careful, the sheet's hot. What did you do with the doll?"

Bernie handed Simon the cutter with a bow.

"It's in the shed," he said. "Do they want it?"

"Goodness no. Hannah, that's the bride, told me to burn it. I'd like to have a look at it."

"Why?"

"Curious, maybe? I have trouble understanding why someone would come to a wedding shower and do something like that to the bride. It was no joke." I thought of the expression on Hannah's face as she talked about what a similar doll had once meant to her.

"Pure meanness." Bernie turned on the tap and washed her hands. "I'd like to have a look at it, too."

"Did you search it, Simon?" Rose asked. "Perhaps a message was enclosed?"

"I haven't opened the box." He made quick work of the scones and once they were laid in neat rows, I popped the baking sheet into the oven and set the rooster timer. "Marybeth, take these out when the timer sounds, please. I'm going to have a look at this doll."

Simon led the way. Bernie and I followed him, and Rose followed us.

It was not long after five, but in July that means full daylight still. The lovely century-old, handmade shed that used to house Simon's gardening equipment had burned to the ground not long ago. A mass-produced, prefab structure had taken its place. The new one had absolutely none of the rustic charm of the original, but Simon had done his best to liven it up with bright red paint on the door and window frames and window boxes overflowing with colorful annuals and trailing vines. He'd built a trellis on the sunniest wall and planted clematis. Early days yet, but in years to come they'd go a long way toward brightening up the bland, unattractive building.

We stood in a circle inside the shed, surrounded by bags of potting soil and fertilizer, hoses and water jugs, empty terracotta pots, and hand tools hanging neatly on the walls, staring at the box.

It was nothing but an ordinary cardboard box. Simon pulled the flaps back; as one we leaned over and peered in. The doll's head lay on top, staring up at us. Even though I'd been expecting it, I shivered.

"Creepy's the word," Bernie said. "Funny how something as innocent as a child's toy can look, in the right circumstances, so evil." She picked up the head, turned it over, and studied the bottom. "It's been cut. Didn't happen by accident, not that I thought it had."

Simon lifted up the body. "Likely cut with scissors, not a knife. You can see the fraying here. These cuts look fresh, from what I can tell."

"What does that mean?" I asked.

"That it was done recently," Rose said. "No doubt to make an impact on this specific occasion."

"It looks new," I said. "Hannah told me she had one like that as a child, and it meant a lot to her. I'm glad it's not the same one."

Nothing else was in the box. Not even any packing material.

"What do you want me to do with it?" Simon asked.

"Toss it in the garbage," I said. "If we'd gotten it under less . . . weird . . . circumstances, I'd offer to sew the head back on and give it to the charity shop, but I also never want to see this horrid thing again."

When we'd finished examining the doll, Rose headed back to the house. Bernie offered to walk with her, saying she had to get straight home. She had some great ideas for her book, which she wanted to get down while they were fresh in her mind.

"Do you think," Simon said to me as we watched them cross the lawn, heads close, arm in arm, "Bernie's book will ever see the light of day? I don't know anything about writing a book, but should she still be coming up with new ideas at this point?"

"If we were talking about anyone else, I'd say no. But Bernie." I shook my head. "If Bernie wants something, she usually gets it." My friend had quit her job in the spring, cashed in her savings, and come to Cape Cod to pursue her dream of writing a novel. I'd lost count of the number of times she'd changed the characters, the setting, the time frame, the entire premise. She'd finally settled on a late-nineteenth-century mystery novel, intended to be the start of a series about two women who set up a detective agency in Boston (or was it New York?). Despite that, she kept heading off in all sorts of different directions. She might, eventually, finish the book, but I feared it would be a scrambled mess when it was done.

Simon put his arm around me and said, "Need any help tonight?"

"No. You go on. You were here early and you must be beat. It's hard work having to chase off all those women wanting to admire more than your roses. Not to mention ones bringing you glasses of champagne." The moment the last sentence was out of my mouth, I regretted it. Simon and I had only been together a couple of weeks. We were finding our way, slowly and carefully. About the last thing I wanted was to come across as the jealous type. But I couldn't help thinking of that McKenzie Reynolds, beautiful, rich, spoiled. And the gleam in her catlike eyes when those eyes first spotted Simon. She was supposed to have come to the wedding weekend with her boyfriend. But I feared that wouldn't stop her setting her cap for someone else.

"Don't work too late," he said.

"I won't."

He held me close and we stood together for a while. Then, no doubt conscious that my grandmother and my best friend, not to mention a veranda full of B & B guests, might be watching, we separated.

I watched him head around the side of the shed, and a minute later the powerful engine of his motorcycle started up. He'd blown me a kiss from underneath his helmet as he sped past.

I put in a late night in the tearoom kitchen, getting plenty of baking done and sandwich ingredients prepared for a regular day of serving afternoon tea tomorrow.

Finally I finished my labors. The prepared food was in the fridge or freezer, the dishes stacked in the dishwasher. I switched out the lights, checked the ovens were off, and let myself out the back door, making sure to lock it behind me, and headed home.

I live in a cottage at the edge of the B & B property, so my commute isn't much. When my grandmother was in her early twenties, she hurried out of a butcher's shop in the town of Holgate in Yorkshire, England, where she was visiting her sister, intent on her errands, not looking where she was going, and collided with a passing American by the name of Eric Campbell. She sent him flying. They married not long after he got out of the hospital, and he brought her home to Grand Lake, Iowa, where they settled down to a long, happy, prosperous life. He died a couple of years ago, and to the consternation of her five children and numerous grandchildren, Rose sold their house and bought a Victorian-era mansion overlooking Cape Cod Bay. She had, she told my mother, missed the sea all those years she spent in Iowa.

Having bought the house of her dreams, Rose immediately realized she couldn't afford the taxes and the upkeep on such a large old property, so she turned it into a luxury B & B. A good part of the reason she can charge what she does for a night's stay is the size and quality of the gardens. According to Tripadvisor the gardens at Victoria-on-Sea are the number-one garden attraction in North Augusta.

There is, I must add, no number two.

Even with the B & B income, she continued to struggle financially, so, against the advice of my mother and all my uncles, I moved to the Cape and opened a tearoom on the premises. So far we're operating in the black, and even turning a small profit.

As part of the incentive to get me to join her in the business, Rose turned over a small cottage on the property for my use. I live there, happily and comfortably, with my labradoodle, Éclair.

It's a quiet life but, so far at any rate, after the frantic bustle of the Manhattan restaurant world, it suits me.

When I let myself into the cottage, Éclair greeted me in her usual over-the-top fashion, and I did the same for her. I pay Rose's housekeepers a bit extra to pop in a couple of times during the day to let the dog out for a short romp and to refresh her water bowl when I can't get away from the tearoom.

Earlier, I'd poached a chicken to make Darjeeling chicken sandwiches tomorrow, and I cut off some of the meat, slapped it between two slices of bread, slathered on the mayonnaise, and ate standing up while cupcake batter whirled in the mixer. I didn't need dinner and was looking forward to dropping into my bed, so I said to Éclair, "Just a quick one tonight, okay?"

She indicated her agreement by letting out a single bark and running to the hook where her leash hung. I took it down, and we headed out.

It was full dark by now. Lights shone from Rose's ground floor suite and some of the bedrooms and over the long, wide veranda where four middle-aged women were playing cards. The sound of waves caressing the shoreline drifted toward us on the soft, warm night air.

As I passed, one of the card players said, "Are you sure you want to do that, Karen?"

"Yes, Sheila. I am sure."

"Okay then. Don't say I didn't warn you."

One of the women called hello to me as I passed, and I waved. Éclair sniffed at the bushes lining the path, her stubby tail wagging with delight. She was a good dog, and I could trust her to stay with me when we walked and to come when called if she did wander off, but I always carried the leash in case we came across a guest with a fear of dogs or a child with no fear at all.

We strolled down the driveway as far as the road and then turned back. The teacups decorating the tearoom patio tinkled cheerfully in the breeze, and the scent of good earth, salty water, and healthy flowers filled my senses.

I work hard here, but no harder than at a restaurant in Manhattan, and at the end of the day I get to enjoy a few moments of peace such as this.

The tearoom isn't my only job. I make the breakfasts for the B & B, and I remembered I should take tomorrow's bacon out of the freezer, so before going home, I climbed the steps to the veranda of the main house.

The card players were still at it. The glasses of wine at their sides were almost empty and only a few crumbs remained on the platter of cheese and crackers. A woman chuckled as she shuffled and another said, "Really, Karen. I don't know where you got the idea you could run diamonds."

"If my partner had bid suitably, I would not have, now would I?"

"Whatever. That's it for me tonight. I'm turning in, it's been a long day."

I smiled as I let myself into the house. Those women were, Rose had told me, a bridge group from Jamaica Plain, who'd arrived today for four days of vacation and cards. I hoped they'd last until Tuesday.

It was early for people on vacation to turn in, and the house wasn't yet quiet. A floorboard creaked over my head; from the drawing room came the sound of someone laughing.

All the rooms at Victoria-on-Sea are decorated as though Queen Victoria herself might drop in at any moment and feel at home. Except for the guest bathrooms and this kitchen. No money had been spent on the kitchen and it was decorated as though the characters from the 1950s TV show *The Honeymooners* would drop in at any moment and feel completely at home. I happen to know what the set of *The Honeymooners* looks like because Rose loves that show.

I took the bacon out of the freezer, and then checked I had sufficient muffins available for tomorrow. Enough to get us started, and if we had an unexpected rush on them, I could always whip up more. Every evening before she retires, Rose prepares a list of dietary requirements and special requests for me. I glanced at it now: a request for gluten-free from room 104. That was never a problem. I took a small loaf of gluten-free banana bread out of the freezer, and I'd offer to do the guest pancakes when they came in.

"Come on, Éclair," I said. "Let's go home."

I let us out the back door and we climbed the three steps to the ground level. This side of the house faces the bay, perched on the top of a cliff. Benches are placed at intervals along the fence so guests can relax and admire the view. A soft glow lit up the sky to the west and the lights from a charter fishing boat crossed the water, heading to harbor.

Two men leaned on the railing at the cliff's edge, between me and my intended route, talking in low, angry voices. The smell of tobacco drifted on the air, and a red ember glowed against the night as one of them pulled on his cigar.

"Dad. I am not having this conversation. Not again." I recognized the voice of Greg Reynolds, the soon-to-be groom.

"Hear me out, son. There's still time."

"No, there isn't. The guests are all here. The wedding's the day after tomorrow. Even if I wanted to back out, which I can assure you, I do not, I would never humiliate Hannah like that."

"She doesn't need to be humiliated. She can say it's her idea." Ralph's words came out slurred. He belched.

I hesitated. I didn't want to be caught eavesdropping, but I'd heard enough that if they saw me now, they'd think that's what I'd been doing. I stepped backward, into the darkness at the bottom of the kitchen steps. Éclair sniffed at the men's shoes. So wrapped up were they in their discussion, they scarcely paid her any attention, and she soon wandered away.

"Dad, no."

Ralph took another drag on his cigar. "Look, Greg. This marriage is a mistake and you know it."

"I know nothing of the sort. I love Hannah and she loves me. I simply can't understand what you have against her."

"I don't want any daughter of Max Hill coming anywhere near my family."

"Hannah's father's been dead for a lot of years. What happened between you and him is ancient history. You can carry a grudge for as long as you want, but it's none of my concern. The whole situation is absolutely ridiculous."

"Hear me out, son. Max—"

"We have nothing more to say, Dad. Good night. If you and Mom would prefer not to attend my wedding, that's up to you." He started to turn.

"One hundred thousand dollars."

"What?" Greg froze.

"A hundred thousand bucks will go a long way toward getting that mural painting business of yours off the ground."

"You'd give me that if I call off the wedding?"

"I would. On the condition you agree never to see Hannah or anyone in her family again."

"What would Mom have to say about that?"

"She doesn't need to know."

Greg laughed, the sound low and bitter. "Like she doesn't know everything. When it comes to money anyway. Her and Grandma. Although there are plenty of other things Mom doesn't know. Or maybe she knows full well and just doesn't care. Sorry, Dad. No. Hannah and I'll make a go of it on our own. She doesn't expect anything more."

"Are you sure about that?"

"What does that mean?"

"Are you sure she's not expecting you to inherit from your grandmother. My mother's not getting any younger, you know."

"Was it you who played that trick with the doll?"

"Why would I do that?"

"Hoping to make Hannah look emotionally unstable

maybe? Give me the excuse you think I need to back out of the wedding at the last minute?"

"I don't need to make her, or her fool of a mother, look any more unstable than they are. No, that wasn't me. And, before you ask, I don't know who brought it."

"If you still have issues with Jenny, after all these years, because she married Max, I'm sorry about it. I really do not care. This conversation is over."

"Don't—"

"You've had way too much to drink tonight, Dad. Go to bed. Sleep it off. Forget we ever had this conversation. Good night."

Greg walked away.

Ralph threw his cigar over the cliff and stamped off in the opposite direction from his son, his steps unsteady. "We'll see about that," he muttered as he stumbled over a patch of grass close to my hiding place.

I cautiously stepped up the stairs and watched him go. From the deep shadows of the shelter of a bush next to the steps leading down to the beach, a figure emerged. Not making a sound, staying out of the light in the doorway, it followed Ralph and melted into the dark at the side of the house.

I called to Éclair and we headed to our own beds.

Family dynamics. Thank heavens all that had nothing to do with me.

# Chapter 6

Unfortunately, the dynamics of the Reynolds family turned out to have a great deal to do with me.

I arrived the following morning at the B & B kitchen at a quarter after six, late for me. Last night, I'd confirmed enough muffins were in the freezer to get the day started so I didn't see the need to be exactly on time today.

Simon was standing at the edge of the cliff, watching the bay come to life. Same spot as Ralph and Greg Reynolds had been last night, but he was in a considerably better mood. "Good morning." He held out his arms, and I fell into them. We kissed as Éclair snuffled at our feet, wanting attention.

Finally Simon broke away and leaned over to pet the dog. Her tongue lolled, and her tail wagged happily.

When he straightened up, I lifted my hands, wiggled my fingers, stuck out my tongue, and moved it up and down, along with my hips.

Simon cocked one eyebrow. "Are you having an incident, Lily?"

"No, I am not having an incident. I'm wanting attention, too."

He reached out and scratched behind my ear. Laughing, I skipped down the stairs and let us into the kitchen.

Simon put the coffee on while I got bacon and eggs out of the fridge. At Victoria-on-Sea, we specialize in serving our guests a full English breakfast. The same sort of meal my grandmother prepared for my grandfather every Sunday of their married life. As the years passed, times changed, and they got older and more concerned with their health, Rose stopped frying the bread in a lake of bacon fat, alongside the mushrooms and tomatoes. My grandfather begrudgingly accepted toast, rather than fried bread, and vegetables lightly sautéed in olive oil rather than animal fat, but he drew the line at giving up his bacon.

I served the same to our guests: grilled bacon or sausages, eggs to order, sautéed mushrooms and tomatoes, a stack of toast, even baked beans out of a can. I'd also do an egg-white frittata on request and offer pancakes or eggs Benedict on special occasions. For those who didn't want a full breakfast, we laid out cereal and yoghurt and a salad of fresh fruit, along with muffins or coffee cake.

"Anything special on today?" Simon asked as the coffee maker gurgled to life.

"Just the usual. Which is good. I enjoyed putting that shower on yesterday, but I wouldn't want to do it every day. Too much emotional baggage." I thought about the conversation I'd overheard last night but said nothing to Simon about it. Our guests did have an expectation of privacy.

"Baggage is right," he said. "I went to the shed before coming in here. I had this feeling I should check on the doll. Make sure it hadn't tucked its head under its arm and wandered off into the night."

"I don't think I'd have been all that surprised if it had. Poor Hannah, what an awful thing to happen to her. I hate to think about someone who'd be that mean."

"Good morning, all." Edna Harkness, the kitchen assistant and breakfast waitress, bustled in. She put her purse under the counter and took her apron down from the hook by the door. "How'd the wedding shower go yesterday?"

"My part went perfectly well," I said.

"Meaning other parts didn't?" she asked.

"Family drama," Simon said. "Nothing like a wedding to get all the old resentments boiling over and everyone acting out. That or a funeral."

"No one acted out at my wedding," Edna said. "And we haven't had my funeral yet. Although . . ."

"Although?" I prompted.

"My brother's ex-girlfriend showed up at the wedding, saying she'd been invited. Which she had—when they were a couple. I assumed she'd know she was no longer expected to attend, not after he dumped her because she'd been cheating on him with his best friend. Former best friend."

"How awkward. What happened? Did she make a scene?"

"No. She sat at the back of the reception hall, scowling at my brother all night. I had a lovely time at my wedding. My brother," she chuckled, "did not."

When the coffee was ready, Simon poured mugs for me, Edna, and himself. He then took a seat at the kitchen table, reached for a sharp knife and the big cut-glass fruit bowl, and began slicing bananas, melons, and oranges for the morning salad. "Couple of these extra bananas aren't going to make it until tomorrow," he said. "I can do some shopping for you, if you prepare me a list. I have to go into town later."

"Thanks. If I have time this morning, I'll throw together a banana bread with them. Looks like it's going to be another perfect day, and I expect a busy day at the tearoom."

Fruit salad finished, Simon drank the last dregs of his coffee, grabbed a muffin, and gave me a quick kiss. "Talk later." He left the kitchen and skipped nimbly up the steps.

I turned to see Edna grinning at me. "What?"

"Nothing. I'm happy you and Simon are together. Took you two long enough."

I harrumphed, and she laughed.

Breakfast service went off without a hitch, and I had time to use the about-to-expire fruit to whip up a quick banana bread to put in the freezer for emergency supplies. At ten to nine, I was pouring myself another cup of coffee, happy to be able to get away a few minutes early to enjoy a brief moment of relaxation by myself before heading up to the tearoom to get started on my second job of the day, when Edna came into the kitchen with a load of dirty dishes. "We might have a problem."

"I don't want a problem."

She put the tray on the counter next to the dishwasher and said, "Doesn't matter if you want it or not, Lily."

I sighed. "I know. I know. Any sign of Rose yet?"

"No. I'll call her, if you want."

"Let me see to it first. What's happening?"

"A guest says her husband hasn't come down as expected, and he's not answering her texts."

I raised one eyebrow. "She texts her husband over breakfast?"

"Apparently. They're obviously not sharing a room. But that is absolutely none of our business. She sent someone up to knock on his door and there's no answer."

"He's probably gone out for a walk and lost track of the time. What does she want us to do?"

"Open his door."

I grimaced. "Should I?"

"They might have reason to be concerned, Lily."

"I don't suppose this wife is a haughty, thin, nicely dressed blonde in her early sixties, and her son's getting married tomorrow?"

"Bingo."

Sophia Reynolds.

After what I overheard at the cliff last night, it wouldn't surprise me if Ralph packed up and headed home without telling anyone. But, if he'd done that, he should have left the room key on the desk and informed Rose he was checking out. Particularly if he had a room to himself. "Let me call Rose first, and if she doesn't know where he is, I'll talk to them. I hate getting involved in people's problems."

"All part of the service." Edna began loading the dishwasher.

I phoned my grandmother, and she answered with a bright enough voice I knew I hadn't woken her. "Good morning, love. Is everything all right?"

"Not entirely sure," I said. "Did you get a premature checkout last night or early this morning?"

"No. As it happens I'm checking the reservation book at the moment. Why are you asking?"

"I'll let you know when I know."

"Very well. I'll be down in a couple of minutes. Please ask Edna to have my tea ready."

"Like that's gonna happen." I hung up.

Rose and Edna continually engaged in a game of wannabe and not-wanna-be master and servant. Edna maintained she was the B & B waitress, not Rose's personal maid. Rose, who'd been a kitchen maid herself in her Yorkshire youth and had never had a personal maid of her own, wanted to have one. Edna was the only prospect.

Edna didn't need this job, and I suspected she largely did it for the enjoyment of the game of wits she played with the strong-willed Rose. Who was, not incidentally, a regular bridge opponent of hers.

"Okay," I said. "I'll see what's happening. If I must. I'll talk to Mrs. Reynolds."

I untied my apron. Éclair recognized the going-home signs and came out from under the table, ears up, eyes bright, tail wagging.

"Sorry, girl," I said. "I have an errand to do first."

Her face fell. I didn't feel too guilty; I suspect that when my back is turned Edna slips the dog slices of uneaten bacon or sausage.

The dining room was still full of guests relaxing over the last of their coffee and planning their day. The four bridge-playing women had maps spread across the table and iPads open at tourist information pages. We'd pushed two tables together to make a table for eight next to the French doors leading to the section of garden overlooking the bay. Sophia; Regina, her mother-in-law; her three children, Greg, McKenzie, and Ivan; and Dave, the best man, were gathered around the table. Their breakfasts had been finished and cleared away, but coffee cups and juice glasses were still in use.

"Good morning, Mrs. Reynolds," I said, trying to sound helpful and cheerful. "Edna said you wanted to speak to me."

"Are you in charge here?" Sophia asked. She looked lovely this morning in a soft peach blouse and white capris. Gold hoops were through her ears and a small diamond on a thin gold chain nestled at the base of her throat. "I thought you owned the tearoom."

"I also help out at Victoria-on-Sea in my grandmother's absence."

McKenzie looked up from her phone. She was ready for a day at the beach, in a long, loose blue wrap and flip-flops, with her hair pulled back into a high ponytail. "Sorry to bother you. Much ado about nothing. My dad's having a sulk, and my mom's all in a tizz. I mean, it's not like that's never happened before. Either the sulk or the tizz."

Sophia glared at her daughter. Greg threw me an apologetic look and the other two men glanced away, embarrassed.

Ralph's mother sniffed. "I agree with McKenzie. Can't Ralph have a moment to himself without you always making a fuss over him, Sophia?"

McKenzie dropped her phone into her cavernous beach bag and pushed her chair back. "You do what you want, Mom. I'm going to have a stroll in the gardens." She plopped an enormous pair of sunglasses on her face. "Do you know if that English guy's working today? I'm so interested in the work a gardener does." She stared directly at me as she spoke.

*Was that supposed to be some sort of a challenge?*

"Is that what you call it, Mac?" Ivan said. "Give it up. He's not interested. What's Jack up to today anyway?"

"Oh, Jack. He'll come when I call. He always does. Toodle-oo!" She left via the French doors, swinging her beach bag and her ponytail.

In the silence that fell over the Reynoldses' table, I could hear one of the bridge players say, "This tour seems to be a lot cheaper than the others."

"Likely because it's not as good. How long is it?" her friend asked.

"They're all rather expensive. Karen and Laurie, are you listening to us?"

Karen's and Laurie's attention had wandered from day-planning, and they were obviously listening in on the Reynoldses' family drama. Caught eavesdropping, they both started and hid guilty looks. "Whatever you girls want is fine with me," they chorused.

"As I told your waitress"—Sophia's sharp voice pulled my attention back—"my husband is not answering his phone. I have an appointment at a spa in town at ten o'clock, and we arranged for him to drive me. My son knocked on his door, but he got no answer. I'm"—her composure momentarily broke—"concerned he might have fallen ill. When we travel we find it more convenient to have separate rooms," she added, although I hadn't asked, "as we keep to very different schedules on vacation."

Regina snorted. Sophia ignored her.

"I told you I'll drive you to the spa, Mom," Greg said.

"That is hardly the point," she snapped.

"Are you wanting me to let you into his room?" I asked.

"I am. Yes."

"Is he the sort to go for a walk in the morning? A set of stairs leads down to the beach, and often people walk far longer and farther than they realize, if the tide's out and it's a nice day."

"My dad's never taken a walk in his life," Ivan said, "if you exclude the golf course. Although, come to think of it, these days he doesn't even walk from one hole to another."

"In his own awkward way, Ivan is correct," Sophia said. "A morning walk would be most unlike my husband." She pushed her chair back and started to stand up.

A streak of black sailed into the room and landed on what had been McKenzie's chair.

Sophia shrieked. The senior Mrs. Reynolds said, "Goodness," and patted her chest.

Robert the Bruce had arrived, and that meant my grandmother couldn't be far behind.

"A cat." Ivan pointed out what everyone had noticed. "Is it allowed in the dining room?"

"All our promotion clearly states a cat is in residence,"

Rose said. "As does the sign by the front door. Good morning, everyone."

Robbie gave Ivan a self-satisfied smirk and washed his whiskers.

People muttered something along the lines of, "Good morning."

"Did you sleep well, Regina?" Rose asked.

"As well as can be expected, thank you for asking," the elderly woman replied. "You know what it's like. Old bones on an unfamiliar bed. But the sound of the sea was comforting. If I could hear it over the cacophony of my granddaughter's snores. In that, if nothing else, she takes after her late grandfather."

Greg and Ivan both laughed.

Sophia cleared her throat. "If we can get back to the matter at hand."

Rose folded her hands over the top of her pink cane and said, "What seems to be the problem here?"

I explained, and she said, "Very well. Lily, fetch the master key ring, please."

I went into the kitchen and got the keys down from the hook.

Edna was putting away clean dishes. "He hasn't come down?"

"No, and his wife might have a point. Guy didn't look in all that great shape to me."

"Call me if you need anything."

Back in the dining room, I lifted the keys to show everyone I had them. "If you all wait here, I'll do a quick check and be right back. Which room?"

"Two oh one," Greg said.

I would have preferred to go alone, but Sophia, Greg, Ivan, and Dave all followed me. From the back of the procession, I could hear Rose and Regina discussing the prospects for the weather tomorrow—the day of the wedding.

Robert the Bruce charged ahead of us, and we all climbed the stairs.

I tapped lightly on the door of room 201. "Excuse me, Mr. Reynolds, I'm sorry to bother you. It's Lily Roberts here. Mrs. Campbell's granddaughter. Can I speak to you for a moment, please."

Silence.

"Ralph!" Sophia shouted. "I've had enough of your nonsense. Open this door, this minute."

Regina stepped forward and rapped firmly on the door with her own cane. "Ralph!"

"Stop that, Grandma," Greg said. "We don't want to have to pay for damage to the door. Let Lily handle it."

Regina harrumphed, but she stepped away to stand next to Sophia without another word.

I desperately hoped Ralph Reynolds hadn't snuck a late-night visitor into his room and was now trying to stuff her into the closet.

I put my ear against the door but could hear no sounds of closet-stuffing, or anything else, coming from within. I knocked again, much louder this time. "I'm coming in, sir." I put the key in the lock, turned it, pushed the door open a crack, and peered cautiously in.

This room was one of the smallest we had, with space for nothing more than a double bed and a small dresser. The bathroom featured a shower stall, rather than a full bath. As were all the guest rooms at Victoria-on-Sea it was decorated as it might have been in Queen Victoria's day, with red and gold wallpaper, a red carpet, and heavy drapes tied back with gold rope. The carved wooden headboard and matching dresser were not antiques but mass-produced imitations. Two prints of red-jacketed riders mounted on badly painted horses hung on the walls. We advertised this room as having a garden view, meaning it didn't look out over the water. Our best, and most expensive, rooms overlook the bay and some of them have private balconies.

Ralph Reynolds lay on his back on top of the bed. He was fully dressed, having taken off only his shoes. His arms were spread to one side, and his head turned away from me, facing the window. An overturned liquor bottle was on the night table next to him, and an upturned glass lay on the carpet half under the bed.

I wasn't entirely surprised at finding him like that, so I was able to recover my wits quickly, and I tried to block the view of the press of people behind me. In that, I failed. Greg shoved the door fully open, and he and Ivan charged past me. Sophia screamed. Regina yelled, "What's happening? Get out of my way, you stupid girl, and let me through."

"Rose," I said, "see to the ladies." I ran into the room and slammed the door shut behind me.

Greg was bent over his father, shaking the man, while Ivan stood in place, frozen in shock. Ralph's head rolled back. He stared up at us, unblinking and unmoving.

Ivan swore.

I pulled my phone out of my pocket and dialed 911.

# Chapter 7

Rose managed to convince Sophia and Regina to accompany her to the drawing room and take seats there while we waited for the authorities to arrive.

Ralph must have died some hours ago; his sons and I could do nothing for him now. After being told the ambulance was on its way, I left Greg and Ivan to wait with their father and went downstairs. Dave, pale-faced, had fallen into a crouch against the door to the room across the hall.

"Is everything all right?" One of the guests, a tall, thin middle-aged man, dressed for the day in hiking gear, called to me from the door to room 104. He had a trail map of the area in hand.

"A guest has . . . taken ill. An ambulance has been called. Please, sir, go about your day."

"Oh, I'm sorry to hear that."

"Is there anything we can do?" A woman peeked over his shoulder. Same age, also thin, and also about to set out for a hike along the cliffs.

"No, thank you. If you'll excuse me."

I left them to their curiosity and went into the drawing room. "I am so sorry for your loss," I said.

Sophia wept softly. Regina's small dark eyes were fixed on the other woman, and the look on her face was not a nice one.

Edna came in behind me, carrying a laden tea tray. "Rose caught me as I was leaving." She put the tea on a side table. For once Edna had brought Rose a cup also. Rose gave her a warm smile in thanks.

"Tea?" Rose asked.

Regina said, "No, thank you." Sophia said nothing. Edna threw me a question and I said, "I've called the . . . authorities. They might want coffee or something."

"I'll see to it."

Rose poured herself a cup of tea and added a splash of milk from the small jug provided.

I heard sirens, heading our way, and went to the windows to see a police car making the turn into the driveway, followed by an ambulance.

"I'll let them in," I said. "And . . . uh . . . show them upstairs."

Sophia continued to weep, and Regina continued to stare at her with such open hostility it shocked me.

"Sure you won't have tea?" Rose asked again. Despite the circumstances, I smiled to myself. Tea: an English-woman's solution to every difficult situation.

As I stepped into the hall, Regina spoke for the first time. "I trust you realize this doesn't change anything between us, Sophia. You will not be getting my son's share of my income."

Simon came at a run when he saw the ambulance and police cruiser turn into our driveway. He'd been digging in a flower bed. Sand was in his hair; dirt covered the knees of his overalls, and his heavy gloves were shoved into a pocket.

He was at the bottom of the steps, watching, when I opened the door. "He's upstairs," I said to the medics. I'd told the 911 operator I believed the man was dead.

Simon threw me a questioning look.

"Can you give Edna a hand, please, Simon. She made tea but someone might want coffee. Take the new banana bread out of the freezer and slice it. It won't be frozen yet."

He gave me a sharp nod and headed down the hallway without a word, and I led the way upstairs. When we reached the second floor, I pointed toward room 201. I'd shut the door behind me when I slipped out, and all was quiet. "The man's sons are with him."

"Thank you, ma'am," one of the medics said. A police officer had come with them and they went into the room.

Through the window at the top of the landing, I saw a second police car pull up to the front of the house. When I reached the bottom of the stairs to offer to show the newest arrivals the way, Regina Reynolds came out of the drawing room. She stood straight and stiff, head up, facing forward, her age-marked hands clenching her cane. Her eyes were not wet and she showed no sign of crying.

"I wish to be with my son," she said.

Officer Jocelyn Bland, whom I knew from other times the police had been called here, was next to enter the house. "Ms. Roberts. Everything okay here?"

"Thank you, yes," I said. "Your colleague and the medics are upstairs."

We turned at the sound of footsteps to see Greg coming down the stairs. "Ivan'll go with Dad to the hospital. I need to call Hannah. Grandma, can I take you to your room? You should lie down."

"I am not going to my room to be put to bed in the middle of the day, like a misbehaved child," Regina snapped.

"What's happening?" Sophia clutched a linen handkerchief, trimmed with pink lace, to her face. Rose hovered in the doorway behind her.

Regina took one step toward Officer Bland. At barely five feet tall, she had to crane her neck to stare into the young woman's face. "You will want to call your supervisors, Officer. My son was in perfect health, and more than one person had reason to want to see the end of him. They may begin by questioning this . . . lady here." She pointed to Sophia.

Rose sucked in a breath. Edna was coming down the hallway with a tray of coffee things and she froze in her tracks. Simon, following with the banana bread and a small plate of butter, almost ran into her.

"You don't know what you're saying, Grandma." Greg reached for the older woman's arm, but she snatched it away. "I'll help you to your room."

"I know perfectly well what I'm saying, Gregory. Your mother has been wanting to be rid of him for years, and finally she did it."

"Please ignore my mother-in-law, Officer." Sophia tried to sound unconcerned, as though she were brushing off the comment, but she couldn't hide the waver in her voice or the touch of fear that flashed across her perfectly put-together face. "She's been addled for years. Age as well as alcohol will do that. My husband was not in perfect health, as she put it; he suffered a heart attack a year ago, and his doctor was not happy with his progress. Particularly as he refused to give up his odious cigars, never mind his own serious drinking habit."

"Nothing was wrong with his heart," Regina insisted. "It wasn't a heart attack, it was indigestion. A bad case of heartburn. What's the world coming to if a man can't enjoy a cigar and a glass of whiskey at the end of a hard day of providing for his family?"

"I don't think we need to get into that now," Greg said.

"If Ralph told you that, he lied," Sophia said.

Greg hesitated, looking between his mother and his grandmother. The two women faced each other, faces set, backs stiff. I could almost see years, likely decades, of mutual antagonism swirling between them.

I threw a helpless look at my own grandmother. From upstairs came the sound of footsteps, and one of the medics appeared, followed by Dave, the best man. They glanced between us, picking up on the tension. "I'm going out to the truck," the medic said.

"Ivan's going to stay with your dad," Dave said to Greg. "Everything okay here?"

"Yeah," Greg lied.

"Need a hand, mate?" Simon asked the medic.

"If you could clear this hallway," Officer Bland said, "that would be good."

"Certainly," Rose said. "Edna, you brought coffee, what a brilliant idea. And Simon has some of Lily's marvelous baking. Shall we take seats and get out of these nice people's way?"

No one moved.

"Greg," I said. "If you'd like some privacy to call Hannah, you're welcome to use the dining room. Has anyone contacted McKenzie yet? Sophia?"

Sophia blinked. "McKenzie? No. Oh, dear. She said she was going for a stroll in the gardens. Did you see her, young man?"

"Yeah." Simon shifted uncomfortably. "She wanted to chat, but I had . . . uh . . . things to do. I gave her directions to the stairs leading to the beach."

"Get a move on, everyone," Officer Bland said. "We need to clear this hallway."

At that, they began to move. Greg went into the dining room, pulling out his phone. Edna and Simon carried their trays into the drawing room, and Rose fussed about, in a very unRoselike way, ensuring her guests were comfortably settled.

Which they most definitely were not.

Regina sat in Rose's favorite chair. Robbie looked as though he was about to leap into her lap, and then he wisely changed his mind and slipped away to hide under the big circular table at the center of the room.

Seeing her place usurped, Rose hesitated before lowering herself to perch awkwardly on the edge of the couch.

Dave took a chair, looking as uncomfortable as the rest of them.

Sophia stood at the windows, looking out. "Officer, I'll accompany my husband to the hospital. When it's time."

Bland was young and she had an unfortunate tendency to blush at inappropriate times. She turned various colors now. "I don't know if that will be possible, ma'am. I'm sorry, but I don't know when that's going to happen, and I can't forget what this other lady said."

"I told you," Sophia snapped. "My mother-in-law gets confused."

"I stand by what I said," Regina insisted.

"What'd she say?" Dave asked no one in particular.

I truly hate being involved in other people's problems. I looked around the room. Everyone grieves in different ways, but Regina didn't seem to be grieving the death of her son at all. Maybe she was in shock and the sharp pain of loss would come later. Sophia had initially wept, but now she seemed more intent on refuting her mother-in-law's accusations. Perhaps immediate concerns had taken precedence in her mind.

Greg slipped quietly into the room. "I told Hannah and Jenny what's happened and they're coming over."

"Why?" Sophia asked.

Greg blinked. "Why? Because this concerns them, too."

"Coffee?" Rose asked brightly. "Edna, please help our guests. I'll have a refill of my tea while you're at it. Milk and two sugars, please."

I indicated to Officer Bland that I wanted to speak to her privately and led the way into the hallway. I shut the door behind us. "Are you going to call the detectives?"

"I have to, Ms. Roberts. The older woman made an accusation."

"I'm not trying to stop you," I said. "Rather, I think you should. Not that I'm saying there's anything to what she said, but this is supposed to be a wedding party. The taller young man, the one who made a phone call, is the son of the . . . man upstairs. He's getting married on Saturday, tomorrow, but the tension between them all has been noticeable." I thought about the headless doll; the nighttime conversation I'd overheard between Ralph and Greg; the silent figure watching from the shadows.

# Chapter 8

Fortunately, it was another glorious summer day and most of the other B & B guests had headed out for the day before the commotion started.

Watching a body being removed under a sheet is never good for one's holiday mood.

When Marybeth and Cheryl arrived for work, they'd seen the vehicles parked in front of Victoria-on-Sea and called me to ask what was happening and if I needed anything.

I told them I'd be in late, but I'd done enough prep last night they should be able to open as usual.

Jenny and Hannah soon arrived, and Greg and Hannah were walking together in the garden. Jenny declined to join the others in the drawing room and took a seat on the veranda.

"Can I get you anything?" I asked her. "Tea, coffee?"

"No, thank you." She gave me a tight smile. Her eyes were dry, but the redness in them told me she'd been crying earlier. She pulled a tissue out of her pocket and blew her nose heartily.

"Had you known Mr. Reynolds for long?" I asked, just to be polite.

"A long time indeed," Jenny replied. "It was none other than Ralph himself who introduced me to my late husband. Max, Hannah's father."

"Oh. That's . . . uh . . . interesting. I didn't realize . . ." I edged toward the door. Greg had told me Max and Ralph had once been friends, but he hadn't mentioned that detail. "If you need anything, my grandmother will be around all day, and I'll be up at the tearoom if not here."

"Thank you." Jenny looked out over the garden. Hannah and Greg were holding hands, walking slowly, their heads close together. As we watched, Hannah stopped to admire a bush bursting with yellow roses. "We were close. Once," Jenny said, more to herself than to me. "Ralph and I. His family and mine. Things . . . changed between us, and we stopped being friends. Strange sometimes, isn't it, how life can come full circle. I worked at a pharmacy in the town where we lived, and I was engaged to Ralph for a short while. Max was an executive at Reynolds Tools. I met him at a company party I went to with Ralph. And . . . well, I broke it off with Ralph shortly after. He didn't take it well. Even more so when Max and I got engaged. Things got tense, to say the least, at the company and Max soon quit. He found a job managing a hardware store. He liked it a lot better than working for—more like trying to control—the mercurial Ralph and his headstrong mother. Small towns can be tight and it's hard to break out of a circle of friends and acquaintances. Even more so, as in his new position, Max still did a lot of business with Reynolds Tools. Ralph carried a lot of anger against not only Max but me. I did my best to stay out of his way. Him and Sophia. He married Sophia soon after our engagement ended."

"Small town?" I asked. "I thought you were from Boston."

"Boston area. When Max died, I had to sell the house, and Hannah and I moved to Lowell, where I still live. We lost touch with the Reynolds family. Until now. Strange how things work out sometimes, isn't it?" she said. "Greg and Hannah, being together. Ralph didn't approve, you know. He didn't think my daughter was good enough for his son." She laughed without humor. "Once, he would have wanted my daughter to be his daughter. No, that's not quite right. It was more, I believe, he didn't want Max Hill's daughter to marry Greg. Poor Ralph. Such a dreadful waste. All of it. The years of anger. Leading to nothing but a sad death on what should have been a joyous occasion for both our families."

I shifted uncomfortably. This was none of my business, but Jenny seemed to need someone to talk to, as though she wanted to hear her thoughts expressed out loud.

Two cars came down the highway, slowed, and pulled into our driveway. The first was a taxi, the second a plain-clothes NAPD vehicle I recognized.

The taxi pulled up to the steps, and Karen, one of the bridge players, paid the driver and got out. She was alone. She hesitated at the bottom of the steps, watching the police car park and two people get out of the car.

Detectives Amy Redmond and Chuck Williams didn't need patrol cars or uniforms or badges to look like cops. He was in his late fifties, overweight, balding, bored with his job, bored with his life. His more-than-ample belly hung over the belt holding up his ill-fitting suit pants, and his tie sported a fresh coffee stain. She, on the other hand, was young and sharp and keen. Tall and fit, with dyed blond hair cut close to her head, and dark watchful eyes. Slim-fitting jeans, white T-shirt under a black leather jacket, and low-heeled black boots. They were a mismatched pair, but no one would mistake either of them for anything other than what they were.

Karen, wide-eyed with interest, watched them approach. Redmond glanced at her as they passed, and Karen forced out a stiff smile.

The police climbed the stairs. Karen followed. She was in her late fifties, much the same age as her friends, brown hair lightened with caramel highlights cut in a neat bob, subtle makeup well applied. She was slim without being skinny, several inches shorter than my five foot eight, dressed in white capris, a loose-flowing pale blue shirt, and small gold earrings. Her glasses were large with thick black square frames. "Goodness," she said to me, "are those people police officers? They certainly look it. What's happening?"

"A guest took ill," I said. "An ambulance had to be called."

"Sorry to hear that." A paperback mystery novel peeked out from the top of her tote bag, and she kept her eyes on the police as she spoke to me. I suspected she found the real police drama passing in front of her of more interest than what was in the pages of her book.

I didn't reply, and she hurried to add, "I hope it's nothing contagious. I'm not feeling very well myself. I didn't feel up to going out on a boat. We were supposed to be going whale watching, so I told my friends to go ahead without me, and I grabbed a cab back here."

"I hope you'll be feeling better soon," I said.

"Thanks. I'll go to my room now." She went into the house, still watching the police out of the corner of her eyes.

"Lily?" Amy Redmond said. "Can you fill us in as to what happened here, please?"

Jenny got to her feet. She held out her hand, and the detectives shook it in turn. "I'm Jenny Hill. I'm from Lowell,

Massachusetts, and I'm here to celebrate my daughter's wedding, which was originally scheduled for tomorrow." She pointed toward the rose garden. "That's my daughter, Hannah, there. With Greg Reynolds, her fiancé. It's Greg's father, Ralph, who passed away."

"Are you and your daughter staying here?" Redmond asked.

"No. We're at the Pierside Hotel. Greg called to tell us what happened. We arrived not more than a few minutes ago."

Officer Bland had come outside when she heard the detectives' voices. She cleared her throat and said, "Detectives, an accusation has been made. The family are gathered inside."

"Accusation?" Jenny said. "What does that mean? What sort of accusation? I assumed Ralph had another heart attack. Isn't that right?"

"Another heart attack?" Williams asked.

"He had one last year. Greg told us about it at the time. We . . . Ralph and I . . . were not close."

"Mr. Reynolds's family are waiting for you in the drawing room, Detectives," I said. "You know the way."

"So we do," Redmond said dryly.

"Dare I hope your grandmother's on an extended vacation?" Williams asked me.

"Sorry, no."

He sighed and went into the house. Redmond lifted one eyebrow at me and followed him.

I glanced toward the rose garden. Greg and Hannah, still holding hands, were approaching. Jenny pushed herself to her feet and put on a fake smile of welcome.

"What's happening in the bedroom?" Williams was asking Bland when I came in.

Karen's curiosity had gotten the better of her need to lie

down and she hovered under the stairs, trying—and failing—to be unobtrusive.

"Guy's been dead for a couple of hours at least," Bland replied. "Medics are packing up, and the coroner's been called. Officer Kowalski's staying with the deceased. One of the man's sons is with him."

"I'll have a look," Williams said to Amy Redmond. "You check on the family, and I'll join you in a couple minutes. Keep them all where they are until we can speak to them. I can't believe we're here again." He shook his head and lumbered off. He put one foot on the bottom step and noticed Karen. "Can I help you, madam?" he asked, his tone clearly indicating he wanted to be of no help at all.

"No. No thank you, I'm good." She waved a room key at him and scurried off to open the door to room 102.

"Before we talk to anyone, Lily," Redmond said, "fill me in on what happened."

I did, trying to be as concise and succinct as possible.

"When Jocelyn called us, she said the man's mother accused his wife of having had something to do with it."

"I heard that, yes. But I don't know anything about it. The guest's room was locked, and I had to use my key to get inside. The man was lying on the bed; no one else in the room. I suppose they might have been hiding in the closet. We didn't search."

"My officer would have. Although in the commotion someone might have slipped out. Was someone in the room the entire time, following the discovery of the body, before we arrived?"

"Yes. Ivan, the elder of the man's sons, stayed with him."

"Go on."

"I wasn't in the guest room for long, but I saw no signs of anything like a disturbance."

"Does the door to that room lock from the outside?"

"It can be locked from the outside with the key, but it locks automatically when the door's pulled shut."

"Okay. Let's see about this accusation."

In the drawing room, Sophia sat alone on the couch, head down, twisting the rings on her left hand. Regina was in Rose's chair, stiff and still, her expression ferocious. Rose perched uncomfortably on the unfamiliar couch. Robert the Bruce sat on her lap, watching everything, and Simon stood protectively next to her. Dave scrolled through his phone. Edna had left after laying out fresh mugs for the new arrivals.

Rose gave us a relieved smile when we came in. "Ah, the good Detective Redmond. Inspector Williams not with you today? What good fortune."

"*Detective* Williams is checking the scene upstairs, Mrs. Campbell. He'll be joining us shortly." Redmond attempted to speak sternly, but she failed to stifle a grin. Williams and Rose had butted heads on more than one occasion. The detective introduced herself to Regina and Sophia, and said, "My condolences. If you—"

"You can begin by asking my daughter-in-law if she killed my son," Regina said. "That will save us a great deal of trouble."

"I'm not answering that ridiculous accusation," Sophia said, before proceeding to answer it. "I saw my husband last night at dinner, and we went our separate ways when we got back here. Allow me to assure you, I did not see him again."

"Did you and he dine alone?"

"No. My eldest son and my"—a glance toward Regina—"husband's mother came with us. My younger son and his friend had dinner with his fiancée. My daughter joined friends of her own. I don't know where they went."

"Ridiculously overpriced restaurant," Regina said. "I told Ralph it looked like a tourist trap to me, but did he ever listen. No, I—"

"Did you, Mrs. Reynolds, and your party return here together?"

"We did," Sophia said.

"Yes," Regina said. "We took a taxi."

"Continue, please."

"I hope you'll excuse my mother-in-law," Sophia said. "She has not been herself of late, as anyone can tell you, and the stress over my son's upcoming wedding has not helped her mental state."

Regina pounded her cane on the floor. "She's been wanting to do away with him for years, and she finally made her move."

"You've never approved of me," Sophia said. "Never. Because I tried to stop you from constantly ordering Ralph about, as though he was still in grade school. Is this how you're getting back at me?"

"Stop this! Both of you." Greg stood in the doorway. Jenny and Hannah hovered behind him. "My dad's lying dead above your heads and all you can do is snipe. I'm sorry, Grandma, but you're out of line. Detective, my grandmother is clearly overcome by her grief and she needs to rest. May I take her to her room?"

Dave leapt to his feet, relieved at the chance to have something to do. "Why don't I do that?"

"I am not a child to be tucked into bed while the adults discuss important matters," Regina said.

"You're acting like one," Sophia said.

"Mrs. Regina Reynolds," Redmond said, "if you have something specific to say, I'd like to hear it. Lily, may we use your dining room?"

"Yes. Of course."

Dave slowly sat back down. Regina huffed. "I've said my piece. It's up to you to find the evidence."

"I'm afraid it doesn't work that way." Williams came into the drawing room. "Detective, a moment of your time." He jerked his head in the direction of the hallway.

"I fear the coffee's getting cold," Rose said brightly. "Lily, love, do be a dear and refresh the pot. Hannah, my dear girl, how nice to see you. Good morning, Jenny. Greg, why don't you offer Hannah and her mother some refreshment?"

I picked up the still-warm coffeepot and carried it out. The detectives and Officer Bland were standing by the front door, talking in low voices. I lingered, eavesdropping, as had obviously been Rose's intent in sending me on the unnecessary errand.

"No obvious signs of trauma," Williams said. "Nothing in the room appears to be disturbed, other than a bottle of whiskey and one glass."

"Medics said the same," Bland added. "Heart attack most likely. Bottle of top-shelf whiskey almost empty, and the glass had been used."

"We'll see what the autopsy has to say," Williams said, "but unless it comes up with something, I'm not wasting my time on family squabbles."

"Lily," Redmond said. "May we be of assistance?"

I held up the coffeepot as evidence of my innocent intentions. "Just getting more coffee. Can I ask you a question?"

"Go ahead."

"How many drinking glasses were in the room?"

"I only saw the one," Bland said. "It was on the floor. Empty. Smelled of whiskey. I can check with the forensic people."

"Why are you asking that, Lily?" Redmond asked.

"Each room contains two glasses. An item on the house-keepers' daily checklist is to ensure there are two clean glasses on the tray with the tea and coffee things. It's entirely possible one glass was taken outside and not returned. For having drinks on the veranda, or something. That happens a lot, but I thought I'd mention it."

"Good to know," Redmond said. "Anything else we should know, Lily?"

"I unlocked the door, and I was the first person in the room. I didn't . . . look carefully, but I did see that Mr. Reynolds was fully dressed. Other than his shoes. He was lying on top of the covers. That doesn't indicate to me he went to bed and died in his sleep."

Redmond grinned. "Nicely observed. Officer, any comments on that?"

"Almost empty bottle of whiskey on the side table," Bland said. "Used glass fallen onto the carpet. We packed those up for you to send to the lab. Strong smell of tobacco on his clothes. The guy was overweight, by a lot. His wife says he had a heart attack a year or so ago, although the old lady claims it was nothing but bad heartburn."

"I've had heartburn bad enough I thought I was having a heart attack," Williams said.

"I'll file that piece of information away for future reference," Redmond said. "We'll check with his doctor about this previous heart incident. What you're saying, Officer Bland, is that a heart attack is possible?"

"I am. He takes off his shoes and sits on his bed to have a drink. He has more than one drink. Doesn't feel well. Lies down, and . . . good night."

"Lily," Redmond asked. "Did you make any observations on the man's state of health?"

I thought. "Overweight, like Jocelyn says. Ruddy face.

Obvious rosacea on his nose. At a mere guess, I'd say his health wasn't good, and he was likely a heavy drinker. He smoked cigars."

"Yeah. Found a box of cigars on the dresser," Bland said. "I packed those up, too."

"We'll have that room gone over," Redmond said, "and order an autopsy. But until we have evidence the guy didn't simply lie down and die due to excessive alcohol consumption and unhealthy living habits"—she couldn't resist a sly glance at Chuck Williams—"I'm not getting in the middle of a family feud. Lily, how long are they booked to stay here?"

"Until Tuesday, I think. Rose handles the reservations."

"We'll check with her. Do you know where they live?"

"Boston area, I've been told, but I don't know precisely where."

"Far enough away, it's unlikely they'll want to leave before we release the man's body. I want to have a look at the scene myself before we go. Jocelyn, will you get everyone's contact info please and tell them we'll be in touch. If the elder Mrs. Reynolds asks what's happening about her accusations, say we're looking into all possibilities."

"Yes, ma'am." Jocelyn Bland turned to do as she'd been asked. "Can I help you?"

I also turned to see who she was speaking to. Karen, the bridge player with the big glasses, stood at the door of her room farther down the hall, peeking out.

"Pardon me," she said. "I'm not feeling too well, so I was hoping someone could give me a couple of aspirin."

"This is not a good time," Williams said.

"I'll check with my grandmother," I said. "If she has any, I'll bring something to you when I'm finished here."

"Thank you. Sorry to bother you." She slipped quietly back into her room and shut the door.

"I wouldn't worry too much about the aspirin, Lily," Redmond said. "I've seen that type many times before. She wants to know what's going on and had to come up with an excuse on the fly when she was caught listening to what's none of her concern. Which reminds me. How many other guests do you have this morning?"

"Six, I think. Four friends here to play cards, including that lady, and another couple. Hikers, I think they are."

"Take statements from them, Jocelyn," Redmond said. "Ask if they saw or heard anything in the night or early hours of this morning. Also ask if they've met the deceased or anyone in his party prior to arriving here."

"Got it," she said.

"I have something else you'll want to know," I said. "About Mr. Reynolds."

"What?" Williams asked.

"I don't know these people, and I've had hardly anything to do with them, but even so I've sensed some dissent around this impending marriage they've supposedly all gathered here to celebrate."

"Meaning?"

"Ralph Reynolds wanted his son to call off the wedding. With only two days remaining until the ceremony. Mr. Reynolds offered him money, but Greg refused, point blank."

"You know this how?"

I explained what I'd overheard.

"Speaking of listening in to conversations you are not party to," Redmond said.

"We run a hotel," I said. "People bring their problems with them, and it's not my fault if they want to discuss those problems in my hearing."

"I'm not criticizing, Lily," she said. "Just commenting. You'd be surprised, or maybe not, at the number of cases we can put to rest because the miscreants don't know not to talk in front of restaurant and hotel staff. Anything else?"

I was about to mention that someone else had been listening to the men last night, but I held my tongue. I couldn't identify anyone, and I wasn't entirely sure what I had seen. Likely someone who, like me, found themselves listening to a conversation they didn't want to hear.

"I'm sure you're anxious to get to work, Lily," Williams said. "We'll have to ask your grandmother to keep that room out of bounds until we've finished with it. Don't let your cleaners in until we give the all-clear."

I sighed. An empty room in the middle of the summer. No way to run a business. I hoped the Reynolds family wouldn't ask for a refund.

At that moment the front door swung open, and McKenzie Reynolds swept in. The very picture of a well-off young woman on vacation, her long blue beach dress flowing behind her like the surf, blue beads around her wrists and neck clattering like squabbling seagulls, hair streaming behind her.

She came to a screeching halt, lowered her sunglasses, and peered at the detectives. "What on earth is going on here?" she asked me. "A couple of police cars are parked out front. I've had, like, a hundred phone calls from my mom and my brothers."

Redmond and Williams said nothing.

"Hi," McKenzie said.

"Hello," Detective Williams said.

"Did you speak to your mother?" I asked.

"Not yet. I've recently started with a new therapist. She says I need to be more mindful of my surroundings. I went for a walk on the beach, when Simon said he didn't have time to show me the garden, and I turned my phone off.

My therapist says I have to do that if I want to be truly mindful. I turned it on now, and—"

"Your mother and one of your brothers are in the drawing room," I said. "Why don't you join them?"

"What are they doing in there? I thought Mom was going to the spa this morning, and don't Greg and Ivan have, like, wedding things to do?"

I didn't reply. Williams and Redmond watched McKenzie.

Slowly, comprehension began to make its way through her veil of self-absorption. "Is . . . something wrong?"

"I'm sorry," I said, "But yes. Something is wrong."

"Where's my dad? And why are the police here?" She stabbed a finger toward Williams and Redmond. "Is that who you two are?"

Amy Redmond nodded and introduced herself.

McKenzie bolted for the drawing room. She threw the door open and screamed, "Dad! What's happened to my dad?"

# Chapter 9

"The wedding has been postponed," Rose said.

"That's too bad, but it's completely understandable," Marybeth said. "I hope the family isn't going to lose the money they've already paid for the reception and everything."

"I don't know about that." Rose said. "It is late notice."

I chopped dark chocolate prior to preparing the ganache for the always popular Earl Grey chocolate tart that would be a feature of today's menu. "Did Regina have any more accusations to make against Sophia?"

"Not in my hearing," Rose replied.

After Sophia had swept McKenzie into her arms and taken the weeping girl upstairs to her room, I slipped away and went to the tearoom to get to work. We had a full reservations book for today, including a bus tour of twenty people due to arrive at three o'clock.

Early in the afternoon, a plain black van pulled into the driveway and drove slowly up to the house.

"The coroner's arrived, Lily," Cheryl told me a few minutes later. "They'll be bringing the body out soon, I suspect."

I grimaced. "Not something people want to see as they relax over their tea and scones."

"No. But they know how to be discreet, and not many of the tables on the patio have a direct view of the front of the house."

I desperately hoped the autopsy would show that Ralph died of natural causes. I've been involved in police investigations before and, for one thing, they have a way of interfering with me going about my job.

The coroner's van had departed by the time the bus tour arrived. One of the best things about having an afternoon tea–focused restaurant is customers don't order individual meals, with all the complications that involves. We offer a traditional afternoon tea made up of a selection of scones, sandwiches, sweets; the royal tea, served with a glass of sparkling wine; a children's menu; a dessert-only course; sandwiches only; and a cream tea, which consists of scones and accompaniments. Along with an extensive tea menu, iced tea or lemonade for children and those who want something cold, and coffee for the non-tea drinkers. I can make gluten-free and/or dairy-free items on request, and keep some on hand in case of unexpected demands, but I find when people make reservations they generally specify that sort of requirement up front.

Meaning, I am rarely hit by surprises. Which, after working in a Michelin-starred restaurant in Manhattan under the ownership and supervision of a celebrity "bad boy" chef, frequented by the rich and famous (and spoiled), is like being in food-service heaven.

Marybeth and Cheryl prepared tea and ferried three-tiered stands of food out to the patio. A light tap at the kitchen door, and Bernie's head popped in. "Can we come in?"

"No. I'm busy."

I don't know why she bothered to ask, and I don't know

why I bothered to answer. She came in anyway, followed by my grandmother.

Because my kitchen is so small, there are no chairs in it. Bernie dragged an unneeded chair (I hoped it was unneeded and one of my guests hadn't found themselves drinking tea and munching on sandwiches while standing up) from the main dining room for Rose, and my grandmother had plunked herself down to give us the news from the house.

"I saw the coroner's van arrive a while ago," I said. "It left not long after."

"Mr. Reynolds has departed," Rose said.

"In more ways than one," Bernie said.

"Bad taste, Bernie," I said.

"Sophia and one of her sons, Ivan, I believe his name is, the elder one at any rate, followed," Rose said. "Jenny and her mother are in the drawing room with Greg, attempting to contact people to tell them the wedding's been postponed."

"What about Regina and McKenzie?"

"When we left, they were in their room."

"Rose filled me in on what happened," Bernie said. "The old lady . . . pardon me, Rose, the distinguished matriarch of the family, accused her daughter-in-law, straight to the cops no less, of bumping her husband off. That'll add a whole new dimension of tension to the family table next Thanksgiving." She chuckled. "Wish I'd been there to see it."

"I saw it, and I would rather not have," Rose said. "I politely mentioned to Regina that I could call some of my hotelier contacts and find her alternate accommodations. She looked quite confused and asked why I'd do that. Was she no longer welcome? When I said I assumed she wouldn't want to stay under the same roof as Sophia, she informed me she would not be driven out of her home, no matter how temporary a home that might be, by, and I quote, 'the likes of her.' "

"Bus group's settled and happy. One order for full tea for four. It sounds to me"—Cheryl sucked in her stomach and wiggled around Rose's chair to get to the shelf of tea canisters—"like those two have clashed before over living arrangements. Often happens between the generations, doesn't it?" I thought of my mother, telling me I'd be insane to go and live with her mother. I refrained from saying so. "It was kinda the opposite in my family," Cheryl continued. "My grandma wanted to move into a retirement home when my grandfather died, and my parents insisted she come and live with us. Which she did, for a short while. It didn't exactly work out, probably because she sabotaged the living arrangements, and then she happily moved into the place she'd wanted to go to all along. Where for many years she was the reigning jigsaw puzzle queen. Speaking of reigning queens, Rose, my aunt Josephine tells me you haven't been at bridge much lately." As she talked, Cheryl scooped leaves of fragrant, deliciously smoky Lapsang souchong into a teapot, added hot water, and set the timer for the proper steeping time of the leaves. Without being asked, Bernie, who knows the routine by now, began laying food on the platters. Sandwiches on the bottom tier, scones in the middle, desserts on top, in the traditional pattern.

"I'm getting bored with it," Rose said. "The players are becoming increasingly unimaginative. And then they changed the time of the regular meetings to Monday evening, rather than afternoon. I don't like going out after supper these days. I prefer an evening of good telly."

"If we can get back on topic," I said. "Is Sophia the one checking out then?"

"No." Rose said. "When I spoke to her, she said much the same as her mother-in-law."

"Awkward," I said.

"If I had to choose between the two of them who to keep," Bernie said, "I'd take the grandmother. That Sophia is a piece of work."

"Regina, I suspect," Rose said, "keeps her head down and her thoughts to herself, as women of that age . . . our age . . . were taught."

"She didn't keep her thoughts about her son's murderer to herself," I pointed out.

"True. Even women of a certain age, some women at least, know when it's time to speak up. Although," she added almost to herself, "sometimes it's better not to be quite so vocal."

"The situation is awkward. To say the least," I said. "It's not helped by having crime scene tape draped dramatically across the door to room two-oh-one, directly opposite Sophia in two hundred and Regina and her granddaughter in two-oh-two."

"At least the body's gone," Bernie said.

I suppressed a shudder. "I'm surprised any of them are going to continue to stay with us."

"They've taken five of my best rooms. I don't offer refunds when people depart prematurely. Whatever the reason," said the ever-practical Rose. "In other news, McKenzie collapsed weeping and had to be escorted to her room by her brother's friend, whose name escapes me."

"Dave," I said.

"Shortly thereafter a young man arrived I'd not met before. He said his name is Jack and he claimed to be McKenzie's boyfriend. Dave took him up to McKenzie's room. From where I then heard a renewal of copious amounts of weeping."

"Not that you were listening at doors or anything," Bernie said.

"Of course not. I had matters to attend to on the second floor, at that end of the hallway."

"You're an astute observer of human nature, Rose," Bernie said. "I like to think I am, too, but I wasn't there. Was McKenzie truly shocked, do you think, or playing for the room? Can't say I thought much of her and her oh-so-dreadfully-bored act at the shower."

"Perhaps a touch of the latter," Rose said. "Although that might have been nothing but force of habit. I do think she was genuinely overcome by news of her father's death."

"Like mother, like daughter," Bernie said. "It wouldn't surprise me if that Sophia had offed her husband after all. I didn't like her one tiny bit."

"Being unlikeable doesn't make someone a killer," I said.

"I guess not," she begrudgingly admitted.

"What's happening with Jenny and Hannah?" I asked.

One of the nice things about being a baker is that I can work and talk at the same time. Hard to do if I was an accountant or bank clerk. Being a baker, I can also rope people into helping. "Bernie, boiled eggs are in the fridge. I need them made into sandwich ingredients."

"Cheryl," Bernie called. "Lily needs the eggs peeled."

"Most amusing," I said. "Get to it or you have to leave. And take Rose with you."

Grumbling, but not meaning it, Bernie edged around Cheryl to get to the sink to wash her hands. I strained the creamy chocolate mixture to get the tea leaves out prior to filling the sweet tart shell cooling on the counter. Next, I turned my attention to making always-popular chocolate chip cookies for the children's tea. I always love the look on our littlest customers' faces when they taste a home-baked cookie for the first time, if all they've had before are those served straight from a supermarket box.

"Full tea for two and children's tea for three," Marybeth called. "Bernie, can you get out of the way. I need to get into the fridge."

"I'm looking for eggs. Where are the eggs?"

"About two inches away from your nose."

"Oh, right. There they are, the pesky little things."

I stifled a groan. It would be faster, and easier, to do it myself, but as long as Rose and Bernie were intent on discussing recent events, I knew I wouldn't be able to get rid of them until they were finished.

"I don't know what Hannah and her mother are going to do now," Rose said in answer to my question.

"That's a weird situation there," I said. Okay, I'll confess, I enjoy a good gossip as much as the next person. "Jenny told me she'd known Ralph for a long time. She'd been engaged to him at one time, and she left him to marry Hannah's father."

"That would have been decades ago. Surely, you're not thinking Jenny killed him?" Bernie's long slim fingers moved fast as she peeled the eggs.

"Not at all. Just commenting on the strange personal dynamics at play between them all."

"Never mind whatever's between Sophia and her mother-in-law," Bernie said. "Rose, you sat with Regina at the shower. What was your take on her?"

Rose thought for a long time while the business of a busy kitchen swirled around her. And the busy kitchen workers tried to squeeze themselves past her and her cane and her chair. "Our acquaintance was obviously brief," she said at last. "We chatted about our families, mostly. Ralph, incidentally, is her only child. She's been widowed for a long time. If I have to comment, I'll say I didn't care for her overly much. She clearly doesn't like her son's wife, and that is entirely their business." She cleared her throat. "One of my own daughters-in-law comes to mind. But

Regina let that feeling show, by expressions rather than deeds, at the shower. In front of me, a complete stranger. I can't say she has . . . had a lot of time for her son, either."

"What does that mean?" Bernie has made sandwiches for me before, and without having to be told, she reached for the pots of fresh herbs growing on the sunny windowsill and selected dill, chives, and basil to add to the egg mixture.

"Hold that thought until I get back." Cheryl hoisted her tray bearing a teapot of fragrant, smoky Lapsang souchong, along with matching jug and sugar bowl, and four tea sets. "I want to hear this."

"If we keep holding thoughts," I said, "they'll never get finished."

Marybeth came in. "I'll cover for you, Mom. We can tag-team the conversation. One of the women in the bus tour examined the offerings and then told me she's on a nonfat diet and do you have any fat-free scones?"

I suppressed a shudder. "No, I do not have any fat-free scones."

"What's a fat-free scone anyway?" Bernie said. "Might as well eat a pile of raw flour."

"For heaven's sake," I said. "Tell her to pick the raisins out of her scone and eat those. I can offer her a bowl of raspberries, and that's about it. But it will be an extra charge as raspberries are not on the menu."

"You want me to say that?"

"No. Please explain that we're generally unable to accommodate individual requests such as hers at such late notice. However, I can do some toast with . . . I don't know what I have that's completely fat-free. Afternoon tea is not known for being diet friendly."

"Want me to run out to the garden and collect some dead leaves?" Bernie added a spoonful of mayonnaise to her chopped eggs. "Is compost fat-free?"

"I can do toast with an egg-white omelet made with fresh herbs," I said. "Ask if she'd like that. And no, no extra charge. I'm not making anything special for anyone else, though."

"People today are far too fussy," Rose said. "In my parents' house you ate what you got and you were happy to have it."

"You walked ten miles to school every day. Uphill. Both ways," Bernie said.

"Something like that." Rose grinned at her. "Although, as I recall, the village school was situated next door to our house. And, even in my time, the sons and daughters of the rich could be as fussy as they liked, although Lady Frockmorton was always conscious of not letting her children take undue advantage of the kitchen staff . . ."

Marybeth slipped out and Cheryl returned. "What did I miss?"

"Nothing," Bernie said. "We were discussing the dining habits of the various classes in England in the mid-twentieth century."

"What?"

"As for Regina . . ." Rose said. "I wouldn't want to have to spend any more time in her company than is necessary. She thought she was being witty when she was simply being catty. And she was very catty indeed about some members of her own family. Other than her granddaughter, the one with a surname as her first name. Ridiculous modern habit. Regina's very fond of her."

"Isn't Mr. Darcy's first name Fitzwilliam?" Marybeth asked. "You know, the *Pride and Prejudice* guy? That sounds like a last name to me."

"She's got you there, Rose," I said. "Sophia made a crack about Regina's drinking. Did you think she was overdoing it?"

"Not that I noticed," Rose said. "She had a glass of

prosecco in front of her while the gifts were being opened, but she didn't down it in record time, if that's what you mean."

"What about Hannah, the bride?" Bernie asked. "Did Regina express any opinions on her?"

"If anything, I got the impression she thought Hannah joining the family was a good thing. Put some long-missing backbone into the Reynolds gene pool, is what I believe she said. Greg, the groom-to-be, is an artist. Regina most definitely does not approve of that as a career choice. Hannah's a schoolteacher, and that, according to Regina, is a suitable occupation for a young, soon-to-be-married woman."

"Speaking of the shower," Cheryl said. "Anything happen about that creepy doll gift?"

"I completely forgot about that." I dropped spoonfuls of cookie dough onto a baking sheet. "I didn't think to mention it to the detectives when I spoke to them earlier. Do you think it might have something to do with what happened later? About Ralph?"

"Unlikely." Bernie cut slices of white bread into circles. "I wouldn't rule it out completely, though. Hasn't Redmond told you before to let them do the thinking?"

"Me? It's you two always thinking about these things."

Rose pushed herself to her feet. "No more thinking for me. The poor man died of heart disease. Far too young, but such is life. I'm going up to the house to do some much-needed work on the accounts."

"Any turnover in the house today?" I asked.

"One room only. A couple from Quebec are leaving, and another couple, this time from New York City, are taking their place. Otherwise, the bridge group will be here for a few more days. They've taken two rooms. I mentioned to them that I am a bridge player of some competence myself, and I'd be happy to join them in a game if one of them doesn't feel like playing at any time. The Reynolds party has taken five rooms until next Tuesday. Other than the single room Greg is in, which is due to be vacated tomorrow, as it was planned that he would go on his honeymoon. Hmm . . . I don't know what to do about that. If they want to stay as booked, I'll be a room short tomorrow. Unless the police free Ralph's room."

"You can't put his son in there," Bernie said.

"No, perhaps not."

"Someone should tell Amy Redmond about the shower doll," Bernie said.

"I agree," Rose said. "Take care of that, will you, love?" She opened the kitchen door.

Bernie indicated her platter of perfectly prepared egg sandwiches on circles of soft white bread. "My work here is done, and I've got a book to write. Take care of contacting Amy, will you, Lily. I'll escort Rose up to the house."

The door shut behind the both of them.

"Why," I asked my staff, "is it always up to me?"

# Chapter 10

Unfortunately, for me, I have Amy Redmond's contact number in my phone. While the cookies baked, I quickly (and reluctantly) whipped up an egg-white omelet, put my phone on speaker, and gave the detective a call.

She answered immediately. "Lily Roberts. I was wondering when I'd hear from you."

"Me? It's Rose and Bernie who are always interfering with your job, not me. I tag innocently along behind, helplessly trapped in the wake of their enthusiasm."

"And innocently place yourself directly in danger. I know. I also know you have good instincts, Lily, and I will begrudgingly admit, although not to anyone else, you've been of help to us in the past. So what's up?"

"I don't suppose you've got autopsy results on Ralph Reynolds yet?"

"That's scheduled for six tonight. If you're wanting an invitation, the answer is an emphatic no."

I swallowed. Probably the last thing I wanted, after accommodating another request for nonfat afternoon tea, was to be witness to an autopsy. "Did anyone tell you about an . . . incident that occurred at the Hill-Reynolds bridal shower held here yesterday?"

"What sort of incident?"

"Nothing anyone would have considered to be of interest to the police under normal circumstances, but in light of accusations and tensions swirling around the sudden death of one of the guests at that shower, I thought you should know about it."

"I have not been told about anything specific regarding any shower. You say here, meaning it was held at Tea by the Sea?"

"Yes."

"Sounds intriguing."

"It'll make more sense if I show it to you. If you have time."

"I do not have the time. But I'll make time. I'm not opening a criminal investigation into Mr. Reynolds's death. Not yet. It seems, so far, to be a case of a man with a bad heart overindulging in things he shouldn't in celebration of his son's marriage. That situation might change depending on the results of the autopsy and the lab reports on the contents of his bottle and glass. In case it does, I'd like to see what you're talking about."

"I'll be at work until—" I was about to suggest Detective Redmond come to see the doll after the tearoom closed at five. Instead, she said, "On my way," and hung up.

I slapped the egg-white omelet onto a plate and sprinkled finely chopped herbs across it.

"She's coming now?" Marybeth asked.

"Unfortunately yes. I shouldn't be long. I hope I'm not long. Everything okay out there?"

"Seems to be. The other members of the bus tour are digging in happily. Do you want me to offer Detective Redmond tea?"

"Absolutely not."

When Amy Redmond says she's "on my way," she means it. It's about a ten-minute drive from the North Augusta police station to Victoria-on-Sea. Five minutes after our phone call, she pulled into the driveway. Detective Williams was with her. I took off my apron and hairnet, went out the back door, and around the corner of the eighteenth-century stone building I'd worked so hard to convert into a warm, welcoming tearoom.

The police waited for me by their car. Fortunately, not many of the guests seated on the patio paid them any attention.

Police activity at a restaurant is never good.

"It's in the garden shed," I told them.

"What's this *it* you've dragged us all the way out here to see?" Williams asked.

"Best if I show you. You need to see it in person to get the full effect."

I'd texted Simon to tell him we needed to get into the garden shed and he was waiting for us. He held two short-stemmed yellow roses, one in each hand. He handed one to me, with a bow, and then one to Amy Redmond, with a deeper bow.

She colored slightly, looking quite pleased, before wiping the expression away and regaining her usual no-nonsense composure. "Let's see it. Whatever *it* is."

Simon opened the door to the shed and we stepped in, two of us carrying our roses. I indicated the cardboard box. "This came gift wrapped. Among the piles of presents brought to the shower. Pointedly, it didn't have a card attached. The bridesmaid looked for it, but she didn't find one. No one claimed responsibility. One of my staff found the present sitting by the gate, so she put it with the rest of the gifts. The box was wrapped but, if it matters, we threw the wrapping out with all the rest. Sorry."

The police studied the box.

"The bride opened it, and what she saw upset her enormously. So much she fled the shower and did not return."

Redmond laid her rose on a shelf and lifted the flaps. The blank, empty eyes of the Raggedy Ann doll stared up at us.

"It's a doll," Williams scoffed. I don't know what he expected—maybe the head of a thoroughbred racing horse as in *The Godfather*.

"You got it in one, mate," Simon said.

Redmond pulled gloves out of her pocket and slipped them on before picking up the head and studying it. For some ridiculous reason I thought of Hamlet: *Yorick. I knew him well, Horatio.* Instead of uttering the immortal lines, she said, "A doll in two parts. I'll admit, a highly unusual shower gift."

"Greg, the groom, opened the box. He lifted out the head. Hannah screamed and tried to get away. Greg threw it aside. Someone knocked over the box and the rest of it fell out. It caused a considerable commotion."

"As I would expect," Redmond said. "Which, presumably, the sender also expected."

"Total chaos," Simon said. "The head landed near a woman, and she just about trampled everyone near her in her haste to get away."

"A practical joke," Williams said. "One in bad taste, okay, but a joke. Any preteen boys in this family? I'd start there." He walked out of the shed, shaking his head.

Detective Redmond did not follow. She examined the head from all angles.

"It's obviously been cut." Simon pointed. "Cleanly, too."

"It shows no signs of wear. Meaning, it's a new doll, likely bought for this specific purpose. You say the bride was very upset, Lily. If this was intended as a message, do you think she got it?"

"I don't know about a message, but she told me she had a doll similar to that one as a child and it had great emotional significance to her."

Redmond put the head to one side and took out the body. "An old-fashioned sort of doll, but it looks industrially made. All machine stitching." She pointed to a tag attached to the right leg. "Here's a label. *Made in China.* So not rare or an antique."

"Hannah said the childhood doll was one of the last things her father gave her before he died."

"Mean. Very, very mean. Whether this has anything to do with the death, natural causes or not, of her prospective father-in-law, might not matter. Not directly. But it does indicate to me that someone in the wedding party or among their guests is not a nice person."

"Detective, are you coming?" Williams called. "We don't have all day."

"Give me a few more minutes," Redmond replied.

"Your time to waste. As for me, Lily, got the coffee on?"

I rolled my eyes at Simon. Redmond's head was down as she studied the details of the doll's dress, so she might not have noticed. Then again, she didn't miss much.

"It can be," I said.

"Some of those cookies wouldn't go amiss, either. The English ones."

"Shortbread. Tell Cheryl or Marybeth to offer you some."

Amy Redmond continued examining the doll. "This is made all of cloth, and rough textured at that, so it's gonna be tough to get any useable prints. But, in case we find some, I suppose a lot of people touched it?"

"Greg Reynolds, as we mentioned. Simon did. I think Bernie helped stuff it back in the box."

"All the usual suspects."

"Uh, yeah. Greg Reynolds grabbed it and dropped it back in the box. People were jumping up and milling about, so I didn't exactly see who did what and when."

"Like I said," Simon added. "Total chaos."

"Same for the box itself?" Redmond asked.

"Yup," I said. "It was gift wrapped. Greg handed it to Hannah and they opened it together."

"I carried the box in here," Simon said. "Before that, anyone could have touched it. Plus, I don't lock the shed during the day."

"Anything noticeable about the wrapping?"

"Sort of sparkly?" Simon said.

I thought. "It was attractive. A silver pattern, with a big matching bow. Suitable for a shower gift, but nothing exceptional. The paper and the bow looked to be store-bought. I didn't examine them in any detail."

She put the pieces of the doll back in the box and bent to lift it up. Simon reached to help her and she snapped, "No touching."

He jerked back and lifted his hands. "Sorry. My prints are all over it."

"Be that as it may, I don't need any more. Lily, can you bring my rose, please." She carried the box out of the garden shed. I scooped up her flower, and Simon and I followed. On the tearoom patio, Detective Williams was talking to Marybeth. She showed him to an unoccupied table.

"Don't have all day indeed," Redmond muttered under her breath. "The autopsy's scheduled for six. I've got time to drop this off at the lab before. Provided I can convince my partner to have his coffee and cookies as takeout."

She turned to me and gave me what I took to be an approving nod. "As I said earlier, your instincts are good, Lily. *Some men*, not being fully aware of the importance of a wedding shower to a young bride, might take this to be nothing but a practical joke. In line with what you had to tell me, and what I observed myself, about the tension in the Reynolds family, and between certain of them and Mrs. Hill, I think this little joke might be highly significant indeed. If this case goes any further, that is."

She headed for her car, and I went with her, still carrying her rose as well as mine. Simon shut the door to the shed.

Redmond popped the trunk of her car and put the box inside. "I'll have a talk with Hannah Hill about this. She might have some idea who sent it. And why."

"If you need someone to be with her—"

"Her mother can take that role. The Hills are not staying here. I thank you for your help, but I won't need any more." She took the rose out of my hand. "Oh, no. He's ordering the full tea. We'll be here all day."

# Chapter 11

As I normally do, I stayed at Tea by the Sea after closing and after Marybeth and Cheryl had cleaned up and said their good nights. Following a hectic day, I always enjoy time alone, surrounded by peace and quiet and good food, doing what I love best—baking.

The kitchen backs onto the main road, and I can hear the sound of passing traffic. Usually I tune it out, but today I was more aware than usual of cars slowing and turning into our driveway. Not long after the police left, with the headless doll and its head in their trunk, Amy Redmond carrying her rose, and Chuck Williams lugging a hastily prepared take-out container of afternoon tea offerings, Ivan Reynolds and his mother, Sophia, returned to Victoria-on-Sea. Shortly after that, Greg left, on his own. And not long after that McKenzie departed in the company of a man around her age who I took to be her boyfriend, Jack.

I assumed Greg was on his way to meet with Hannah. I felt dreadfully sorry for them both. Despite how her bridal shower had ended, and despite all the negative emotions being expressed by certain other people, they were clearly in love and looking forward to their nuptials. Now, the wedding had been postponed. Never mind the money they'd likely forfeit, but the disappointment had to be crushing. I'd been told the wedding was to be held at the yacht club in North Augusta. Those premises did not come cheap. Two hundred guests had been invited. Many of them would already have arrived at hotels and B & Bs nearby, making a holiday of the occasion. Now everyone had to be contacted to be told the wedding was being postponed. They'd all have questions. Poor Hannah. Poor Greg.

It might be a long time before the families were in the mood to celebrate, and longer still to organize another grand affair.

For everyone's sake, I sincerely hoped nothing would come of the autopsy.

But that was not to be.

I was cleaning up the last of my night's work around nine o'clock, ready to head home for an exciting evening of slipping into my pajamas and watching something boring on TV with my dog and a microwaved dinner, when three vehicles turned into the driveway. Two were SUVs with the markings of the North Augusta Police Department, and the other a plain car I recognized from earlier today.

The only reason, I thought, Williams and Redmond would come with uniformed officers would be if they intended to open an investigation.

I shoved dishes into the dishwasher, set it, cast my eyes around the kitchen to ensure I hadn't left anything perishable out or the ovens on, pulled off my apron and hairnet, threw them on the butcher block, and left the tearoom at speed.

The sun had dipped below the waters of the bay, leaving the western sky streaked with shades of gray and orange.

Many of the lights in the B & B were on, giving the grand old house a warm, welcoming appearance. I hurried through the garden, trees dark against the sky, white daisies glowing in the dying light, flowers fragrant as they settled down for the night.

When I reached the house, Rose was letting our unexpected visitors in. I ran up the steps after them.

"We're here to speak to the Reynolds family," Detective Williams said as the two uniforms stood stiffly behind him.

"I myself was about to retire for the night," Rose said. "I don't know if anyone is in. But I can check their rooms, if you like."

"Cars belonging to Ralph Reynolds, Greg Reynolds, and Ivan Reynolds are parked outside," Officer Bland pointed out.

"People often take cabs if they're going out for dinner." Relief crossed Rose's face as she saw me edging around the police. "Lily, I'm glad you're here. Would you mind, love?"

"Not at all," I said.

I raised one eyebrow at Amy Redmond in a question. Her face was expressionless, and she did not acknowledge me in any way. That in itself told me plenty.

I ran upstairs. When I hit the landing, a low buzz of conversation was coming from room 202. Sophia's room.

I knocked lightly on the door, and Greg opened it. "Lily. Good evening. What's up?"

I glanced over his shoulder. Room 202 is our best and biggest room, decorated in a highly feminine style of soft shades of peach and sage green with white French provincial furniture.

Greg's mother reclined on the king-sized bed on top of the covers, fully dressed except for her shoes, propped up against a mountain of pillows. The double doors leading to the spacious balcony were open and the night air off the sea and the sound of surf hitting the rocks filled the room. Ivan sprawled in a chair by the doors to the balcony, a bottle of beer clenched in his hand.

"I'm sorry to bother you," I said. "The police are downstairs. They'd like to talk to you."

"Why?" Ivan asked.

"I don't know."

"Okay. Thank you," Greg said. "We'll be right down."

"Is the elder Mrs. Reynolds in her room?" I asked.

"I think so," Greg said. "I checked on her when we got back from dinner, and she was there then. She didn't want to join us this evening."

*No kidding.*

"McKenzie and Jack, the perpetual loser, went somewhere by themselves after we left the restaurant," Ivan said. "Don't know where."

"The detectives didn't ask," I said. "But I suspect they'd like to talk to her as well. Is Dave around?"

"He's in our room," Ivan said. "Wanted to catch the end of the game."

Sophia swung her legs off the bed. "Let's get this nonsense over with. Ivan, call McKenzie and tell her to get back here. Now."

I went down the hallway to room 200. I knocked, and a voice said, "What is it?"

"Lily Roberts here, Mrs. Reynolds. I'm sorry to disturb you, but you're needed downstairs."

"What on earth for?"

"The police are here."

"Tell them to talk to Sophia."

At that moment Sophia and her sons came out of her room. Her face tightened in anger, and she said, "If you're too drunk to put in an appearance, Regina, I'll make your excuses."

Greg grabbed her arm. "That's not helping, Mom."

"It's not?" But she allowed him to lead her away.

"Very well," Regina said through the closed door. "I'll be right down. Goodness knows what she'll say if I'm not there to set the record straight."

Ivan opened the door to room 203 and called, "You're needed downstairs, pal. Cops are here."

By the time I arrived downstairs, Williams was ushering the Reynolds family into the drawing room. The four bridge-playing women had returned from dinner and were watching events with undisguised interest. Redmond spoke to them. "Are you ladies guests here?"

"Yes," a short, slightly plump one replied. "We are. We're from Boston, and we're here on a bridge vacation. I'm Laurie Kilpatrick."

"Were you here, in this house, last night?"

Four heads nodded in unison.

"Did one of my officers take your statements?"

"Oh, yes. It was very exciting!"

The friend with the big black eyeglasses jabbed the speaker in the ribs. "Show some respect, Marie. A man died here yesterday. That's what you want to talk to us about, Officer, right? Sorry, we can't help you. We didn't know him. I mean, I didn't know him. I can't speak for us all."

"Karen's right," Laurie said. "We don't know anything." Her friends nodded in agreement.

"Then you can return to your rooms. Officer Kowalski will assist you, if you can't find the way yourselves."

"At least," Marie, the oldest of the women, said in what she probably thought was a whisper, "we get a young and handsome one."

Redmond threw Kowalski a grin, and he turned various shades of scarlet as he followed the bridge group down the hallway. They passed Regina, slowly descending the stairs.

The elderly lady hesitated when she saw the little group before saying, "Hello . . . uh . . . ladies."

"Mrs. Reynolds. My condolences on your loss," Karen said. Her friends also mumbled words of sympathy before they continued down the hallway to their rooms.

Regina watched them go, and then turned her attention to the detective. "I demand to know what's going on. It's late; it's been an exceptionally exhausting day, emotionally and physically, and I'm ready for my bed."

"Thank you for joining us," Redmond said.

"Do I have a choice?"

"You always have a choice," Redmond replied. "Until you don't."

The matriarch sailed past us in a cloud of expensive perfume, recently applied. She might claim to be ready for bed, but she was still dressed in the clothes she'd had on earlier.

"Lily," Redmond said, "you and your grandmother may join us. This incident happened on your property, therefore you're directly concerned."

Before we could move, the front door flew open once again and Bernie and Matt Goodwill fell in. Matt is our neighbor, and he and Bernie recently started dating.

"This is not a public event," Redmond said with an exasperated sigh.

"We were . . . uh . . . just heading back to my place," Matt said. "When we . . . uh . . ."

"Saw all the lights were on and decided it wasn't too late to drop in for a nightcap," Bernie finished with a dazzling smile.

"Good try," Redmond said. "Let me guess. If Lily didn't call you, Rose did."

"Only being neighborly," Matt said.

"Tonight you can be neighborly from your own property," Redmond said. "I can't order you to leave, as this is a private home, but I will strongly recommend it. I'll also remind you, Lincoln Badwell, you are not going to be party to any part of this conversation. Or any other. If you happen to overhear anything, you cannot repeat it."

Lincoln Badwell was an international bestselling true-crime writer. Matt used a pseudonym, thinking the name of Goodwill didn't exactly suit the sort of books he wrote. He gave Detective Redmond a smile that almost out-dazzled Bernie's. "I never use anything you tell me, Amy. You know that."

"Which is only because I never tell you anything. Not about an active case that is."

"So the death of Ralph Reynolds is an active case?" Bernie asked.

Redmond rolled her eyes to the heavens. She spoke to the uniformed officer hovering beside the door. "When Ms. McKenzie Reynolds arrives, show her in. No one else. Got that?"

"Yes, ma'am."

"Why don't we have a nightcap at your place?" Bernie said. "If Lily needs us, she can call."

"Great idea," Matt said.

I mouthed, "All okay, but thanks," to Bernie and she nodded.

My friends left, walking very, very slowly. The uniformed officer shut the door behind them, and I followed Detective Redmond into the drawing room.

Rose had snagged her favorite seat, and it was Regina's turn to perch uncomfortably on the edge of a chair. Sophia huddled into herself on the couch, next to her son Ivan. Her younger son, Greg, stood by the window, staring out over the darkening garden. Dave spoke to him in a low voice, Greg shrugged, and Dave took a seat at the desk. Detective Williams stood in front of the fireplace, cold and empty on a summer evening.

Williams cleared his throat. "At the request of the NAPD, an autopsy was conducted earlier today on Mr. Ralph Reynolds."

Greg turned away from the window. Sophia emitted a muffled sob and buried her head in her hands. Ivan put his arm around his mother. Regina sighed deeply. How sad, I thought, that the two women could not be of comfort to each other in their shared grief. Rose and I said nothing.

"The cause of death was heart failure," the detective said.

"It's a wife's job," Regina sniffed, "to ensure her husband maintains good health habits. Unfortunately, my son was allowed to, occasionally, neglect his well-being."

Sophia, wisely, said nothing. That had been a heck of a mean comment.

"Grandma," Greg said. "Please. Not now."

Regina pursed her lips and said no more.

"Be that as it may," Redmond said, "the pathologist has some concerns."

"What sort of concerns?" Greg asked.

Before she could answer, we heard voices in the hallway, and seconds later the door opened to admit McKenzie, wearing a short, skin-tight dress with lots of bling, and mega-high-heeled shoes. Her eyes were heavily outlined in black and her lipstick a deep, dark red. She was accompanied by the man I'd earlier assumed was her boyfriend, Jack. He was in his early thirties and extremely good-looking. About six feet tall, slim, with prominent cheekbones, hair a mass of black curls, large brown eyes under thick lashes, and a day's worth of stubble on his strong jaw.

Behind them, Karen, one of the bridge women, was trying to peer into the room. Her eyes fell on Sophia, and I saw a flash of interest, before Officer Kowalski shut the door in her face.

"What's happening?" McKenzie looked between her

brothers, her mother, and her grandmother. "Ivan called to say I was needed here, but he wouldn't say why. We left without even finishing our drinks."

"Please, Ms. Reynolds, take a seat," Williams said.

"You are?" Redmond asked the man who'd come in with McKenzie.

"Jack Weber, of Boston. I'm McKenzie's plus-one for the wedding. Which"—he glanced at Greg—"I'm sorry to hear is temporarily postponed."

McKenzie lowered herself slowly to the seat next to Ivan. She tugged at the hem of her dress, trying to keep it down. Jack went to the window and stood with Greg. "You okay, man?" he said in a low voice.

"Not really. Not much I can do about it, though."

"To continue," Williams said. "Ms. Reynolds, we were discussing the results of the autopsy on your father. The pathologist has sent samples to the lab for further analysis, but as a preliminary observation, he believes a substantial amount of digoxin was given to Mr. Reynolds which aggravated his already serious heart condition."

"Digoxin? What's that?" Dave asked.

"Heart medication," Sophia said. "Ralph was taking it regularly. It's possible he misjudged the dose."

"It's also possible someone gave it to him," Regina said.

"I'm sorry," I said. "Not my place to ask questions, but what do you know about this drug, Detective? Can one take too much inadvertently?"

"Unlikely," Redmond said. "The amount needed to kill, in one go, would be substantially more than a regular dose. It has a taste, but isn't particularly foul."

"Added to a glass of expensive whiskey," Williams said. "Yeah, if someone was paying attention they'd notice the whiskey was off. But, after consuming a substantial amount . . . people aren't always paying attention to what they're drinking."

"The autopsy revealed that Mr. Reynolds had enjoyed a considerable amount of alcohol last night," Redmond said. "Much of it had been drunk after the time you told me you went out for dinner."

No one said anything. I studied the faces of the family. Shock, incomprehension, denial. No sign of guilt. Not that I know what guilt looks like.

I wanted to ask if it was possible Ralph had deliberately consumed the excessive amount of the drug that killed him. But I held my tongue. Not in front of his family.

"In addition," Redmond added, "preliminary analysis of the bottle found in Mr. Reynolds's room indicates the substance had been added to that bottle."

Silence. Rose and I exchanged glances.

Ivan laughed. "Surely you're joking, Detectives. Sorry, but is this April Fool's Day and I haven't noticed? You can't possibly be suggesting someone murdered my father."

"That," Regina said, "appears to be precisely what they are saying."

"Pending," Jack said, "further investigation. It might turn out to have been natural causes after all. Am I correct, Detectives?"

"What are you, a lawyer?" Williams asked, his tone not entirely approving.

"A musician actually. But I can read between the lines, and in this case I have."

"Crazy," Dave said.

Redmond told us the name of the brand of whiskey found in Ralph's room and said, "Mrs. Reynolds, was your husband a regular Scotch drinker?"

"Regular," she said dryly, "might be the right word."

"Meaning?"

"He was a heavy drinker, yes. That brand you mention is considerably more expensive than he could normally afford, but . . . our son's wedding is a special occasion. Ralph did like to treat himself when he had an excuse. Any excuse. Isn't that right, Regina?"

"In this instance, my daughter-in-law is correct, Detective. Ralph enjoyed the finer things in life and he had little impulse control. He needed assistance at times with that."

I wondered what she meant, but again I kept quiet.

"When last I spoke to him, he was well on the way to a good drunk," Greg said. "I told you, Detective, I ran into him last night, out for a breath of air. What I didn't say, and I suppose I should have, is that it was obvious he was well into the sauce."

"What time was this?" Ivan asked.

"Not long after I got back from dinner with Hannah, Jenny, and Samantha. Nine thirty, ten maybe."

Lights washed the driveway as more cars arrived. Outside, doors slammed and people called to each other.

"To that end," Redmond said, "we've called in a forensics team. That should be them now. They'll go over Mr. Reynolds's room in greater detail. And, I have to inform you, your rooms also."

"Surely not!" Regina exclaimed. "The idea's preposterous."

"Do you have something to hide?" Sophia asked.

Regina's look in return was pure poison.

Sophia stood up. She held out her key. "Search all you want, Detectives."

Williams took the key. "We will."

"Look, I didn't really know Ralph," Dave said. "I've met the guy exactly once before coming here at Greg's stag. You don't need anything from me, do you?"

"What room are you in?" Redmond asked.

"Two-oh-three."

"He's sharing with me," Ivan said. "Although he's Greg's

friend, not mine. Greg, 'cause he's leaving before the rest of us, got a room to himself."

"In that case," Redmond said to Dave, "we will be searching your room."

Dave pulled a face, but he said nothing more.

"Because I'm aware it's getting late," Redmond said, "and you people have nowhere else to go tonight, we'll search your rooms first. One at a time, beginning with you, Mrs. Reynolds. I'll go up with you. If the rest of you will remain here with Detective Williams until it's your turn. First, Lily, a moment of your time."

Everyone stared at me. I stood up slowly. "Me?"

"Is there another Lily in here?" Williams asked.

I followed Redmond into the hallway. Men and women in white overalls and booties were coming into the house, lugging equipment, climbing the stairs. Farther down the hallway, the doors to the other rooms were open and curious heads peeked around corners.

I suppressed a groan. Tomorrow, the news would be all over social media. I wouldn't be surprised if some guests checked out prematurely. I've found, in other instances when the police have been interested in the goings-on at Victoria-on-Sea, that there are two groups of people: those who want to get as far away from the police investigation as possible, as soon as possible; and those who want to see everything, hear everything, and generally interfere in everything.

"I assume," Redmond said to me in a low voice, "the rooms were cleaned today and the trash taken out?"

"Yes."

"We'll have to search the garbage."

"The bins are at the back of the garage. You're in luck. Yesterday was garbage pickup so there won't be a week's worth for your people to go through."

She smiled at me. "I'll take luck where I can find it. You are also in luck, Lily, as I've decided we don't need to search your kitchen. Either of your kitchens. Therefore, you can remain open."

"That's nice to hear. Why?" It *was* nice to hear. On other occasions, I've been shut down under suspicion of poisoning a guest. If word of that gets around, it's not good for business.

I couldn't help but notice that Redmond had said, "I've decided," and she seemed to be issuing the orders, while Williams, technically her superior, went along with it. A change in the balance of power, perhaps. Such was not unwelcome. I'd thought before that Chuck Williams was too inclined to cut corners, too quick to take the easy way out.

"If something was added to Mr. Reynolds's drink, it was in the bottle he, or someone in his party, brought with them. It did not originate in your supplies. It's getting late. We can lock up behind us when we're finished here. You and your grandmother can retire. Or, I should say, you can call Bernie and consult with her."

"Something like that. You know Rose won't go to bed while the police are poking around her house."

"I know. Thought I'd make the suggestion anyway."

"One thing I should mention. You've probably thought of it, but . . ."

"Never assume I've thought of anything at all. What?"

"The house isn't locked during the day. Even at night, guests have keys to the main door so they can come in after Rose has gone to bed. Keys can be copied."

"Meaning someone, not in the family, might be responsible for what happened to Mr. Reynolds."

"Yes."

"I have considered that," she said. "The Reynoldses are not from around here, but they have a great many friends and extended family staying in the area for this wedding.

Friends, family. Enemies? It's possible. Anything is possible. Earlier, I asked Sophia Reynolds and Jenny Hill to provide me with a copy of their guest lists. It amounts to a heck of a lot of people, not to mention it was no doubt common knowledge where the wedding was being held, so anyone with ill intent could have followed him here. I'll be in touch with the police in their town and the surrounding area, to find out if Ralph Reynolds has come to their attention on previous occasions. As well as Boston, where his family's company has their offices. As for now, the immediate family has to be my focus. The other guests staying here have been asked if they saw anyone in the house who shouldn't have been here. It's a hard question—considering they don't know who's a fellow guest and who wandered in off the street and found an unlocked door."

"One other thing," I said. "I'm sure you've considered that it's possible he did it himself."

"It's a possibility, yes."

"The missing glass might put paid to that theory. If someone joined Ralph for a drink that night and slipped something into the bottle, they took their glass with them."

"An officer spoke to your housekeeper. She says she checks the refreshment tray every day and if there had not been two glasses, she would have noticed and supplied clean ones. As you pointed out, glasses and the like tend to wander in places like this." She grinned. "Sometimes even in places like my own apartment. And that's without trying to cover up a crime."

"Are you ready for me?" Sophia came into the hallway. She didn't look, I thought, overly nervous. The police would find nothing incriminating in her room. Whether that was because nothing was to be found, or she'd earlier disposed of it, would be up to the detectives to find out.

"Call me if you need anything, Detective," I said.

"Thank you, Lily."

"There's something I should tell you, Detective," I heard Sophia say as they headed for the stairs. "I didn't like to say, not in front of my son . . ."

"Say what?" Redmond asked.

I stopped walking and pretended to be wiping a speck of dust off a picture frame with the hem of my shirt.

"Jenny Hill," Sophia said. "Greg's fiancée's mother, she and my husband had what you might call a history."

"What sort of history?"

"They were in a relationship at one time. Engaged to be married, in fact. The wedding never happened and they each went on to marry other people. In Ralph's case—me. I only mention it because Jenny's husband died of a heart attack. Very sudden it was. He had no history of heart problems, and he was only in his forties. At the time people said his death was . . . suspicious."

Redmond let Sophia proceed her up the stairs, and I heard no more.

# Chapter 12

Nine thirty on the morning following the searching of the Reynolds family's rooms at Victoria-on-Sea found Bernie and me sitting on my porch watching the bay come to life. Nothing had been found. That is to say, nothing had been found that necessitated being rushed to the lab or an evidence locker under full lights and sirens, and no grim-faced (or weeping) suspect had been marched out of the house in handcuffs.

One at a time, the Reynoldses, as well as Dave, were taken to their rooms to watch their possessions being searched. The forensics people then did what they had to do in what had been Ralph's room.

Finally, in the early hours of the morning, the police and all their equipment departed. Jack left, Dave and the family turned in, and the lights in the other guests' rooms were finally switched off.

"Detective Williams told me I can have room two-oh-one cleaned tomorrow and open it to guests," Rose had said as I walked with her to her rooms, while Robbie ran on ahead. "A great relief for my reservations book, as young Greg has asked if he can stay on until his father's remains can be taken home. I do believe it's time to put our investigators' hats on, love."

"Please, no," I said. "This time, whatever happened to our guest has nothing to do with us. Neither you nor I, thank heavens, are under suspicion. Let the police handle it."

"As they so capably have done on those other occasions."

"They would have arrived at the solution eventually. I think. Redmond would have. I think."

I repeated all that to Bernie as we sipped our coffee and watched Éclair checking under bushes and around fence posts. I emphasized, to my friend as I had to my grandmother, this had nothing to do with us, and I intended to stay well out of it.

"Agreed," Bernie said.

"What?" I slapped the side of my head. "I must be losing my hearing. I thought you agreed with me."

"I did, Lily. For once. We're not involved. We don't want to be involved. Rose isn't suspected. No one's suggesting you keep a supply of deadly poison in your tearoom. You have a business to run. I have a book to write. Matt's offered to give me a hand getting over some tricky points, but . . ."

"But . . . ?" I prompted.

"But . . . I don't want that sort of help. I like him, okay, Lily, but . . ."

"More buts."

"Yeah. I like him, but I don't see it turning real serious. On his part, either. I don't want his help with my book and then me owing him when . . . if . . . we break up."

"I've helped you with it."

"Totally different. You and I will never break up." She gave me that Warrior Princess grin. "You'd never dare."

"Got that one right."

"Besides, you're not a professional writer like Matt is.

Aside from anything else, I worry he'd start to take over. Even if he didn't mean it. He's, like, a mega-bestseller and I'm . . . not. Do you know what I mean?"

"I think I do."

"Back to the case. Like you told Amy Redmond last night, the B & B isn't exactly a secure facility. Anyone could have walked in, found Ralph's room, and put something in that bottle."

"The doors lock automatically when they're closed."

"Maybe he didn't shut it fully. Maybe he was in the bathroom and didn't have the latch on and someone slipped in? That might be—"

"We're not investigating."

"Yeah, right. Except—that gives me an idea. Remember what happened with the doll gift at the shower? It created a heck of a commotion, right? Do you suppose someone set it up so they could nip up to the house and—"

"I suppose nothing, Bernie. And neither do you."

"Okay. Right. Back to the beginning of my train of thought. This is no locked-room mystery. Anyone could have come into the house unnoticed. Heck, Ralph might have unwittingly brought the tampered bottle with him. Did you think to ask—?"

I stood up and called to Éclair. "Time for work. Time for you to go."

"Go where?"

"Home, Bernadette. To work on your book."

"Oh, that. You're right." She drained the last of her coffee.

I put Éclair into the house, assured her someone would be around later to give her a walk, and walked with Bernie to her bicycle.

Simon was in the rose garden, deadheading the plants and selecting the most perfect flowers to decorate the tables in the tearoom. We gave him a wave and he waved back.

"Might rain later," Bernie said. "So the weather report said."

"I hope it holds off until closing. The plants need the rain, but we need the patio space." In a soft rain with little wind, people could still sit under the awning and the umbrellas and enjoy the garden. But not in the face of weather more severe.

"I don't suppose you know what Ralph Reynolds did for a living?" Bernie asked me.

"He worked at his family company. Reynolds Tools, I think's the name. I don't know what he did there, though. I suppose they make tools, of some sort, or did at one time. Not exactly a field I know anything about. Why do you ask?"

"If I have some free time later, like when I'm on a break, I might look him up. Not that I'm investigating. Just out of curiosity." She gave me a broad wink. "And to keep my hand in."

I didn't even bother to groan. Bernie had majored in business in college, with a minor in computer science. As a forensic accountant, she knew how to parse a set of books down to the finest details, searching for that one supposedly insignificant line that would put a criminal away for a long time. I suspected that, as a computer buff, she also knew how to go places she wasn't supposed to go.

That diligence, and skill, had helped us in the past. But, considering we were not getting involved in the Reynolds case, I didn't want to know anything more about Ralph and his family than I already did. "If you find something," I said, "don't tell me."

The rain held off, and we had a busy day at Tea by the Sea. At three o'clock, I was doing standing yoga stretches in the kitchen, trying to work some niggling kinks out of my back.

"Cream tea for two," Cheryl said. "You okay there, Lily?"

"Just stiff. I got next to no sleep last night." As we'd prepared for opening, I told Marybeth and Cheryl the Reynolds case was now a murder investigation. They already knew—they'd seen it on social media.

Cheryl took down a tin of our special lavender Earl Grey tea and scooped out the mixture of dark leaves, rich and fragrant with oil of bergamot and the slightest hint of lavender. "The cream tea's for them."

"For who? I mean, for whom?"

"The engaged couple. He asked what tea went best with true love. I made up something on the spur of the moment, and this tea seemed the most suitable." She sighed. "Isn't that sweet? I remember when my Jim used to talk to me like that."

"TMI, Mom." Marybeth carried in a load of used dishes. One lonely salmon sandwich remained on the three-tiered tray. Everyone too polite, I assumed, to take it. I had no such hesitation and popped it into my mouth. In the restaurant business you take your meals when you can get them.

"Too much information," Marybeth continued. "I don't want to know anything about you and Dad's love life."

Cheryl winked at me. "Come to think of it, I don't think Jim ever talked to me like that. When he proposed he said something along the lines of 'Off-season's coming, and business will be slow. Good time to get married.'"

Marybeth rolled her eyes at me.

"Which only proves, honey," Cheryl said, "you don't need romance to be happy. Not if you have love."

"Whatever."

I said nothing. I knew Marybeth wasn't happy in her own marriage. She'd married too young, to her high-school boyfriend, and had children too soon. She thought she'd missed out on too much in life—adventure, romance, travel. I'd once told her she'd get the child-rearing part of life out of the way early and then have decades free to enjoy herself while those who had children later in life were buried under surly teenagers and college tuition fees. I don't think she entirely believed me.

The rooster timer dinged and I took a sheet of warm, fragrant scones out of the oven. "Greg and Hannah are in luck. Nothing fresher than these ones. How do they seem, Cheryl? Aside from being sickeningly romantic?"

"Okay," she said. "I won't say they're happy, but they're not crying, either."

On sudden impulse I took off my apron and hairnet. "I'll take this out to them. Say hi. I feel bad for them. First that awful scene at the shower and then his dad dying."

In a normal day, I rarely—if ever—get out of the kitchen to have a chance to see the fruit of my labors being enjoyed. I felt myself smiling as I walked through the main dining room, carrying my tray of fresh, warm scones, clotted cream, butter, and Edna-made strawberry jam. All around me, people were eating and drinking, laughing and chatting. I'd decorated the rooms in my restaurant as though they were a drawing room in an English castle or country home. The main dining room featured pale peach walls hung with paintings of gentle pastoral scenes or scarlet-clad riders at the hunt, a rich red carpet, chairs upholstered in peach and sage-green damask, wooden tables with starched and ironed white cloths. The smaller tables featured a single rose in a crystal vase, the larger ones a full, lush, Simon-arranged bouquet. A chest of drawers painted a crisp fresh white displayed the items we offered for sale: teacups and sets of fine china, tins of good quality loose-leaf tea, assorted locally made jams and preserves.

"You don't want that last tart, do you, dear?" a man asked a woman.

"Actually, honey," she replied. "I do. Arm wrestle you for it?"

I went through the vestibule, past the welcome desk, and out into the garden. The patio was full, all the tables occupied. I spotted Greg and Hannah in a far corner, at a table for two tucked against the flower-filled low stone wall. They were holding hands across the table, staring into each other's eyes. I felt momentarily uncomfortable, not wanting to interrupt them. Hannah looked up and saw me and gave me a smile, so I approached. "Cream tea?"

They took their hands back to make space on the table.

"Great. Thanks," Greg said. "Oh, Lily. Hi."

"Hi. Sorry to interrupt, but I wanted to say hello. I hope everything was satisfactory at your shower, Hannah. Until . . . the way it ended."

"The way it ended was not your fault," she said. "Everything was marvelous. Even Sophia managed to keep a lid on it." Her eyes widened. "She did pay you, didn't she? My mom wanted to contribute, but Sophia insisted on everything being bigger and more expensive than we wanted to pay so—"

"Yes," I said quickly. "She paid. And she tipped generously as well." I arranged the dishes on the table. Kindhearted Cheryl had given the couple one of our best tea services: plain ivory china with a thick gold trim, from the aptly named Royal Doulton Romance collection.

Greg snorted. "That doesn't sound like my mom." He nodded to the teapot. "Would you like to do the honors, Lily?"

"I'd be happy to." I lifted the pot and poured. The scent of tea and lavender rose into the air. "What happens now, if you don't mind my asking? Have you been able to reschedule your wedding?"

"Too early for that," Greg said. "We need to find out what's happening with Dad first. What a mess."

"I woke up this morning," Hannah said, "so dreadfully excited. My wedding day. The day I've been looking forward to for so long." Her face fell. "And then, I remembered."

Greg held his hand out, palm up, and she put hers into it. He curled her fingers into his. "A wedding," he said, "is nothing but an expensive formality. A reason for us to party and our family and friends to party with us. In our case, it's also a reason for my parents to spend a lot of money they can't really afford to show off to their friends. It's not like we missed our falling-in-love day, or the day we met. Now that would have been a tragedy indeed."

Hannah's face lit up. I walked away. They'd be okay, I thought. I only hoped what had happened wouldn't hang over their heads for much longer.

"Table of four just arrived, Lily," Cheryl said. "No reservation. Hope it's okay that I seated them."

I took a sheet of mini vanilla cupcakes out of the oven. "The sign says we're open until five." It was ten to five now. "What are they having?"

"Royal tea."

"Too bad. That means they'll be inclined to linger."

"Can't be helped. Several tables are still occupied. Everyone seems to be in the mood to linger today."

"Not me," I said. "I've got a stitch in my back that's been bothering me all day. I want to go for a short walk in the garden, loosen things up a bit. Can you manage?"

"Of course." She began assembling the three-tiered food stands.

I slipped out the kitchen door. In the shade of the big

old oak tree, I gave my back a good long stretch. I keep telling myself I need to get back to yoga class. But, with converting a crumbling stone cottage into a pleasant tearoom, setting up the tearoom, and now the season in full swing, yoga had not been at the top of my priority list. I took a deep breath of the fresh salty air and walked slowly around the side of the building.

"I suppose you're happy now," Greg Reynolds said, his voice sharp with anger, the words bitten off.

"Happy? Your father is dead. No, that does not make me happy."

I stopped in my tracks. The voices were coming from the edge of the driveway, near the gate to the tearoom patio.

"I'm not talking about Dad. No matter how awful you were to each other. I mean my wedding being canceled."

"Canceled, or postponed?"

"You know what I mean."

Sophia sighed. "No, I am not happy. Certainly not considering the circumstances. It's no secret I don't believe Hannah's the right woman for you, but you clearly love her, and she you, and so you have my blessing. As I believe I've told you on more than one occasion."

I peeked around the corner. Greg's car was parked at the side of the driveway. Sophia was in beige slacks, a summer-weight sweater, and sturdy walking shoes. She must have gone for a walk and her son came across her as he was returning to the B & B after dropping off Hannah.

"Yeah. Okay, Mom," he said. "I'm sorry. It's just . . ."

"It's hard for us all, Greg. Harder still with the police poking around, implying someone killed your father. The very idea's preposterous. I won't say everyone loved your father—"

"Because that wouldn't be true, would it, Mother?"

Slowly, I edged backward, trying to be perfectly quiet.

This was absolutely none of my business, and I had no desire to be caught eavesdropping.

"Thanks," I called when I was several feet from the corner. "I'll be back soon." I retraced my steps, this time walking as nosily as I could.

Greg and his mother smiled at me when I came around the corner. "Lovely day," Sophia said. "I was enjoying a pleasant walk. You're lucky to live in such a beautiful place."

"Thank you. We like it a great deal." I silently repeated my vow not to get involved in this family's problems as I passed them.

# Chapter 13

My vow to not get involved didn't last long.

I spent a couple of productive hours after the tearoom closed getting baking done for the following day. Satisfied I had enough to get us started, I cleaned the kitchen, locked up, and was strolling up the driveway by seven o'clock, looking forward to a walk with Éclair followed by a quick supper in front of the TV, a nice relaxing bath, and an early night when, once again, a car bearing the two detectives passed me, followed by a cruiser.

*Dare I hope they'd come to tell the family a suspect had been arrested?* A suspect who had nothing to do with Victoria-on-Sea?

Unlikely, not if the detectives had brought uniforms with them.

Thoughts of a pleasant do-nothing evening shattered, I broke into a jog and reached the frontmost car as the doors were opening. "Evening, Detectives. What brings you here? Again."

"Questions, Lily," Amy Redmond replied. "Always questions."

"Until we're satisfied." Chuck Williams glanced around at the scattering of cars in the guest parking area. I didn't recognize most of them.

"It's early still," I said. "Everyone's likely out at dinner."

"I called Ivan Reynolds a short while ago," Williams said. "His mother and grandmother didn't feel like making the effort to go out for dinner tonight so they ordered takeout. The gang's all here."

"Chuck," Redmond said, "why don't you round up whoever you can find. I want to talk to Lily for a moment."

He grunted in acknowledgment and climbed the steps to ring the bell. Officers Bland and Kowalski followed. The door opened so quickly it was obvious Rose had seen them coming and had been lying in wait. "Not you again," she said. "I'm considering petitioning the state to have the town line of North Augusta moved slightly north. I'm sure the police in the next town over are more accommodating of an elderly lady's need for privacy and rest."

"Huh?" Williams said. "What does that mean?"

Rose sighed. "Do come in, Inspector." She saw me watching and threw me a questioning look. I shrugged in response.

"I'm afraid the kitchens are closed for the evening," Rose said as she stepped aside to let her uninvited guests into her house. "So you needn't stay long."

"What's happening now?" I asked Redmond when the front door to the house had closed.

"As we said, questions and more questions. This one, I want to ask of you, Lily. You're observant."

"I like to think so," I said modestly.

"Tell me what you observed, if anything, between Jenny Hill and Ralph Reynolds."

"What I observed? Nothing. She and her daughter aren't staying here. Thursday afternoon, at the shower, the men came late, after tea, in time for the gift opening . . ." My voice trailed off. Redmond noticed. "And?" she prompted.

"Okay. I might have observed that Jenny and Ralph weren't exactly friendly toward each other. I have to point out Jenny and Sophia weren't besties either. Although, in my opinion, the animosity came from Sophia and Ralph only. Jenny, on her part, tried to be nice. What does it matter?"

"Everything matters," Redmond said, "in building a case. Anything specific about this apparent failure to get along?"

"It was a bridal shower, meaning the bride and her mother should be the stars of the show. Sophia acted as though she was the one in charge. Which, I guess she was, as she paid for it. Not Jenny. Maybe Jenny resented watching Sophia throwing her money around. I can't say. It's obvious the Reynoldses are better off financially than Jenny and Hannah. Although, as I said, Jenny was the one attempting to be nice. Not Sophia and Ralph. Why are you asking about Jenny?"

"Someone told us Jenny had been heard making threats against Ralph Reynolds."

"Who told you this?"

Redmond hesitated, obviously debating how much to tell me. Then she said, "Dave Farland, Greg's best man, claims to have heard the two of them arguing shortly before guests arrived. Jenny was furious, accusing Ralph of attempting to sabotage her daughter's happiness. She, according to Dave, threatened him."

I'd earlier told the detective what I'd overheard at the edge of the bluff between Ralph and his son. Yes, Ralph had been intent on preventing the marriage. If Jenny knew that, and she likely did, how far would she go to stop his interference? I decided it didn't matter one whit what

Ralph or Sophia, or even Jenny, wanted. Greg and Hannah intended for the marriage to go ahead. "What of it, Detective? For heaven's sake, this isn't the nineteenth century. What's Ralph going to do, threaten to banish his son and his bride to the colonies? Send him to a monastery?"

"Personal disagreements never have to make sense, Lily. Not to outsiders, although they can make perfect sense to the participants."

"You can't accept hearsay."

"I can, and will, accept anything I want. Hearsay isn't valid in court, but we use it all the time in putting together a case."

"Surely, it means nothing. We all get mad and make idle threats. Well, most of us do, at any rate . . ." My voice trailed off.

"That's true. But when someone threatens to stop someone else, one way or another, and I quote, and the second someone ends up dead less than twenty-four hours later, I take it seriously, yes."

I thought of the figure I'd seen slip out of the shadows to follow Ralph, after an angry Greg had stormed off. Had Jenny overheard Ralph trying to bribe his son into abandoning Hannah at the altar and decided to take action? I answered my own question with a firm no. Greg had turned his father's offer down. And forcefully at that, not wavering for a moment. "Okay. Okay. Say I buy that. I don't, but Jenny and Ralph had an argument about the wedding. It would appear that Ralph accepted a drink from the person who meant him harm. He wouldn't have invited Jenny up to his room for a drink a few hours later, would he?"

She studied my face. "I'm not coming to any definite conclusions, but it's also been brought to my attention that Ralph and Jenny were involved at one time. In a romantic relationship. From what I understand, they were engaged, the wedding date was set, the arrangements made. And then she left him to marry another man. Maxwell Hill, Hannah's father. Ralph didn't take being dumped almost at the altar well, but he married Sophia shortly after that. Admittedly, that all happened a long time ago."

I nodded. I'd heard the same.

"His marriage to Sophia, according to his mother for what that's worth, was never a happy one. His children haven't come straight out and said the same, but they obviously agree."

"So?"

"So, perhaps, if he still had feelings for Jenny, he invited her up to his room. For old times' sake. And, I have to ask, did she still have feelings for him? But feelings in the opposite direction? Max Hill worked at Ralph Reynolds's company. He quit, or was fired depending on who you ask, after Jenny broke her engagement to Ralph. He'd been an up-and-coming business executive. He ended up managing the small-town branch of a national hardware chain. He died ten years later. Does Jenny hold Ralph responsible for that?"

For no other reason than because I liked her, I felt compelled to defend Hannah's mother. "That's all pure speculation. You can't accuse a woman of murder based on that."

She raised one perfectly sculpted eyebrow. "I can't? We'll see. I believe I've kept everyone waiting long enough."

I followed her into the house. The two uniformed officers stood beside the open doors leading to the dining room. Karen, the bridge player with the big glasses, huddled beneath the staircase, anxious to eavesdrop on the drama, but trying not to be noticed and ordered to leave.

She gave us a weak grin and held up her phone, pretending she'd come out into the hall to make a call.

Redmond and I went into the dining room. As well as the Reynolds family, with the exception of McKenzie, Hannah and her mother were there, as was Samantha, the bridesmaid. Dave was nowhere to be seen. Take-out containers from the local Chinese restaurant, barely touched, were piled on the serving table next to the kitchen. Disposable plates, plastic cutlery, and crumpled paper napkins covered several tables, along with bottles of wine and beer and glasses taken from the bedrooms. Unlike the food, the wine and beer had been touched. And quite heavily judging by the level in the bottles and the number of cans scattered around the room.

I stifled a groan. Highly unlikely Sophia would encourage her family to clean up after themselves before turning in. Edna would not be happy to arrive at work tomorrow to see the dining room in this state.

Detective Williams was helping himself to an egg roll as we came in. He dipped it into a small container of lurid orange sauce. Rose had taken a seat at a table for two by the French doors. Robbie sat on her lap, ears up, tail twitching slowly. She stroked him methodically. Two sets of eyes watched events with much interest.

"So pleased you could join us, Detective Redmond," Regina said. "Now, can we get this over with as quickly as possible? It is getting late. Your partner said we were to wait for you. I told him—"

Williams swallowed a huge bite of egg roll and wiped sauce off his face with a paper napkin.

"I'm here now," Redmond said.

Undeterred by the detective's sharp tone, Regina continued, "I told him a lady of my age needs her beauty rest."

Rose grinned to herself. That's pretty much what she'd said.

"As if that's going to help," Sophia said under her breath. She might have meant the comment to pass unnoticed, but Regina's face tightened.

"Enough of that." Greg pushed his unfinished plate to one side. "We're all here now, get on with it."

I thought it significant that Greg and Hannah had taken a table for four, with Jenny and Samantha, rather than joining the rest of his family around the big table.

Ivan got up and helped himself to a beer. Regina waved her empty glass at him. "While you're at the bar, dear . . ."

"That might not be wise. We need to keep our wits about us," Sophia said.

"My wits, thank you, Sophia, are always about me," her mother-in-law replied.

I don't know much about police methods, although I have learned a few things since coming to North Augusta, but I suspect there's not much the cops like better than a group of suspects freely airing their dirty laundry and revealing minor (and major) resentments in front of them.

Ivan ducked his head and filled his grandmother's glass. He handed it to her without looking at his mother. Regina, however, gave Sophia a look of triumph.

Sophia looked away.

"Where's Dave Farland?" Amy Redmond asked.

"He went into town with McKenzie and Jack earlier. They're going to have dinner and hit a few bars. He says he's getting tired of hanging around here," Greg said.

"He's not the only one," Ivan mumbled.

"Why has he not left then?" Williams asked. "Gone home."

"He's being supportive," Greg said. "Which is his role as my best man. Besides, he and I work together, so I know he doesn't have any jobs to hurry to get back for. At the moment, I mean." A quick, nervous glance at his grandmother. "Contracts are starting to come in."

"As you are aware," Williams said, "I regard the death of Mr. Ralph Reynolds to be suspicious. I have further questions for you all. "Did anyone of you—?"

"We'll speak to you one at a time," Redmond said. "If we can use your drawing room once again, Mrs. Campbell?"

"Certainly," Rose said.

Redmond half turned and nodded to Bland, telling her to keep an eye on the people in the dining room.

"Okay," Williams said. "Good plan. Let's start with—"

"Mrs. Hill," Redmond said. "If you'll come with us, please."

Jenny threw a worried glance at Hannah as she said, "Me? I don't know anything. I wasn't even here when . . . when Ralph died."

"It's okay, Jenny," Greg said to her with a smile. "They'll be talking to us all in turn. It's routine procedure."

Hannah gripped her mother's hand in encouragement and Jenny stood up slowly. "If I can help, I will."

I threw a look at Rose. She tilted her head to one side, in the direction of the hallway, sending me a message. Reluctantly, I gave her a small nod. "Why don't I put the coffee-pot on?" I said.

"Good idea," Williams said. "This might take a while. Some cookies would be nice, too."

Rather than going directly into the kitchen, I slipped into the hallway in the wake of the detectives and Jenny Hill. Bland gave me a nod and a smile as I passed and said, "Coffee'd be good, thanks."

I moved to close the dining room door, but Bland put out a hand. "It's okay the way it is." From the dining room entrance, she'd be able to see into the hallway and watch the door of the drawing room in case she was needed.

Karen still hovered under the stairs, her eyes as bright

and wide with interest as Robbie's had been. "Can we help you?" Detective Redmond said in a cool voice.

"No. I'm just . . . uh . . . looking for a cup of hot tea. Oh, there you are, Miss . . . I'm sorry, but my stomach's quite upset. My friends went out to dinner, but I didn't feel well. I'd like some herbal tea. Do you have any?"

"Packets of tea should have been refreshed in your room this morning," I said. "Were they not?"

"Uh . . . I didn't check. Sorry. Sheila, that's my room-mate, might have used them all. She likes her tea."

"If you wouldn't mind checking first," I said. "Then you can let me know if you need any, and I'll see if I can find something."

She scurried off down the hallway to her room. Redmond watched her go, a look of disapproval on her face. "Crime-scene groupie," she muttered.

They went into the drawing room along with Officer Kowalski. He shut the door.

I was pretty sure Rose had been signaling to me to slip into the secret room and listen to the goings-on in the drawing room. Not only did I not want to—part of that not-wanting-to-get-involved thing—I couldn't.

If Officer Bland half turned and glanced into the hall-way she'd see me creeping into the linen closet. And, more to the point, not coming out bearing fresh linens. Plus, I couldn't be sure crime-scene groupie Karen wouldn't sneak out of her room when she thought the coast was clear in an attempt to listen to the various conversations swirling around.

Nothing I could do but make coffee and put the kettle on. I didn't keep any cookies in the B & B kitchen, and I didn't want to use the muffins and coffee cake I'd pre-pared for tomorrow. Besides, plenty of take-out food was still left. Not to mention the wine and beer.

Coffee on and kettle filled, I slipped out the rear door and climbed the three steps to ground level. Outside, all was dark and quiet. The beam of light thrown by the lamp over the door shone on the cliffside pathway. On the far side of the fence protecting walkers from the drop, the waters of the bay murmured softly as the tide came in.

The dining room drapes were open, and I could see everything clearly as I hurried past. Greg and Hannah had pulled their chairs closer together and clasped hands on the top of the table. Samantha, the bridesmaid, had gotten up and was talking to Ivan by the serving table. The Reynolds family sat in silence.

Regina happened to look up as I slipped past. She saw me, but did not acknowledge me. Just another servant, going about her tasks.

I hurried to the cottage and called to Éclair. She needed a walk, even if it was only as far as the big house. It was unlikely anyone would need me, other than to make the coffee, but I wanted to be nearby if anything happened.

My dog also needed her dinner, so I quickly opened a can of dog food and served it up. While Éclair dined, I texted Bernie: **Cops back. More questions for everyone. No other news**

Bernie's reply was instantaneous: **Having drinks with Matt. Need us?**

Me: **I don't even need me. Just providing info**

Bernie: **[Thumbs-up emoji]**

Finally Éclair finished her meal and looked up at me with a hopeful smile. "You're in luck," I said, taking the leash off its hook. "You can come with me."

She yipped and ran for the door.

Outside, the dog sniffed at the base of bushes and fence posts, all ready to settle in for a long leisurely walk. "Sorry, girl, but this is a short one," I said. "I have to get back." I snapped my fingers, called her name, and she, reluctantly, tore herself away from the important business of gathering the news of the neighborhood.

When I passed the dining room windows a second time, some people had moved position. Jenny was back, sitting at the table with Hannah, Greg, and Samantha. Her head was down, her shoulders hunched. Her daughter rubbed her back, while Greg kept his hand on Hannah's arm. Jenny looked up as I passed and we exchanged glances. Her large, dark eyes brimmed with worry. I gave her what I intended to be an encouraging smile. She turned away, not looking encouraged.

Sophia's chair was empty. Ivan was piling his plate with another round of Chinese food. Most of the rest of them had pushed half-eaten plates aside.

In the kitchen, the coffee was ready and the kettle hot. I made tea in an old-fashioned Brown Betty pot and poured the fresh coffee into a carafe. Cups and mugs were kept in the drawers of the serving table in the dining room. I put the drinks on a tray along with cream, milk, and sugar and carried the lot out. Again, taking the route via the hallway rather than the door leading directly into the dining room. I didn't order Éclair to stay and she trotted after me.

At the sight of us, Karen stepped out from the door to her room. "There you are. I was coming to look for you. I found those tea packets, like you said. A chamomile will do me good, I'm sure." She spoke to me, but her eyes wandered to the dining room. She attempted to crane her neck to see around the corner. From the drawing room came the sound of low voices, but I couldn't make out any words.

At that moment the front door opened to admit the three remaining women of the bridge group.

"What's going on?" Marie asked. "There's a police car outside."

"Have they come to arrest the murderer?" Laurie asked, the excitement in her voice palpable.

"I don't know," I said.

"A coffee'd be nice." Marie threw a pointed look at the tray I was carrying.

"Not for me, thanks," Laurie said, even though I hadn't offered. "I can't have caffeine after noon or I'll never sleep."

Victoria-on-Sea isn't a full-service hotel, and I didn't want anyone mistaking it for such. "This is for the police," I said. "You should have everything you need in your room."

The bridge players peered into the dining room. I wasn't surprised they were interested. The scene was like something out of a movie. The tall, young, stern-faced cop, standing at the doorway, back straight, feet apart, hands on hips, silently watching everyone and everything. The elegant formal dining room. The dark night outside; the sound of the sea in the distance. The feuding families, gathered in their own private worlds, all of them trying to hide how nervous they were. Voices, either low in questioning or sharp in reply, coming from behind a closed door. My grandmother, black cat alert on her lap, long fingers moving through the fur, taking it all in without appearing to be doing so. Like an elderly English version of Benoit Blanc.

Only one of the bridge players had no interest in the official goings-on. She'd spotted Éclair the moment she came in, and immediately dropped to her haunches and held out her hand. "Aren't you a darling. Are you a little girl or a boy?"

"Girl," I said. "Her name's Éclair."

The woman laughed. "Perfect. I could gobble you right up. Yes, I could. Munch munch munch."

Éclair graciously allowed herself to be scratched.

"Trust Sheila," Laurie said. "She never met a dog she didn't want to take home with her."

"Got that one right," Sheila said.

A shout came from behind the drawing-room door. Instinctively we all looked toward it. It appeared to be Ivan's turn under the bright lights, and he wasn't bothering to keep his voice down.

Marie winced and smoothly changed the subject. "How are you feeling, Karen? Tummy better?"

"Much better, thanks." Karen tore her attention away from the goings-on in the dining room. "Did you have a pleasant dinner?"

"It was great. Nice place close to the pier." Marie indicated the closed door to the drawing room. "We planned to watch a movie together. Shall I assume that's not in the cards tonight?"

"Sorry," I said. "The police have taken that room for their own use."

"I'd love to know what's happening, but it really is none of our business, right, girls?" she said. "The night is still young, although we are not. How about a couple of hands of bridge before turning in?"

Even Éclair's attention couldn't distract Shelia from the sound of that. She pushed herself to her feet with a soft grunt. "I'm in."

"I'd rather not," Karen began. "I'm still feeling a bit queasy. Plus I'm at an exciting part in my book and—"

"You can't bow out," Sheila said. "You just said you were feeling better, and a proper game of bridge needs four people."

"Probably not tonight," I said. "But another time if you need a fourth, my grandmother's a good player."

"She told us that. I'd love to have her join us one night." Sheila linked her arm through Karen's and led her away. "Our room, ten minutes. Although I'd just as soon not partner with you tonight. You've been off your game."

"Stomach bug setting in," Karen said.

"Yuk," Laurie said.

I took the tray into the dining room.

# Chapter 14

One by one the Reynoldses and their friends and frenemies were interviewed by Detectives Redmond and Williams, and then allowed to return to the dining room. Ivan did his best to demolish the leftover Chinese food, but no one else ate much of anything. Other than Regina, who made good use of the wine, despite (or perhaps because of) Sophia's disapproving glare.

When Greg's interview was over, he returned white-faced and tight-lipped. He gave Hannah a feeble smile and suggested he drive her and her mother to their hotel. They could come back for their car in the morning.

"Sorry," Bland said. "The detectives' instructions are that no one's to leave until they're finished."

"I'm not proposing we flee the state," Greg snapped. "Mrs. Hill is clearly tired and she needs to rest."

"Sorry," Bland repeated. "The detectives might have follow-up questions."

"We're all tired," Sophia said. "Why, poor Regina is positively exhausted. She's aged ten years since this all began. But we'll do whatever we have to do to help the police. I would have thought you'd want to do so also, Gregory."

Jenny laid a hand on Greg's arm. "It's all right, dear. I'm fine."

Éclair visited everyone in turn, hoping for scratches and admiration. Only Hannah and Samantha obliged, and eventually the dog took a place on the carpet next to Rose's chair. Robbie bristled at the new arrival, but didn't object further, and Éclair settled down, while keeping a watchful eye on her nemesis.

I leaned over and whispered in Rose's ear. "If you want to go to bed, I'll stay with them and make sure everything's locked up when they leave."

"Thank you, love, but no. The tension in this room is most entertaining."

"As you like, *Madame Blanc*," I said.

She began to raise one eyebrow in question before she got the reference. She grinned. "I rather like that."

I amused myself by cleaning up the dining room. "Does anyone want to take the rest of this food with them?"

"Leave it," Ivan said. "No better breakfast than leftover Chinese food."

"We have other guests staying here," I said. "I need to set this room to rights."

Hannah stood up. "Let me help you, Lily. We've made such a mess. I'm sorry."

"I can manage," I said.

"Please, I'd like to."

The room was once again clean and tidy, properly set for breakfast, when Redmond and Williams came into the dining room. They'd spoken to Samantha last, but when her interview was finished they hadn't come with her. I'd strained my ears as best I could whenever I happened to stroll casually past the still-closed doors to the drawing room on my way to the kitchen, but I could hear nothing other than the low murmur of voices.

Redmond said something to Bland and she gave the detective a sharp nod of acknowledgment. The three police officers crossed the room, every eye on them, and stopped in front of Jenny Hill.

Hannah sucked in a breath and threw a terrified look at Greg. Greg rose slowly to his feet.

"Jennifer Hill," Williams said. "We'd like you to accompany us to the station, please."

"What's this about?" Greg said. "If you have more questions, surely they can wait until a decent hour."

"Please," Detective Redmond said.

"Are you saying she killed my son?" Regina asked.

"We are saying nothing," Redmond said. "We have further questions for Mrs. Hill that can be asked at the police station."

Jenny's eyes were wide with fear. "I . . . I don't know . . ."

Hannah leapt to her feet with such force her chair fell over. "What did you say to them, you miserable old bat?" She thrust a finger toward Sophia. "You've always had it in for us."

"Hold on there," Ivan said.

"You, you're no better than the rest of them. Greedy, grasping bunch of—"

"Please, Hannah," Greg said.

"They're a pack of liars," Hannah yelled at the police. "Every last one of them. The only Reynolds with an ounce of decency is Greg. You can't believe anything they say. Any of them."

Bland laid her hand on Jenny's arm. Hannah swatted at it.

"Careful there, miss," Williams said.

Greg put his arms around Hannah and edged her away. A weeping Samantha got to her feet and wrapped them both in a hug.

I looked around the room, studying them all. The slightest of smiles touched the edges of Sophia's mouth. Ivan's face was impassive. Regina shook her head. Rose's eyes were wide with shock. Both Éclair and Robbie felt the tension in the room, and had risen to their feet.

"Does Mrs. Hill need a lawyer?" Greg asked.

"That is up to her, of course," Redmond replied. "But it might be advisable."

"Can we come with you, to the police station?"

"You can follow," she said. "Let's go, Mrs. Hill. Don't make this harder than it needs to be."

I was pleased that Bland didn't put handcuffs on Jenny. She gave Hannah one last, long look and then allowed the cop to lead her away. Her head was high and her steps firm. She couldn't help herself from throwing a look at Sophia as they passed. The other woman had the grace to dip her head.

"I'm calling you a cab," Greg said to Hannah. "Sam, you look after Hannah. I'm going after them, and I'll contact our family lawyer on the way."

"I want to come with you," Hannah said.

"No. Please. I'll keep you posted. Promise. Sam?"

"We'll be okay," Samantha said. "Go."

"Family lawyer?" Ivan said. "I hardly think Dad's lawyer can be asked to represent his murderer. Alleged murderer."

"Thanks for your support, bro," Greg said. "Always knew I could count on you."

"I'll call the cab," I said, pulling out my phone.

"Thanks," he said. "We'll wait on the porch." He put his arm around Hannah and together he and Samantha helped her from the room. I made the call as I followed them, conscious of the eyes of the Reynolds family on us. The taxi driver said he'd be here in ten minutes.

"If there's anything we can do . . ." I said to Greg.

"Thanks. I'm sure it's nothing. My mother, and my grandmother, tend to exaggerate sometimes."

"My mother," Hannah said fiercely, "is not a murderer. The idea's ridiculous."

"The cops will soon realize that, babe," he said.

Once again heads were popping out of doorways. A couple of guests stood at the top of the stairs, dressed in their nightwear, peering down. The bridge women clustered at the door to the room occupied by two of them. They must have been playing while listening to what was going on. They were still dressed, and Sheila held her cards in her hand.

"Can I be of assistance to anyone?" I said in a loud voice.

The people at the top of the stairs slipped away.

"No," Marie said. "We're fine. Come on, girls. I do believe I said three clubs." They also faded away.

"Ghouls," Samantha said.

"People are curious," I replied.

We stepped outside into the fresh night air. Headlights swept down the driveway, and at first I thought the taxi had been quick to arrive. But Jack was at the wheel, and McKenzie Reynolds leapt out before he brought the car to a complete stop. Dave followed her.

"What's happening now?" McKenzie yelled. "Where's Jenny going with the cops? Is everyone okay? Greg, where's Mom and Grandma? Hannah, why are you crying?"

"Shut up, McKenzie," Greg snapped. "Just go inside, will you."

"No need to take that tone with me, brother. I've a right to ask, you know." She turned to me. "You. What's going on here?"

I didn't bother to answer.

"Greg?" Dave asked.

Greg shook his head.

"Leave it, Mac," Jack said. "Let's go inside."

"But—"

"Come on. All the lights are on, so I bet some of your family are still up."

Reluctantly, McKenzie followed him inside. Dave spoke to Greg in a low voice, and Greg quickly filled him in.

"Do you need me to come with you?" Dave asked.

"Yeah, that might be an idea. Thanks."

A few minutes later another set of lights turned off the highway into our driveway. Greg helped Hannah into the taxi, Samantha ran around the car and got in the other side. Greg didn't wait for it to pull away before sprinting to his own car, Dave hot on his heels.

I went back into the house. The dining room door was open and I could hear McKenzie's piercing voice demanding to know what was going on.

I took my phone out again and went into the kitchen to make a call in private.

It rang several times before being answered. "What! What! What's happening?"

"It's Lily here."

"I know it's Lily," Bernie said. "I can see your name on the display. Do you know what time it is? I just got to bed."

"Time? It's ten after ten."

"Yeah, well I had a long day. What's up?"

"Be here tomorrow morning. Six thirty sharp. We have a case."

# Chapter 15

I'd called Bernie on the spur of the moment, but over the rest of the long night, as I tossed and turned, and Éclair snored lightly beside me, I decided it had been the right thing to do.

I liked Jenny. I liked Hannah. I tend to think of myself as anything but a romantic person. Maybe my previous relationships, the last most of all, cured me of that. But I liked the connection between Hannah and Greg. The couple were obviously truly in love, and it was no fault of theirs that their families had problems going back decades.

I couldn't think of a worse start to a marriage than the mother of one part of the couple being sent to prison for the murder of the father of the other.

Thanksgiving dinner at their house would not be a pleasant affair.

If I could help Greg and Hannah, and Jenny, in any way I could, then I would.

Not that I had the slightest idea where to start, but I was confident that Bernie would.

\*   \*   \*

"I'll start with a deep dive into Ralph Reynolds's business affairs," Bernie said as she sliced bananas. "This looks, on the surface, to be a personal killing, but if he was into shady practices, involved with shady characters, he might have found himself on the wrong side of one of those shady characters. And, as has been pointed out previously, anyone could have slipped into the house and up to Ralph's room. Did he think said shady character was calling to offer his congratulations and invite the guy in for a drink?"

"Ralph would have had to be mighty dumb to do that."

"One thing I learned in my previous job: there is no bottom to the level of stupidity to which some people will drop."

Bernie had been waiting for me by the kitchen door of the B & B when Éclair and I arrived at five minutes after six. As I put the coffee on and got baking ingredients out of the cupboards, and set Bernie to work, I explained the goings-on of the previous night.

"You should have told me to come over," my friend said. "I am, as you know, a keen observer of human nature. I would have been able to tell immediately who the guilty party is by a twitch of their eyebrow at an inappropriate moment."

"You keep telling yourself that, Bernie," Edna said. "Those pieces of banana are too big. Cut them finer. And don't eat them all or we won't have enough."

Edna also had news to share this morning. Her husband, Frank, was editor-in-chief of the *North Augusta Times*. The paper had reported Ralph's death, and that the police were investigating. They hadn't yet called it murder but, she told us, they would use that word this morning. "Jenny Hill wasn't arrested. Simply brought in for questioning. They kept her most of the night, and then released her to her prospective son-in-law about an hour ago. She's been ordered not to leave North Augusta."

"Does Frank have any idea what they have on her?" Bernie asked. "They must have something to go on. Of all the potential suspects, Jenny's the only one deserving of extra . . . attention, shall we say."

"Not that he told me." Edna loaded her tray with cereal boxes and individual containers of yoghurt to lay out in the dining room. "What do you know, Lily?"

"Nothing except Jenny and Ralph have a complicated, but not all that unusual, history and some people have a nebulous idea she wanted revenge for something that happened a long time ago. I can't believe Amy Redmond would arrest her—"

"Bring her in for further questioning," Edna said.

"That. On such vague grounds. Must be something more."

"Not necessarily," Bernie said. "Questioning means just that. Ask questions. Hope for answers that will lead you to another, more important question. And so on from there."

"How many people are we expecting for breakfast, Lily?" Edna asked.

"I've no idea, so let's plan on them all coming down. Fortunately, we've nothing special requested for today."

Rose's nightly note had said, "nothing," meaning no individual requests, which I was always pleased to see.

I poured blueberry muffin batter into the prepared baking cups, and sprinkled a mixture of sugar and nutmeg on the top to give them a nice crunchy texture.

"Mornin' all." Simon came into the kitchen as I was slipping the sheet into the hot oven. "Looks like it's going to be another nice day. Hey, Bernie, what brings you here so early?" He headed for the coffeepot.

Behind his back, I gave Bernie a quick shake of the head.

"Couldn't sleep," she said. "I'm stuck in the middle of this book, unsure of how to propel it forward. I'm at what we writers call the soggy middle. I want to talk some plot points over with Lily, and what better time to catch her than when she's making breakfast."

He added a generous amount of cream to his coffee and stirred two heaping spoonfuls of sugar into it. "Me mum's a keen mystery reader. Can't get enough of the stuff. The darker and grimmer the better."

"Your sainted mother is no help to me now, is she?" Bernie said with a grin. "Being in England and all."

Simon gave me a quick kiss on the cheek. "It's going to be a mighty hot day, so I want to get some of the heavy work in early. I'll take this with me this morning. I'll bring the mug back later to exchange for one of those muffins."

He left.

Edna stared open-mouthed at Bernie. "You are one heck of a good liar."

"I am indeed." Bernie preened. "Why didn't you want him to know what's going on, Lily? Simon's been of help to us in the past."

"I'll admit that's true. But, well you know what men are like. Wanting to rush to the rescue and all that. It's . . . different now. Now that we're sort of semi-involved. Kinda."

Bernie rolled her eyes. "Sounds like a lifetime commitment to me. Make up your mind, Lily. Men like Simon don't come along every day."

"I agree with Bernie about that," Edna said. "He'll be angry if he finds out you deliberately shut him out. But that's your affair. Back to the point at hand, as Jenny Hill was not arrested for the murder, but simply brought in for questioning, in the presence of a hastily summoned lawyer, the paper will not be mentioning any names. If she is arrested, that will change."

"Fair enough," I said.

"Unfortunately, the paper did have to say where this death took place. Victoria-on-Sea. Fortunately, the story's not getting a lot of traction. The Reynoldses and Hills are not from around here. Locals don't care and tourists have other things on their mind than following the small-town news."

"Thank heavens for small mercies," Bernie said. "Okay, that's the fruit cut. You will note the perfection of the small slices. My work here is done. I'm going home to get stuck in and find out what I can about the family. Families."

"Earlier, I overheard Sophia say something about Jenny's late husband dying suddenly," I said. "She tried to imply Jenny might have had something to do with it. Maybe you can look into that."

"I thought we were trying to clear Jenny. Not dig up more evidence against her."

"I'd like to help her, if she's innocent. If she's not . . ."

"When did that happen?" Edna asked. "His death, I mean."

"Hannah was ten when her father died. Must have been twenty some years ago."

"I can get Frank's summer intern onto that," Edna said. "If the death didn't get much press, if any, and it was twenty years ago there won't be a lot to find. Their local paper might have something in their records."

"That'll be a help, thanks." Bernie washed her hands at the sink.

Voices came from the dining room as the first breakfast guests arrived.

"Meanwhile, the task of feeding people never ends." Edna slipped out to see to them.

I dropped sausages into the frying pan.

The next sound I heard was the rapid *tap tap tap* of a cane making its way down the hallway. A moment later, the door opened, and Robert the Bruce flew across the room to land in the center of the table. Under the table, Éclair leapt to her feet with a bark. Robbie hissed in return. He then sniffed at the fruit bowl. I picked him up and put him on the floor.

"Morning, love," Rose said. "Bernadette."

"What are you doing up so early?" I asked suspiciously. Not only was she up, but Rose was dressed for the day in a pair of loose purple pants and an orange T-shirt decorated with yellow and green flowers. Her makeup had been applied and her iron-gray hair arranged into stiff spikes. An aura of heavily applied perfume and too much hair spray fought with the kitchen scents of fresh baking and sizzling sausages.

My grandmother and my friend gave me identical innocent smiles.

"Despite your continued declaration that we were not going to get involved," Rose said, "I assumed you'd want to help Jenny Hill. If only for her daughter's sake. You have a romantic streak in you after all, love."

"I have nothing of the sort. I don't want to see an innocent woman railroaded. That's all."

"Not that Detective Redmond is likely to allow anyone to be railroaded," Rose said.

"Williams would," Bernie said. "If it means he can get home in time for dinner."

"I'm not so sure," I said. "Redmond's increasingly taking over, and he doesn't seem to mind. I think he's okay following her lead."

"I don't trust him," Bernie said.

"Nor do I," Rose said. "But time will tell. As usual

Bernadette and I were on the same page, and I called her last night."

"Got her call about two minutes after yours," Bernie said.

The fat in the frying pan popped and sizzled, and I flipped the sausages.

Like peas in a pod—or sausages in a frying pan—those two. I might look like Rose: blond-haired, pale-skinned, pink-cheeked, with a heart-shaped face and blue eyes, but in temperament she and Bernie were exactly the same. Compulsive, adventurous, risk-taking.

"Now, where do we begin?" Rose settled herself at the table. Robbie leapt nimbly into her lap.

"I see the gang's all here," Edna said as she came into the kitchen. "I was wondering what was taking you so long to show up, Rose. I have five orders for the full English breakfast and one for two poached eggs, medium. The bridge women are in, as is the couple. No sign of the Reynoldses yet."

"I was asking where we begin," Rose said. "I do believe I'll begin with a cup of tea, Edna."

"Kettle's hot," she replied.

# *Chapter 16*

Teamwork. The essence, I've decided, of good detecting is teamwork.

Bernie was investigating the affairs of the Reynolds and Hill families. Edna had put her husband's staff checking into the events surrounding the death of Max Hill, Hannah's father. Rose planned to invite Regina to tea later, with the intention of finding out exactly what the other elderly woman knew about the goings-on in her family. "No one," she'd said to me, "knows more secrets than a so-called old woman. Like the servants of days long past, they're almost invisible, and believed to be not too bright, so people talk freely in front of them."

"A mistake I would never make," I'd replied.

As for me—I had a tearoom to run.

"I heard the bride's mother was arrested for killing the groom's father," Marybeth said to me when she and Cheryl arrived for work.

"Not arrested," Cheryl said. "Questioned and released."

"How do you know that?" I asked. "I checked earlier and nothing had been mentioned in the online news."

Marybeth winked at me. "Town gossip. The sister of a civilian clerk at the police station told me when she picked the kids up for day camp."

"A civilian clerk gossips with her sister about what's going on at the police station?"

"Sisters. She has five. and they're really close. The news'll be all over town by now."

"Why do they keep her on? Shouldn't that be a firing offense?"

"She's the chief's wife's niece. Also a first cousin to the mayor, I think. Is that right, Mom?"

"Everyone's a first cousin to the mayor. If not first cousin, then second or third. Including us. Never mind that. I would have thought, Marybeth, after what happened with me when that stupid TV show was filming here, you'd know better than to repeat mindless gossip."

Marybeth hugged her mother. "You're right. I'm sorry."

"The problem with gossip, is that the juicier it is, the faster it travels. Regardless of the truth, which if it isn't worth gossiping about, doesn't travel far at all." Cheryl freed herself from the hug. Her face was full of the memory of when she herself had been a murder suspect. The issue had been complicated by the fact that she and none other than Chuck Williams had once been in a relationship which had not ended well.

"We've a full reservations book for today," I said. "So let's get to it. Not only that, we also have a private tea for two to cater at two o'clock today."

"Cater?" Cheryl said. "We don't cater. Do we?"

"Only on special occasions," I said. "And if it suits my own nefarious purposes."

At quarter to two, I left a busy Tea by the Sea with a packed picnic hamper. Inside were two sets of china from my personal Royal Doulton Winthrop collection, an Old Country Roses teapot containing leaves of Darjeeling, four freshly made scones, egg salad with herby mayonnaise sandwiches as well as salmon pinwheels, pistachio macarons and fruit tarts, and small containers of clotted cream, and jam.

I never make scones for the B & B breakfasts, nor do I bring out my good china, and I prepare the tea with store-bought tea bags, not carefully selected leaves from custom suppliers. If I didn't do that, what reason would guests have to come to my tearoom?

I went into the kitchen and put the kettle on to make the tea. While it heated, I carried the hamper into the drawing room. I arranged two chairs next to each other, with a small table between, and dragged the coffee table in front of them to make a proper setting for tea. In times past, afternoon tea was sometimes called "low tea," meaning it was served on a low drawing-room table as opposed to "high tea," a working family's evening meal served on a high kitchen table.

I arranged the dishes and the food and stepped back to admire my handiwork. The presentation appeared suitable for afternoon tea with Queen Victoria and Anna, Duchess of Bedford. Although the servings of food were substantially more than those ladies would have expected.

Back in the kitchen, I poured hot water over the tea leaves before texting Rose: **Let the show begin.**

She replied: **[fingers to the lips emoji]**

I waited a couple of minutes and precisely at two o'clock, I carried the fragrant, steaming teapot to the drawing room.

Rose and her guest had taken the two chairs I'd arranged. For once Robert the Bruce had not been invited to join my grandmother.

"This is quite delightful," Regina said. "Rather like being at Buckingham Palace. I heard the late queen was fond of her afternoon tea. Is the new king also?"

*As though Rose, simply because she's English, would know that.*

"My contacts back home tell me he is," Rose replied, as though she had friends who moved in the king's innermost circles. "He's devoted to tradition, as was his mother. If you'd be so kind as to pour the tea, please, Lily."

"My pleasure," I said. I poured the light, floral liquid, flavored with a slight tone of muscatel, into two delicate cups and placed each on the table between the chairs.

"Thank you for inviting me to join you, Rose," Regina said. "I simply could not bear yet another outing with my family. McKenzie and Sophia are spending a day at the spa. Sophia claims she needs relief from the tension of the past few days. What she means is she wants to spend my money while she still can."

My back to Regina, I wiggled my eyebrows at Rose. She kept her face impassive.

"Greg, the hopeless romantic, is off somewhere fussing over Hannah," Regina continued. "Ivan's gone into town to see what he can do about making arrangements to get Ralph home. Poor lost Ralph. My only child. Lily's your granddaughter, I understand. How many children do you have, Rose?"

"Four sons and one daughter, Lily's mother. I have five grandchildren and two great-grandchildren.

"Ah yes, grandchildren."

I slipped out of the room, closing the door silently behind me.

We'd chosen our teatime carefully. At two o'clock on a sunny day, no one should be hanging around the house. As Regina had conveniently confirmed, the Reynolds family had all gone out. The bridge women asked Rose for recommendations about a historical tour and she'd not only laden them with brochures, she phoned to make the booking herself. The other couple staying here checked out after breakfast, and new arrivals wouldn't check in until after four. The weekend housekeeper was upstairs, accompanied by the roar of the vacuum cleaner.

An earlier owner of this house had, for reasons of their own, installed a secret room behind the linen closet next to the drawing room. Rose discovered it during renovations and later showed it to me. We never intended to spy on our guests, but we'd thought it great fun to know about the secret room. No one else, not even Bernie, did.

It proved convenient on other occasions when police and murder suspects had met in what they thought was the privacy of the drawing room.

I slipped into the linen closet, removed napkins, place mats, and tablecloths from two of the shelves and put them on the floor. I reached for the back wall and pulled the concealed lever. The bottom two shelves slid silently aside, and I duck walked into the secret room, pulling the door closed behind me. We'd made the room moderately comfortable with a chair ruined when a guest dropped a lit cigarette between the cushions, and a small, dim lamp. I switched the lamp on. We'd tested the light to be sure nothing leaked out.

The room had obviously been constructed for the sole purpose of listening to goings-on in the drawing room, as the separating wall was excessively thin. Not only that but a few discreet holes had been drilled through the lathe and plaster. A large painting of an eighteenth-century sailing ship heading out to sea hung over the holes on the drawing-room side in an ornate frame heavy enough to discourage anyone from causally rearranging it.

I made myself comfortable and listened.

". . . delicious," Regina was saying. "There is something about afternoon tea, isn't there, Rose. Such a treat."

"It is. I'm sorry Hannah's shower was disturbed by that misplaced gift. Rather a rude joke, don't you think?"

"I'm not so sure it was a joke. It had the desired effect, didn't it? Poor Hannah was most upset. Her special day had been ruined."

"As was her wedding day," Rose said.

"Sadly, yes. Hannah deserves to be happy. As does Greg."

"Have you known Hannah and her mother long?"

"Seems like forever. Jenny and Ralph were engaged to each other at one point. Did you know that?"

"No. How odd. What happened? If you don't mind my asking."

A mouse crept out from a crack in the wall. I watched it. Small black eyes watched me. Whiskers twitched. I waved my hand in the air. It didn't move. I made shooing gestures. It still didn't move. I'm not afraid of mice, not exactly. But if it jumped on me I might not be responsible for my actions.

"It's all ancient history now," Regina said. "They were young, she met another man, she broke off with Ralph, and married the other man. Max Hill. He died when Hannah was a child. Jenny and Hannah moved away, and we had no more contact with them until about a year ago when Hannah and Greg got together."

"Please do have another scone. Isn't the jam wonderful? It's made from local berries, by a woman I know personally."

"I will, thank you," Regina said.

"How did Ralph take the breakup?" Rose asked.

With her down-to-earth, working-class Yorkshire accent, only slightly faded after sixty years living in America, her tiny frame, her outlandish clothes, and playful hair and makeup, Rose is a woman people are comfortable talking to. She also just happens to be very good at gently steering a conversation in the direction she wants it to take. Notably Rose had not taken the opportunity to launch into a lengthy discussion of her own family.

"Not well," Regina said. "To put it mildly. He rushed into a marriage with the totally unsuitable Sophia. And it all went downhill from there."

"I've observed, if you don't mind me saying so, that you and your daughter-in-law don't get on overly well."

Regina snorted. "You noticed that, did you? Hard not to, sometimes. We hate each other. Always have. Her own family had been quite well-off at some time, I believe, and she'd been brought up expecting life to provide for her. Her father was a lawyer, partner in a very prestigious firm. He got caught with his hand in the cookie jar. He was lucky to escape jail, but he was unable to practice law from that point on, and so the family's income and status declined. Sophia's expectations declined along with them. She married Ralph when he was at a low point, on the rebound I believe the young people say, because she mistakenly thought he had money. More fool her. More fool him to stay with her all these years. Loyalty to the children most likely. Ivan arrived less than nine months after their wedding."

I thought about what Regina said when she arrived for tea. That Sophia was out spending *her* money. Not Ralph's money or even the couple's money. I sent a mental instruction to Rose to ask about that. Not that I expected her to pick up my thoughts from behind the wall, no matter how many holes had been drilled through it.

The mouse took a step toward me. I bared my teeth and shook my foot at it.

It might have yawned.

"I should have acted to stop the marriage," Regina said, "but by the time I realized he was serious about her, it was too late. Poor Ralph. I did love him, Rose. He was my only child. But, I hate to say it, he was too much like his father. Weak. Vacillating. Is that salmon, do you think, in that sandwich? Not tuna? I can't abide tuna."

"Yes. Salmon. More tea?"

"Please. This is delicious. Not like the tea we get at home."

"I myself have been widowed for four years now. I miss my darling Eric every day. How long has it been for you, Regina?"

"Seven years. Seven years of bliss."

Rose coughed lightly. I was surprised she didn't choke on her salmon sandwich.

"You think me blunt," Regina said.

"I think you honest."

"At our age, dear, we have no need to beat about the bush. No one to impress. Although we still have people to disappoint and I always enjoy that. I'm glad you had a happy marriage. My own was not the same. My father was a successful man. He built a successful business from the ground up. He was also very traditional, like your king. Times were different as well, back then. He selected Ralph's father from among his junior executives to marry me. His intention was to groom my husband to eventually take over the firm. Instead, my father died of a heart attack in his early fifties, not long after my marriage. And my husband, Joseph, poor stupid Joseph Reynolds, proved totally incapable of running the company. Even after, particularly after, he changed the company's name to reflect himself."

"Oh dear," Regina said. "Did your father's business then fail?"

"No. Because someone in the family had a lick of common sense."

"Dare I guess that someone was you?"

"You may. I ran the entire operation from behind the scenes for decades. It thrived; it grew. We prospered. Eventually Joseph began ailing and he couldn't pretend to be in charge anymore. By then Ralph, our son, was a vice president. I've worked hard all my life. Dedicated my life to the firm my father built. Following my husband's death, I began having a few minor health concerns myself, nothing serious but enough to remind me my days were coming to an end. So many things I hadn't done in my life. So many places I hadn't been. I decided to step away, to retire, to hand the business over to my son."

"How did that turn out? If you don't mind my asking."

"As well under Ralph as it had under his father. Only when it was too late, did I come to realize that it was not Ralph, but Max Hill who actually ran the company. When Max left, because a vengeful Ralph pushed him out, Ralph was simply out of his depth. So I stepped up once again. There appears to be something wrong with the men in Joseph's family. First Joseph himself, then Ralph, and now Ivan. Weak and vacillating and indecisive, the lot of them."

"Ivan? You mean your grandson? Greg's brother?"

"He's supposedly been learning the ropes under his father's guidance. Instead, he's been learning nothing, and now even Ralph's useless guidance is gone. I was hoping to go to Italy in the fall. All the great art I've never seen. My plans will have to change, and I'll have to take control, once again."

"What about Greg?"

"Greg has been a disappointment to me in an entirely different way. He has no interest in the business. He wants to be"—she snorted—"an artist. And not only an artist but a large-scale mural artist. Painting the exteriors of buildings, that sort of nonsense. I cling, perhaps foolishly, to the hope he'll tire of that and want to get involved in the family business. If not him, then Hannah. She is Max's daughter after all. I like Hannah a great deal. It would be better if she married Ivan, but we cannot control the direction of true love, now can we? Much as we might wish to. My father made that mistake. Those tarts look lovely. Like little jewels. Almost too perfect to eat."

Almost, but not quite. Regina munched away for a few minutes. Rose poured another round of tea.

Finally, to my infinite relief, the mouse decided he was bored with my company and slipped away, disappearing into the crack from which it had come. I (quietly) let out an enormous sigh of relief.

Deep in my pocket, my phone vibrated. I checked it.

Marybeth: **Are you going to be much longer? We've had more groups with children than expected and are running out of vanilla cupcakes and cookies.**

Me: **Back soon. Check freezer**.

I glanced at the time as I put my phone away. Almost an hour had passed since I left the tearoom. Trying to operate a restaurant and be a detective at the same time wasn't easy. I'd have to trust Rose to report the rest of the conversation to me later.

I crouched down, ready to crawl out of the linen closet, when the front door opened and footsteps came into the hallway.

"McKenzie. I saw you drive up. We're in here!" Regina called.

"A tea party," McKenzie said from the other side of the wall. "Isn't that lovely. Hi, Mrs. Campbell."

"I'm sorry," Rose said, "but your grandmother and I seem to have consumed everything."

"Not a problem. Mom and I had lunch at the spa."

"Hello," Sophia said.

"How was the spa, McKenzie dear?" Regina asked.

"Okay. I've been to better," McKenzie said.

"Why don't you pull up a seat and join us for a few minutes," Regina said. "Tell me all about your day."

"I guess I can do that," McKenzie said. "I'm meeting Jack in town later."

"Don't let us keep you, Sophia," Regina said. "I'm sure you have things to do. Give Ivan a call, will you, and ask what's going on. I do hope we can go home soon. And take my dear son with us. No, not here. Call him from the privacy of your room. While you're at it, get Greg to come back as soon as possible. I have business matters to discuss with my grandsons that will not wait."

"Am I invited to take part in this discussion?" Sophia asked.

"Don't be silly, Sophia. When have you ever shown the slightest interest in the company? Now, McKenzie, tell me what treatments you had. Did they have a proper steam room? I love a steam room."

The sound of Sophia's heels on the floor and then the staircase just about shook the house. My little mouse friend must have wondered if an earthquake had hit.

"Did you hear anything more about what's happening with Jenny?" McKenzie asked her grandmother. "Is she in jail? How's Hannah managing? I called Greg earlier but it went straight to voice mail and he hasn't replied to my texts."

"Greg hasn't called me with an update, either. Most inconsiderate of him. He must know we're wondering. Thank you for the tea, Rose," Regina said. "It was delightful. My compliments to your granddaughter. You might consider a restaurant career, McKenzie. I don't mean doing the cooking, of course, like Rose's granddaughter does, but maybe as an investment opportunity."

"I'm glad you enjoyed the tea," Rose said. The floorboards squeaked beneath her feet as she stood up. Rose had spent the early parts of her life as a kitchen maid in a grand manor house. She could tell when she'd been dismissed.

# Chapter 17

We gathered in the tearoom kitchen at five thirty so I could get some baking done for tomorrow while we talked.

Bernie called earlier saying Matt had suggested he, Bernie, Simon, and I go into town later to have a drink and listen to some live music. I demurred at first, claiming pressure of work. But Bernie reminded me that "all work and no play makes Lily a dull friend."

I might have continued to demur had a text not come from Simon, suggesting the same thing.

Simon. I liked Simon a great deal. He liked me a great deal, or so I thought (hoped?). We didn't have much of a future together—he was due to go back to England in the fall when the gardening season ended. He had a job lined up to do overwinter care of the greenhouses at a Grade II-listed estate. I couldn't see myself leaving Tea by the Sea and Rose to go with him.

Even if we didn't have a future, wasn't it okay to simply enjoy each other's company while we were together?

Not only did all work make Lily a dull friend, it made her an unappealing romantic partner.

I agreed to the night out.

We had no last-minute customers, so Cheryl and Mary-beth were able to clean up the dining rooms and patio, lay things out for tomorrow, and head home on time.

Bernie dragged a chair from the restaurant for Rose, and my grandmother settled herself comfortably, her hands resting on the top of the cane propped between her legs. I put Bernie to work making chicken sandwich filling out of a chicken about to come out of the poaching pot. I rubbed butter cubes into a mixture of flour, baking powder, and salt prior to forming it into scones.

Edna texted to say she had something to report. Rose called her, put her on speaker, and placed the phone on the butcher block in the center of the kitchen.

"We hit pay dirt," Edna said.

"Of what nature?" Rose asked.

"The local paper in the town in which Ralph, Sophia, and Regina live folded some years ago. As is, unfortunately, happening all over the country. Its place was taken by a big corporate chain, as is also happening all over the country. No one in the company had much interest in decades of records of high school tournaments, fender benders, and bar fights in small-town USA, so one of the laid-off reporters lugged all that paper and microfiche home and stuffed it into storage in his basement. He says he intends to sort through it and publish a history of the town one day. That may or may not happen, but it doesn't matter for us. Zack, Ralph's intern, has a future in this business. If there is a business for him to have a future in. With a substantial amount of dogged determination, he managed to finally speak to someone at the giant faceless corporation who gave him the old reporter's home number. Fortunately, the old guy still has a land line, and he was more than happy to talk about the old days and old cases. Also fortunately, he seems to have a good head for keeping records. He didn't remember the specific case, but once he had the year and the names he was able to track the records down. And then the memories started coming back." She paused.

"And—" Bernie and I said.

"Spit it out, Edna," Rose said.

"I'm dragging out the tension. As I believe you have been known to do sometimes, Rose."

Rose growled.

I dropped the scone dough onto a floured surface and began folding it prior to cutting out the shapes. "We're listening."

"Nineteen years ago, Maxwell Hill died of an apparent heart attack, age forty-one. Leaving behind his wife, Jennifer, and daughter, Hannah. I use the word 'apparent' because there was some suggestion that the heart attack might have been not entirely caused by natural causes."

"Meaning?" I asked.

"Meaning little, I have to admit. There was never any evidence to support that claim, so it was not reported in the paper. The police never opened an investigation. Our contact found it on a note he'd made to himself. Being a dogged reporter, determined to get to the bottom of any story, he did some poking around. He found out two things that might be of interest to us. First, the unsubstantiated rumors likely originated with Sophia Reynolds. Before her marriage to Ralph, Sophia and Jenny were good friends."

"Interesting," I said. "Particularly as Ralph and Jenny were engaged before Jenny met Max. Who she left Ralph for. And Ralph then married Sophia on the rebound."

"Tangled relationships," Bernie said. "Means plenty of emotion seething under the surface."

"And," Rose added, "sometimes on the surface. Please continue, Edna."

"Sophia was active on various charity committees when

her children were young. Much less so these days, but that's irrelevant for this conversation. She had a high profile among what was, admittedly, a small group of people. Small, but influential in that community. The newspaperman's pretty sure it was Sophia who ever so gently put those rumors out."

"If Jenny found out about it, she'd have reason to be angry," I said. I thought back to the bridal shower. Sophia had been patronizing and rude to Jenny. Jenny had not responded in kind.

"She might not have," Edna said. "Her focus would have been on her husband's death and her own and her daughter's future. But—the second reason the rumor had some legs was due to Jenny's occupation. Do you know what that is?"

"No," Rose and I said.

"Yes," Bernie said. "Let me tell. Let me tell."

Edna chuckled. "The floor is yours."

Bernie waved her knife in the air. "Jenny Hill is a pharmacist."

"That is interesting," I said. "That means she, more than just about anyone, would know about medication. What to take, how much of it to take, and what not to take if you have a certain condition."

"Yes," Bernie said.

"These days that sort of information is easily available on the Internet for the mildly curious as well as the evil-intentioned to discover for themselves," Rose pointed out.

"And the mystery writer," Bernie said. "That might be an avenue to explore in my book. Perhaps Tessa could have some knowledge of folk medicine from her years—"

"No," I said. "She does not. Back to the matter at hand. Did this old-time reporter have anything to say about the state of the Hill marriage? I mean, might Jenny have had reason to want to get rid of her husband?"

"Apparently not. She was well-known in the community and respected for her position. He, Max Hill, was the manager of a hardware store, part of a big chain. The reporter says he looked to see if anything was waiting to be dug up, but he found nothing. And so he dropped it. Soon after her husband's death, Jenny sold their house and she and her daughter moved away. The rumor was never mentioned again, as far as we know. The police didn't open an investigation, and the reporter let it go as unfounded. Neither Jenny nor her daughter Hannah have come to the attention of the police again. Until now, in North Augusta."

I slipped the tray of scones into the oven. Bernie had gotten just about nowhere in the preparing of the chicken filling.

"You need to talk to Amy Redmond, Lily," Bernie said. "Find out what the Reynolds family said last night that made them take Jenny to the station for further questioning. My money says they, Sophia at any rate, repeated that old rumor, and the cops wondered if there was a pattern to be found."

"Me? Why me?"

"Because you've developed a rapport with her," Bernie said.

"I have not."

"Let me point out," Edna said, "that the local police didn't open a case into Max Hill's death. Doesn't mean they were satisfied the rumors had no merit. Even the most dogged of small-town newspapermen doesn't always know what the police are thinking." She laughed lightly to herself. "My Frank excepted. He can read the North Augusta police chief as clearly as Lily's menu. Chuck and Amy will have been in touch with their colleagues in the Boston area about the families and wedding guests. They might have learned something we don't know."

"Only one way to find out," Bernie said. "And that's to ask. Right, Lily?"

I grumbled. Plain scones browning nicely in the oven, I started a batch made with orange peel and cream rather than currents and milk. I use the special ones for our royal tea, accompanied not with jam, but Edna's marvelous orange marmalade.

"It is interesting," Rose said, "that in both the previous case and the current one Sophia Reynolds was on the scene."

"You think Sophia killed both men?" Bernie asked.

"Not necessarily. But she does seem happy to point the finger at Jenny."

"Regina told me Ralph was devastated when Jenny left him in favor of Maxwell Hill," Rose said. "According to Regina, he married Sophia with haste, and his and Sophia's marriage never was a good one. I wouldn't be surprised if Sophia blames Jenny to this day for her own unhappiness."

"Let us not forget that Regina pointed the finger at Sophia," I said. "Lots of finger pointing going on here."

"That's all I have for my report," Edna said. "I have dinner to finish, so I'll leave you bunch to your investigations. If you need anything else, let me know. I was a huge Nancy Drew reader in my long-ago youth. I always dreamed of following in her footsteps and becoming a girl detective."

She hung up. Bernie put down her knife and grinned at Rose and me. "That was interesting, but not the only interesting thing learned today."

"Let Rose go first," I said. "She had an interesting tea with Regina."

"Interesting," Rose said, "but not entirely earth-shattering. We know Regina and Sophia don't get on.

Regina believes her son would have made a better match with Jenny than he did with Sophia. Which is largely irrelevant as no doubt if such had happened Jenny would have managed to disappoint the haughty Regina in due course. Perhaps more to the point, Regina's point anyway, Regina clearly would have preferred Max Hill continue working at the family company. He was, again according to Regina, a better businessman than Ralph."

"She told you, a total stranger, all this?" Bernie asked.

"She told me precisely because I'm a total stranger. Regina Reynolds is a woman who likes to believe she's frank and straightforward. I believe she's as devious as they come. But she had no reason not to be honest with me."

"This really is a true-life version of the Capulets and the Montagues," I said. "All we need is a meddlesome friar and a nurse."

"As for the family she does have, I suspect the only one of her grandchildren Regina has much time for is McKenzie. Who's, in my opinion, totally useless. But being a girl, and pretty and charming at that, likely Regina had less expectations of her than she did of her brothers, despite the fact that she herself was a superior businessperson than her own husband and son. Greg and Ivan are great disappointments to her." Rose outlined what she'd learned about the history of the family's company, Regina's marriage to Ralph's father, and Regina's under-the-table control of the business.

When she finished, Bernie's face was a picture of disappointment. "Don't know why I bothered. I spent most of today trolling through the business news and gossip and learned much the same. Regina might think her control was under-the-table, as you put it, but it was always common knowledge to those who care. I do have one thing to add: if what she told you is what she believes, the company is in far worse shape than even Regina's aware of. It is, in fact, shortly to be totally bankrupt and sold at fire sale prices to its competitor. Said competitor is offering pennies for shares that were at one time worth close to a hundred bucks each. Ralph was semiretired, handing over the reins to his eldest son, Ivan. Ivan, on his part, has been outmaneuvered at every turn by their competitors. Street rumor says he, simply, has thrown in the towel. And that was before he came to North Augusta for his brother's wedding and the subsequent death of his father. Pointedly, Ivan is still here, in North Augusta, not in Boston desperately trying to save his great-grandfather's company."

"We can consider it unlikely Ivan killed his father then," I said. "It's causing more disruption at a time he doesn't need it."

"Don't be so quick to assume such a thing," Rose said. "Regina claims Ralph was a bad manager, but was he that bad? Perhaps he realized what was happening under Ivan's leadership and they argued about it. Ivan lost his temper at being lectured and—"

"As good a guess as any," I said. "But we have to remember Ralph wasn't killed in any spontaneous loss of temper. Surely adding poison to his whiskey bottle was premeditated. Or at least done by someone in control of their thoughts and actions."

"Any nefarious goings-on at that company?" Rose asked.

"Nothing I could find," Bernie said. "Although I have some inquiries out that are still to be answered. Frankly, if Ralph and/or Ivan had the wits to try a little creative accounting, they'd be better off."

"Creative accounting," I said. "And other *creative* business practices. Might that be why Regina was a better manager than her husband or son?"

"Possible," Bernie said. "I can dig back further and see what I can come up with along that line."

"What would it take, do you think, Rose, for a mother to kill her own son?" I asked.

"I can't imagine why you're asking me that, love, but I'd say it would take more than is humanly possible. Outside of a Greek tragedy, such is unimaginable."

"Is it? Unimaginable to you, but not necessarily to everyone. The company is important to Regina. She told you that. She's given up much in life to take care of it. How far might she go if she realized the company is in danger?"

"Far too late," Rose said. "If we're hypothesizing, let us hypothesize that if she was going to do such a thing, she would have acted as soon as Ralph took full control, or at least when Max Hill left, once she realized what was happening."

"I'm not so sure I agree with Rose," Bernie said. "Not being a mother, I have no practical experience, but remember Ralph wasn't a child. He was an adult. The product of what, for all practical purposes, was an unloving, arranged marriage. An adult son who turned out to be a huge disappointment to his coldhearted mother. Maybe Regina decided Ralph had to be eliminated so she could take over again?"

"Except that, like Ivan, Regina hasn't rushed back to Boston to try to keep control of things," Rose pointed out.

"She doesn't realize just how desperate the situation is," Bernie said. "Or how badly Ivan's handling it."

"Regina does like to be in control," I said. "I've just remembered something else. She told you, Rose, that Sophia was at the spa spending her money. Not the family's money or Sophia's late husband's money. Regina's money."

"Clearly no love is lost between the two of them," Rose said. "If one of them had died, I'd suspect the other."

"Had Sophia finally had enough?" I asked. "Did she think eliminating Ralph would get her out from under his mother's thumb?"

"There's this thing called divorce," Bernie said.

"Yes, but a divorced wife isn't going to inherit anything. That might be an avenue worth exploring. Did Sophia expect to cash in on Ralph's will?"

"If so," Rose said, "she's going to be severely disappointed. Judging by what Bernie said about the value of the company, Ralph had nothing to leave her. And, as it would appear, neither will Regina in her turn."

The rooster timer crowed, and I took a tray of golden, fragrant scones out of the oven.

"Those smell nice," Bernie said.

"So they should. Is that chicken sandwich filling making itself?"

Bernie glanced down at the barely deboned fowl. "I guess not, eh?" She picked up the knife.

"Any scandal in the Reynolds family?" I asked hopefully. "Illegitimate children, secret affairs, foreign bank accounts, mob connections?"

"The family is, or I should say was, moderately well-off, compared to many," Bernie said. "But not seriously rich enough to attract the attentions of the gossip press. I came up blank there, although I'll have another go tomorrow with some new search parameters."

"Despite all we learned today," I said, "we still have nothing to go on."

"A negative can prove positive," Bernie said.

"What does that mean?"

"I don't know. But I like the spin it gives to our efforts."

"Other people are involved in this," Rose pointed out. "Apart from the Reynolds and Hill families."

"We're doing the best we can, Rose," I said. "We can't investigate everyone who'd been invited to the wedding, and thus gathered on the Outer Cape. Never mind those who wish they were but weren't."

"Not only do we not have the resources to do so, but we

don't even know the names of such people. However . . . and you two call yourself detectives."

"I have never, ever, called myself anything of the sort," I said. "Nor do I ever intend to."

Rose studied our faces. Bernie's forehead crinkled in thought, and then she laughed. "Of course! Got it. Our bad. Who's invisible at a wedding?"

"The previous boyfriends and girlfriends?" I said.

"They're not invisible, rather elephants in the room, sometimes. No, the bridesmaids and the groomsmen."

"Samantha . . . some last name, and Dave Farland."

"Dave, in particular, had the opportunity to kill Ralph. He's staying in the house. He's sharing a room with Ivan. You might want to discreetly ask Ivan if Dave was in their room all evening."

"The police would have checked that," I said. "They would have asked everyone involved to provide alibis for everyone else."

"Alibis can be faked. They can be broken. The absence of an alibi isn't proof of anything," Bernie said. "Rose is right. Not looking into them is a serious oversight on my part. I can check up on Dave, as I have a last name, and I can trace him from his relationship with Greg. Probably same with Samantha, but a surname would help a lot."

"Harder to believe she did it," I said. "She had no reason to be in the house at that hour, and her presence would have been noted."

"Some sort of loyalty to Hannah, perhaps? In the same way Jenny was angry at Ralph for what she saw as his interference in the wedding."

I shook my head. "Far too much of a stretch, Bernie. I mean, really, no friends are that close. And I include you and me in that. You didn't kill Wesley Schumann because he was wrong for me."

"Don't think I didn't consider it," Bernie said. "Was Ralph the sort to have affairs? Might he have suggested Samantha pay a visit to his room and have a drink?"

"Still no motive," I said. "She could have said no, if she didn't want to. Besides, Ralph was . . . well, old."

"A lot older than her at any rate. And overweight. And not rich. Not handsome. But, no accounting for taste," Bernie said. "I'll see if I can find anything on her, although between the two of them, Dave is definitely my preference."

"All of which will have to wait," I said. "It's six thirty, almost seven. We're meeting the guys at eight. I've time to make a quick batch of chocolate chip cookies before going home and fixing myself up. You might have barely enough time to get that chicken deboned, the speed you're going."

"I'm taking the time to be methodical."

"Right. Rose, would you like to come with us? We're going to hear some live music."

"I used to love nothing more than an evening of music and dancing. Is it Les Brown and His Band of Renown? Glenn Miller perhaps?"

"I rather suspect not," I said.

"Too bad." The expression on her face indicated she was traveling far, far away. And long ago. "How your grandfather could dance."

# Chapter 18

I get up at quarter to six, seven days a week. I often work until late into the night. Also seven days a week. My customers are rarely difficult, but when they are I have to step in.

And now, on top of that, I was trying to solve a murder.

By the time I put the cookies into containers and locked up the tearoom, about the last thing I felt like doing was dressing up for a night on the town.

"It'll be fun," Bernie said. "You'll be glad you came."

I turned to look at her. "How'd you know I was thinking of not going?"

"After all these years, Lily Roberts, I can read your mind." She stopped walking, closed her eyes, and extended her arms at her sides. "If I concentrate hard . . . yes, yes, I see it now. You're thinking I'm right. As I always am. You're also thinking Simon will be disappointed if you don't show. And that would not be a good thing." She opened her eyes and gave me that wide Warrior Princess grin. "Am I right? You needn't answer. Of course I am. I always am. What are you going to wear? I'm thinking flirty but casual. We're going to a bar in North Augusta, not clubbing with the rich and famous in Manhattan. I miss clubbing in Manhattan. Do you?"

"No."

"Okay. Fortunately, I came dressed for the occasion so I don't have to go home and change. I can help you select something suitable."

I did not allow Bernie to help me dress. Instead, I told her to take Éclair for a short walk through the gardens. Flirty yet casual and North Augusta–suitable. I had nothing like that, so I put on a pair of slim-fitting, ankle-length pale jeans and tucked a scooped-necked scarlet silk blouse into a thin blue belt. Bernie announced the outfit perfect, but then suggested I needed a long necklace that would snuggle comfortably into my (admittedly limited) cleavage. Éclair had nothing to contribute to the conversation.

"Did you pass any guests on your walk?" I asked, not bothering to search for a long necklace that would snuggle anywhere.

"No sign of the Reynoldses, if that's what you're asking. Sophia and Regina's lights are on, but they might not have bothered to turn them off before going out. I suspect they'll be learning the lessons of economy before much longer. The bridge women are playing on the veranda. Don't you think you'd eventually get tired of playing cards all the time?"

"I've heard bridge people can be highly focused."

"Rose comes to mind. One of the players flagged me down and asked if there's been any developments in the police investigation. I considered telling her they found a blood-smeared queen of spades clutched in the dead man's hand. But I refrained."

"Which one was it?"

"I don't know their names. They're all of an age. They look alike, come to think of it. I wonder if that's a bridge player look? Maybe I'll start to look like that if I take up bridge. Never mind. The one with the round black glasses."

"Karen. I saw a mystery novel in her bag the other day. Like everyone who reads mysteries, she probably intends to write one someday, so she's interested in observing police procedures. Hey, Bernie, she is exactly like you."

"Most amusing."

We'd made plans to meet the guys at the bar, and so we could relax over a couple of drinks, Bernie called for a cab. I told Éclair to guard the house, and my friend and I walked toward the driveway to meet our ride.

We said hello to the bridge-playing women and attempted to walk quickly past. But we weren't quick enough, and Karen waved us down. She laid her cards on the table and stood at the railing. "Lily. We were wondering what's happening about that woman who was arrested last night. She seemed . . . I mean, I don't know her. But she didn't look like a killer to me."

"As if you know what a killer looks like, Karen," Sheila said. "Speaking of killers, I have a killer of a hand, so let's get on with it."

"I don't know anything more," I said, picking up the pace. "Sorry. Enjoy your evening, ladies."

As we approached the steps, Greg came onto the veranda. He was nicely dressed in pressed khaki slacks and a blue-and-white-striped open-necked shirt, balancing his car keys in hand. "Good evening."

"Hi," I said. "Everything okay?"

"Yeah, we're good. As good as possible, I guess, under the circumstances. I doubt anyone else will do it, so I will. I'd like to thank you, Lily, and your grandmother, for your patience and understanding. My family's problems are not yours, but they've disrupted your lives all the same." He looked over my shoulder toward the bridge players. They weren't even attempting to appear to have resumed their game.

"Don't apologize," I said. "All part of the hoteliers' job." Although, from what I learned from the other B & B owners in the association Rose belonged to, they didn't seem to have nearly as many deadly instances at their properties. I didn't want to speculate as to why that might be.

"Heading into town?" Bernie asked. "We can make some restaurant recommendations, if you like."

"Thanks, but I've made a reservation at a place Mrs. Campbell suggested. My grandma wanted me to take her out, but I'd made plans already. I'm having a nice, romantic, intimate dinner with my fiancée. And her mother."

Bernie and I laughed.

"We're going to a movie after. Jenny's a big movie buff, and there's something playing in Provincetown she desperately wants to see. Can't say it's the sort of movie I usually enjoy, but we're hoping the night out will take her mind off her troubles."

"So there's no . . . news?" Bernie asked.

"Nothing I'm aware of. Jenny isn't being held by the police, but it doesn't mean she's in the clear. Those detectives are still nosing around, and friends of Hannah have said the cops back home have been asking questions about them." He shook his head. "Bad business, in more ways than one. Are you two going into town? I can offer you a lift."

"Thanks," I said, "but we've called a cab and that might be it coming now."

"As long as the rest of you seem to have forgotten we're in the middle of a game," Shelia said, "I'm going up to my room for that bottle of wine I bought earlier."

"Bring four glasses down, will you," Marie said.

\*   \*   \*

"Now remember," I said to Bernie when we got out of the cab. "Not a word to Simon or Matt that we're looking into the Reynolds murder. All we're doing is asking questions and doing some work on the computer, and neither of them can help us with that, so no need to worry their pretty little heads."

"My lips are sealed. Until they ply me with drink that is."

The sign on the window told us tonight was Blues Night. We pushed our way inside to be greeted by a wall of sound. It was an ordinary drinking and eating establishment, nothing special. The bar itself filled one wall, tonight worked by three bartenders. The tables were old and cheap, but clean, the chairs also. The place smelled of greasy food, spilled beer, too many people stuffed into too small a place on a hot night. The scarred and scuffed wooden floor didn't warrant close examination. Waitstaff of all ages, dressed in sneakers, jeans, and short-sleeved shirts, worked the room, maneuvering deftly between tables, bar, the kitchen. The place was packed when we walked in. Fortunately Matt and Simon had arrived ahead of us, and they'd snagged a table near the small bandstand. A microphone and an arrangement of instruments were set up, but no one was onstage.

Matt leapt to his feet and waved us over. Simon took his motorcycle helmet off the chair next to him and put it on the floor. Both men greeted us with big welcoming smiles. Glasses of beer were in front of them. Once we'd exchanged greetings, and Bernie and I'd taken our seats, a waitress appeared instantly. She was short and scrawny, well into her fifties, with a life-worn face, a mop of frizzy, graying hair, deep bags under her eyes. But her smile was wide, her eyes friendly, and her accent from the Deep South. "What can I get y'all?"

"What time does the band start?" I asked her.

"Nine o'clock, honey."

"Are you wanting dinner?" Matt said. "I do. I'm starving."

"So am I," Bernie said.

The waitress handed around menus. "Burgers are the best on the Outer Cape."

"Says who?" Simon asked.

She gave him a broad wink. "Love me an Englishman, darlin'. Welcome. Who says they're the best? The cook, of course."

"Then I'll have one. With all the fixings and chips. That's what we call fries in England."

When the waitress left, after giving Simon another exaggerated wink, Bernie said, "I've been slaving away in Lily's kitchen all evening, but she's such a taskmaster, she won't let me have a single bite."

"Let me think." I pretended to do so. "One chicken deboned in two hours. Good thing we don't depend on you to keep the place going."

"Hey. I took that perfectly sliced chicken meat and turned it into a delicious, herby, mayonnaise-y, not to mention attractive, sandwich filling."

Matt laughed and lifted his beer in a salute.

"What were you doing in her place for two hours, if not helping cook?" Simon asked.

"Girl talk," Bernie said.

"More mysterious than the origins of the universe," Matt said.

We all ordered burgers and fries, enjoyed our dinner, and chatted about nothing in particular. Matt asked if the police had been around today, and I truthfully told him no.

The burger might not have been the best in the Outer Cape but it was mighty good, and piled high with all the oozy fixings I love. I wiped my fingers on my napkin as I leaned aside to let the waitress clear my empty plate. Across the crowded room, I spotted someone I recognized heading for the bar and gave him a wave. Dave noticed and changed direction to approach our table.

"Hi," I said.

"Hi." He nodded to my companions.

Matt stood up and stretched out his hand. "Matt Goodwill. Lily and Rose's neighbor."

"Dave Farland. I'm here for my buddy's wedding. Which seems to have been derailed. For the time being anyway."

"We ran into to Greg at Victoria-on-Sea as he was heading out," I said. "He was meeting Hannah and her mom. Are you on your own?"

"Yeah. He invited me to join them, but they're going to see some esoteric European movie about the meaning of being human. With subtitles. Not exactly my scene. Blues"—he nodded toward the stage—"is my scene, so I thought I'd drop in. See if the band's any good."

"Would you like to join us?" Bernie asked. "If you're on your own, I mean."

"Might as well. Thanks." He sat down and called for the waitress to bring him a beer.

Bernie winked at me. I pretended not to notice. But Simon did and he raised one eyebrow. I pretended not to notice that also.

"Are you staying on in North Augusta to support Greg?" Bernie said. "That's nice of you."

"I haven't known Greg for long, but we've become pretty good friends, and I think Hannah's a great girl. I gather he and his brother don't get on all that well, so he asked me to be his best man, and I was happy to. The wedding never happened, so I figure he needs my support more than ever. He's certainly not getting any from his own family." He looked at Matt. "You heard what happened?"

"Yeah," Matt said. "Tough deal all round."

"Did you know Ralph well?" Bernie asked.

"Never met him before Greg's stag affair last week," Dave said. "Don't speak ill of the dead and all that, but I can't say I liked him much. In person he pretty much confirmed everything Greg's told me about him. Thoroughly miserable old guy. Determined to make everyone around him equally miserable. I wouldn't say so to Greg, but I figure he's better off without the old man nagging him all the time."

"Nagging him about what?" Bernie asked.

"His life choices, what else? His dad was pretty much retired now, but he used to run the family business. His mother's family business, I gather. No big deal, a small local distribution company, but you'd have thought by the way he went on it was Ford Motor Company. Ivan, Greg's brother, is the CEO now, but Ralph wanted Greg to work there, too." He drank his beer.

"Greg had other ideas?" Bernie asked.

Not particularly interested in the Reynolds family drama, Matt was telling Simon about his planned trip to North Dakota later in the week. A research trip for the new book. I pulled my attention back to Dave.

"He sure did. Greg's an artist. A good one. That's how I know him. I do the same sort of stuff. We've got some good ideas for some big projects, but . . . it's hard to make a living while starting out as an artist."

"I so know about that," Bernie said. "I'm a writer. Working on my first novel."

"Right," Dave said. "That's why you do waitressing gigs at the B & B and the tearoom."

"For the income," Bernie said.

Simon gave her a sideways glance.

"Good luck with it," Dave said. "Anyway, Greg and his old man didn't get on, but that's common enough. Maybe he's lucky his dad cared about what he got into. My father's a cop. I don't think he knows what I do. He sure doesn't care. Long as I don't get arrested." He stared into his beer. Bernie and I exchanged glances, but before we could ask Dave anything more, like did he kill his friend's father, Simon said, "Look who's here."

I turned to see Ivan, McKenzie, and Samantha coming through the doors along with three men, one of whom was McKenzie's boyfriend, Jack.

Jack and the men peeled off and headed for the stage. McKenzie spotted us and approached our table. "Cool. Nice to see you guys." She leaned over and gave us all showy air kisses. I couldn't help but notice that the brush she gave Simon was more of a real kiss than swiping at air.

"Hi," Samantha said.

"Mind if we join you?" McKenzie didn't wait for us to agree, or not, before searching for a chair to drag up to our table. She spotted one and grabbed it without asking if it was taken. Ivan gave a what-can-you-do shrug and went in search of chairs for himself and Samantha, and we all squeezed over to let the new arrivals in. The waitress came over, and they ordered drinks. Matt asked for another round for us.

McKenzie crossed her legs, kicked Simon's helmet and peered under the table. "Oh, someone has a motorcycle helmet. Is that yours, Simon? Must be. I saw a motorcycle parked next to the garden shed at the B & B."

"Yes, it is."

"I'd love to go for a ride someday. I love motorcycles. The wind in my hair. The feeling of complete freedom." She stretched her arms over her head. "Will you take me sometime? Pretty please."

He colored slightly. "If I have time."

Onstage, Jack and his friends were warming up their instruments.

"Is Jack playing here tonight?" I asked.

"Yeah," McKenzie said. "He arranged a gig at this place and called the other guys to get down here ASAP. He wants to stay close to me while we're waiting for the cops to release my dad's body. Isn't that nice of him?" She looked at Simon as she spoke. "Not that we're a serious item or anything. Just casual, you know."

Simon drank his beer and didn't reply.

"Where's my other dear brother?" McKenzie asked Dave, and Dave told her.

McKenzie howled with laughter. I got the impression this wasn't her first bar stop of the night. "Oh my gosh. That's too perfect. She got him into foreign films? What do you suppose is next? Abstract art? Decorating his minuscule studio apartment in Art Deco?"

"I like Art Deco," Samantha said. "I also like abstract art. You might like those things, too, McKenzie. If you knew what they were."

"Well pardon me for teasing," McKenzie huffed. "I absolutely adore both my brothers," she told me. "They always know when I'm having fun with them."

Dave snorted and took a long drink. He raised his hand to call for another beer.

Onstage, Jack spoke into the mic. "Good evening, North Augusta. How's everyone on this fine night?"

A scattering of people in the audience mumbled, "Okay."

"Don't let your enthusiasm get ahead of you, now," he said. A couple of people cheered and several laughed.

Jack introduced himself and his bandmates and they swung into their first set. A deep, slow, bluesy number.

They were surprisingly good. Extremely good, in fact. Jack played lead guitar and he was also the main singer.

His voice was rich, strong, and emotional, perfectly suited to the songs they performed. The rest of the band, I realized, were not of the same quality as Jack, but he easily carried them along.

Gradually conversation around us fell off as people began paying attention.

McKenzie had pulled her chair between Simon and me. He leaned around her and whispered to me, "Guy's got a great voice." McKenzie grabbed his arm and pulled him toward her. "He sure does."

Simon gave her a stiff smile before edging away.

From the other side of the table, between Matt and Simon, Samantha gave me a shrug. Dave and Ivan drank their beer and said nothing.

The set ended to raucous applause and even a few cheers. While his bandmates headed for the bar, Jack came to our table.

"Hi, all. Nice to see you here. What'd you think?"

"You chaps are brilliant," Simon said.

Jack's smile was genuine. "Thanks. We try."

McKenzie tucked her arm into Simon's and cuddled up to him. "Told you so," she said. Simon shifted slightly to one side. His ears turned a lurid pink.

"Can I buy you a drink?" Matt asked.

"That'd be great, thanks," Jack replied. "Bourbon on the rocks."

Another chair was found and space made between McKenzie and me. Putting me even farther away from Simon.

"Do you get a lot of gigs in the city?" Bernie asked. "I hope you do, you guys are good."

"A few. Enough to pay some of the bills at any rate. I don't suppose any of you have any contacts in the music biz?"

Bernie laughed. "I'm a forensic accountant. If you want

someone to handle your millions, when you start to make them, call on me. Otherwise, no use to you. Sorry."

"I'm a baker," I said. "Simon's a gardener. We're even less use to you than a forensic accountant."

Jack smiled at us. He hadn't expected anything else. The waitress placed a fresh round of drinks on the table. Jack lifted his glass in a toast and said, "Cheers."

A couple of early-twentysomething women in excessive amounts of makeup and short sparkly dresses sitting at the bar were giving Jack flirtatious looks. He didn't seem to notice, and they soon turned their attention to his bandmates.

"You could be in the big leagues," Bernie said. "I mean that, seriously. If you want to that is. Some artists are happy just doing their art. I mean, you've got an appreciative audience here."

"Big leagues." Jack thew back most of his drink. "I can't say I wouldn't grab the brass ring mighty quick if it was offered to me. But it hasn't been offered. You need a great deal more than talent these days, or even luck. Contacts and money's all that counts."

"You need money to make money," Bernie said.

"Yeah. Seed money to get the right gigs in the right places, make demo records and get them distributed. Get the notice of the people who can make a difference." He waved his glass in the air. "The sort of people who don't frequent bars like this one." Jack glanced at McKenzie as he spoke. She'd wiggled her chair closer to Simon, who was doing a failing job of trying to keep a respectable distance. I tried to read Jack's face. He'd glanced at her when they began discussing the money involved in getting a music career started, but he didn't seem all that concerned that she was flirting so outrageously with Simon. Maybe it was normal behavior for her and he was used to it. Maybe he didn't much care. I wondered if he was with her because he wanted her to help him get his foot in the musical door, financially speaking. If so, from what I knew about her family's situation, he was going to be seriously disappointed.

As, eventually, was she.

Bernie caught my eye, jerked her head toward McKenzie, and rolled her eyes. Simon was just about falling off his chair by now.

Jack put his glass down and stood up. "I need to talk to the guys about the next set. Catch you later. You planning to stay to the end, Mac?"

"Might as well," she said, "as the company's so good and the drinks are flowing so nicely."

Matt attempted to come to his friend's rescue. "So, McKenzie. What do you do for a living?"

"As little as possible," she said.

"McKenzie dabbles in jewelry," Samantha said. "You know the homemade hobby stuff people buy for their coworkers for the holidays, because they don't know what they like. Or for their grandmothers."

Ivan coughed into his glass. Dave looked at Samantha with what might have been approval.

McKenzie finally tore her attention away from Simon and peered at Samantha through narrowed eyes.

Samantha pushed her chair back. "It's late enough for me. Perhaps I'll see you lot tomorrow."

"Would you like me to walk you to your hotel?" Ivan asked.

"No, thanks. It's not far; it's early, and they tell me this is a safe town."

"You can ask my father about that," McKenzie said.

"How's Hannah doing?" I asked Samantha.

"Okay. Under the circumstances."

"Tell her I'd love to have her and Greg to my tearoom again. As my guests. And her mother. If . . . uh . . . she's free."

"You mean if she's not in jail," McKenzie said.

"Low blow, Mac," Ivan said.

"That's not what I meant," I said. Although it had been. McKenzie shrugged.

"Anything new happening regarding your father's case?" Matt asked.

"Not that the police are telling us," Ivan said. "All they have is questions. No information."

"Normal enough," Matt said.

"I don't know Hannah very well, just through Greg," Ivan said. "And I don't know her mom at all, but I don't see a woman like her killing a man, do you?"

"You'd be surprised," Matt said, "at what people can do if they think they've been pushed far enough."

"Matt knows all about that sort of thing," Bernie added.

"Are you a cop? Lawyer?"

"I'm a writer," Matt said.

Ivan's look was one of instant dismissal. "The cops have had a lot of questions for me about our family business. We're big in tools, you know."

"Not that big," Dave muttered.

"In what?" Simon said.

"Tools. Hardware. You're a gardener. I bet you have some Reynolds garden equipment in your shed."

"Yeah, I do. Didn't make the connection."

"In my great-grandad's day, the company made all our stuff here in good old USA. Most of it's manufactured overseas now, so the business is more about negotiating contracts, managing supply chains, running just-in-time inventory, and getting the product where it's needed when it's needed. Better profit margins this way. Also fits my skill set better than overseeing a factory. The cops have been asking about the company, but I assured them we're totally legit. Not a whisper of underhanded deals has ever touched us." Ivan smiled at everyone around the table, quite pleased with himself.

"You might want to check further into some of that," Bernie said.

Stung at her failure to appreciate his business acumen, Ivan snapped, "What does that mean?"

"Nothing. Like I said. I'm a forensic accountant."

"I thought you were a writer," Dave said. "And an assistant cook and waitress."

"A woman of many talents," I said.

"None of which," Simon mumbled, "involve cooking."

"Professionally speaking, I'm an accountant," Bernie said. "Therefore, I have a suspicious mind. Although I've given up the accounting gig for a while. I'm writing a book."

"Yeah," Ivan said. "Like everyone else."

Samantha had picked up her purse but made no further move to leave. "I'm glad they're looking into more than Jenny. Any idea that Jenny Hill, of all people, killed a man, is preposterous. I've an idea, McKenzie, you can walk me back to the hotel."

"I'm fine here, thanks." McKenzie waved the waitress down and asked for another glass of wine, without asking if anyone else wanted anything.

"I thought maybe you'd like to check up on your future sister-in-law," Samantha said. "None of this is easy for Hannah, you know."

"She's fine," McKenzie said. "She's got Greg."

Samantha's dark eyes stared at McKenzie, until the other woman turned to look at Jack, another drink in his hand, chatting to his bandmates and a circle of admirers. Not very subtly, she wiggled her chair a few inches away from Simon.

"Lucky her," Samantha said.

"How's your grandmother bearing up?" Matt asked Ivan. "And your mother? It's got to be hard on them."

If that was an attempt to move the conversation away from McKenzie, it failed spectacularly.

"Bearing up is hardly the word," she said. "Grandma's about as grief-stricken as she was when Granddad died. Meaning not much. As for Mom: she's pretending to be all the grieving widow but—"

"Leave it, Mac," Ivan said. "These people don't want to hear about our dirty laundry."

*Sure we do,* I thought.

"Sure they do," she said. "Doesn't everyone want to hear the down and dirty about other people's families? Makes them feel so superior."

Matt, true-crime writer, a man who made his living out of the down and dirty of other people's families, threw a look at Bernie. She opened her eyes wide and pressed her lips into a circle.

"I don't know why my mom's even putting up the pretense of grief," McKenzie continued. "It's not as though they had a happy marriage. I suppose at some time they might have actually liked each other. I mean they have three kids, right? Although, giving her grandchildren might have been nothing more than Mom's way of trying to get into Grandma's good books. Never worked though. It must have been a heck of a shock to Mom when she realized how much control Grandma had over Dad. Including controlling all his money. Yeah, he had his income from his job at the company but anything extra? Grandma gave him an allowance. Can you imagine? I'm not supposed to know that, but I do. Grandma never hesitates to brag about herself. She even holds the mortgage on the house."

"McKenzie," Ivan said in a low growl.

"Is anyone surprised Greg wants no part of that?" Dave said.

McKenzie took another long drink of wine. Samantha remained where she was, making no further move to leave.

"I'd have expected Mom to pop the champagne once he finally shuffled off this mortal coil. I mean, come on, brother dear. Everyone knew Dad's been fooling around on her for years. And not going to much trouble to hide it."

I remembered our speculation earlier as to whether Samantha had been the one paying a late-night call on Ralph in his room. She showed no signs of shock or of being upset to hear what McKenzie was saying. The slight smile on her lips and sparkle in her eyes indicated nothing more than she was enjoying listening to good gossip.

"In any other family, Grandma would have threatened to cut his allowance, but Grandma didn't want him to marry Mom in the first place. Grandma wanted Dad to marry a woman with money. If not money, then some business sense, like she has. I sometimes wonder if he ever loved Mom or just wanted to show Grandma he could make up his own mind." She giggled. "That never works out."

She stopped talking at last. Silence fell over the table as we all shifted uncomfortably under the barrage of McKenzie's cattiness toward her own parents.

"Strange about that last present Hannah opened at her shower." Samantha focused on McKenzie. "We never did find out who gave her that, did we? You'd think whoever played a prank like that would fess up. That they'd want everyone to know who'd been responsible for such a great joke."

"My father's death," Ivan said, "has taken up most of our thoughts."

"Yeah. I see that. But I haven't forgotten. I think I've seen the exact same silver wrapping paper another time. Recently, too. I can't quite put my finger on where that had been. Do you remember, McKenzie?"

"Why are you asking me?"

"No reason. Have another drink, why don't you?" Samantha stood up and walked away.

"Well, pooh her," McKenzie said as the waitress put her drink in front of her. "She's no fun."

"Sometimes," Bernie said, "life is about more than fun."

McKenzie lifted her glass in a toast. "Yours might be. I intend to make sure mine isn't. That fat girl in the ugly blouse is getting a bit over-friendly with my man. I'd better sort her out, right quick." She stood up and headed for the bar.

Ivan had the grace to look embarrassed. "My sister sometimes talks too much. Pay no attention to anything she says. She likes to think of herself as a party girl. My grandmother indulges her. She's really not that much of an airhead." His phone rang, and he dug into his pocket. A deep frown crossed his face when he saw who was calling and he groaned. "Not again. I have to take this. And then I should head back. Nice chatting to you. Night all."

Ivan stood up and walked away, talking into his phone. "I'm in a public place. I can't hear you." He didn't bother to leave any money for his and his sister's drinks.

Dave was next to leave. "Band's getting ready to start again. I'm going to grab a seat at the bar."

"Odd family," Simon said when the four of us were alone once again.

"Did you think Samantha pretty much came out and accused McKenzie of giving Hannah the headless doll?" Bernie asked me.

"Yes. Doesn't mean she did, though. McKenzie didn't confess. It did serve to remind me, however, that the doll's a part of this puzzle we shouldn't forget. I wonder if the police found any fingerprints on it."

"Why do you want to know that?" Simon asked. "You're not investigating, are you?"

# Chapter 19

As Simon and I both get up early for work, we didn't stay at the bar much longer, just long enough to listen to another set. Which was even better than the first.

McKenzie didn't return to our table or join Dave at the bar. She ended up sitting with a group of women who'd been making friendly with Jack's bandmates.

Matt and Bernie (neither of whom had to get up for work at some unnatural hour) decided to head for the pier for ice cream. Simon and I declined.

"I'll take Lily home," Simon said.

I eyed him warily. "I hope you don't intend to put me on that bike?"

He chuckled and took my hand. "Let's grab a cab. I can pick the bike up tomorrow. I only have one helmet with me anyway. We should plan a day out soon. Take the bike along the coast. Best way to see the scenery."

I shuddered. I'm from Manhattan. Driving a car is a feat of daring for me. Never mind sitting on the back of a motorcycle, clinging to the driver, as he makes sharp, fast turns on cliffside paths as gigantic, overloaded trucks whiz past.

"McKenzie would like to go with you," I said, unable to help myself.

"Right piece of work that one is," he replied, gripping my hand all the tighter.

"A great garden," Simon said, "looks good no matter the time of day, or the time of year. Even in winter it should have a different sort of appeal: sculptural branches, long grasses, burlap on the bushes lightly dusted with snow."

I said nothing. Was he reminding me our time together was short? That he wouldn't be here to see the gardens at Victoria-on-Sea in their winter display? Was he hinting he'd like me to ask him to stay on?

Or was he merely making polite conversation, commenting on the properties of a well-established garden, as together we watched Éclair's stubby tail wagging as she sniffed around the rosebushes?

"Even at night, a good garden should shine, although only in reflected light."

I let out a small sigh of relief. He was just commenting. No need for me to search for deeper meanings. "It should appear to glow from within."

"And this is a great garden," I said.

"The number one garden attraction in all of North Augusta," he chuckled.

We stood close together, holding hands, enjoying each other and the night, watching Éclair sniff about the property on her final outing of the day.

"You've done a wonderful job with it," I said.

"Not me. All I've been doing is maintaining it. Uncle Gerry put in all the serious work of planning and planting over the years."

"Nevertheless," I said. "Shall we sit out for a bit? It is such a lovely night. I've a bottle of wine in the fridge."

"Sounds like a plan to me," he said.

I called to Éclair. She came willingly, if not eagerly, and we strolled in companionable silence back to my cottage. It wasn't all that late, not much after eleven, but the grounds were quiet. Greg's car was not in the parking area, but several others were. The bridge women had packed up their game and gone in. The downstairs guest rooms and the upstairs ones facing the gardens were dark, but the light in the second-floor hallway shone. From behind Rose's curtains we could see the flickering blue glow from her television. On the neighboring property, Matt's place, the only light was the one above the front door.

Simon settled himself in a chair on my porch, and I slipped inside for the wine and two glasses.

The night was as calm and soft as the bay in front of us, stretching to the horizon in a sheet of black glass. Behind us, a sliver of moon did little to dim the brilliance of the stars.

I opened the bottle, poured the drinks, and handed Simon a glass. He caressed my fingers as he took it. A jolt of lightning ran down my spine.

He breathed deeply and closed his eyes. He moved the glass to his other hand, and reached for my fingers. He stroked them lightly as he talked. "I can understand why Rose bought this place. Iowa's no place for an English-woman, so far from the sea, and she lived there for what, fifty or sixty years?"

"Something like that. She missed the ocean, yes, al-though more likely what she missed was the idea of the ocean. I've never been to England, but I've seen a map and Halifax, where she's from, isn't near the coast. She says she and her family went to the seaside on holiday every year when she was a girl. It's more about the house itself, I think, rather than the location. The poor little kitchen maid dreaming of being the mistress of a grand old home."

"She wasn't a serf, Lily. By the late fifties, early sixties, she would have earned a good wage and have been treated well by her employers, if only because they'd have not wanted to lose her to a shop or factory job."

"I didn't say the workings of my grandmother's mind make any sense." I sipped my wine.

Éclair jumped to her feet and ran to the gate, ears up. She let out one sharp bark.

Simon opened his eyes. "Did you hear that?"

"Hear what? I guess not. I don't hear anything."

He took his hand back, put down his glass, and sat up straight. "Sounded like a shout."

I listened, but I could hear nothing other than the sounds of the night. I might think Simon was imagining things, except that every muscle in Éclair's body was taut as she pushed at the bottom of the gate.

"Look at the dog," Simon said.

"It might be a squirrel, or something. Or a guest having a stroll. Although she's so used to people wandering about, she doesn't usually react. And not like that."

Simon stood up. "Probably nothing, but I'd like to check." He opened the gate. Éclair shot out as though she'd been fired from a cannon, and headed for the big house.

Then, at last, I heard it too. A low cry. A woman, calling, "Help!"

# Chapter 20

Éclair reached her first and then Simon. By the time I arrived, Éclair was beside the woman, frantically licking her face, while Simon hovered above saying, "Are you okay?"

"Yes. Yes. I . . . think I am." Sophia Reynolds blinked rapidly as she struggled to sit up.

Simon edged the dog to one side, and then dropped to his haunches next to Sophia and put his hands lightly on her shoulders. "Careful, there. No need to hurry. Take your time."

Sophia gave him a weak smile. She lifted her hand to the back of her head. Her fingers came away wet and she started at them. Éclair moved in for a closer sniff, but I pulled her away, and ordered her to stand back.

"Let me see," Simon said. Sophia bent her head forward. Simon parted her hair and examined the back of her head. "I can't tell too well in the dark, but you might have a nasty cut there. Do you think you can stand up and let us help you to the house?"

"I . . . yes, I think so."

Simon took one arm and I took the other and together

we helped a shaking Sophia to her feet while Éclair wagged her tail and sniffed at her legs.

"Did you trip on something?" I looked around for a misplaced rock, a patch of disturbed earth.

"I did not trip. Someone attacked me."

"Are you sure?" Simon's tone was full of skepticism.

I could see no one hiding in the shadows. If an intruder was lurking, Éclair was more occupied in trying to offer comfort to Sophia than searching out trespassers.

"I'm sure," Sophia said, her voice firm. "I heard someone behind me. I started to turn and then . . . they hit me." Instinctively her hand returned to her injury. "I fell forward, but the cut's on the back of my head."

Simon glanced at me. He gave me a nod.

"Let's get you up to the house," I said. "Check it out under the lights. Do you want me to call an ambulance?"

"No. I'm fine. I just need to sit down."

We walked slowly, Sophia between Simon and me, Éclair running ahead. Simon helped Sophia settle into a chair on the veranda, close to the light above the door, and then he carefully examined her head once again. "Bleeding seems to be stopping already. You're going to have a heck of a lump though. You'd better get some ice on that."

"You didn't see who was behind you?" I asked.

"It's dark, the person wore dark clothing. The shape was indistinct. I thought, at first, it was my daughter, McKenzie. Same height, about. But . . . no, it wasn't McKenzie." She shivered and wrapped her arms around herself.

"In case something's been damaged," Simon said, "you shouldn't be alone. Not overnight. Can we call McKenzie for you?"

Sophia blinked rapidly. "I don't know if she's back yet.

Ivan is. He stepped into my room shortly before I went out. He was in town having a drink with McKenzie and Jack when Regina called and ordered him to return to Boston immediately. Immediately, as in tonight. As though Regina can order my children to do anything. He needed to talk to me about that. He wants to stay here, with me, as he should, until we can take Ralph home. Following that discussion, I knew I wouldn't be able to get to sleep so I went for a walk. And"—she indicated the back of her head—"this happened. I want to call the police. My husband's been murdered. I've been attacked. The incidents have to be related."

I looked at Simon. We nodded to each other at the same time. Sophia was right: if she'd been attacked, this couldn't be a coincidence. It was possible she'd tripped and fallen and mistakenly believed someone had been responsible, but she seemed convinced such wasn't the case. I'd attempted to take a few surreptitious sniffs of her breath. For what it was worth, I hadn't smelled any alcohol.

She took her phone out of her pocket and made a call. "Ivan, it's Mom. I'm downstairs, on the veranda. I need you to come down immediately. Why? Because I said so, that's why."

She hung up.

"I'll call the police," I said. "And then get that ice."

I went into the house, wanting to get out of Sophia's hearing range before speaking to Detective Redmond. Yes, I happen to have her number in my phone. No point in wasting time on 911.

"Sorry to be calling so late," I said. "But something's going on here that might relate to the death of Ralph Reynolds." I told her what had happened. What appeared to have happened at any rate.

"I hear some hesitation on your part, Lily. Do you have reason to doubt what Mrs. Reynolds says? You didn't witness the incident yourself, and you say you didn't see anyone hanging around."

I rummaged in the freezer with one hand and found a container of ice cubes. "I can't say, Detective. Tensions in that family have been, to put it mildly, bubbling to the surface. I don't think Sophia's lying. She didn't give herself that lump on the head. It's possible she tripped in the dark and thinks someone caused it."

"I'll be there in ten."

"Okay."

I folded a handful of ice cubes into a clean tea towel, dumped the rest of them into a bowl, and carried them out. Not only Ivan had come down but Regina also. Ivan wore a time-worn T-shirt far too large for him over boxer shorts, but his grandmother was still fully dressed.

Simon took the tea towel from me and gently pressed it against the back of Sophia's head. She muttered her thanks.

My phone buzzed, and I put down the bowl.

Rose: **What's happening? I hear voices**

Me: **Minor incident. Simon and I have it under control**

Rose: **What sort of minor incident?**

Me: **Tell you tomorrow. Good night**

"Are you sure, Sophia?" Regina was saying when I put my phone away. "You have only a minor injury, if that. Have you been drinking?"

"No, I have not been drinking, and I'll thank you not to suggest such to the police. I am unhurt, because these people arrived on the scene quickly. They and their dog obviously scared her away."

"Her?" Ivan said.

"You arrived on the scene quickly, Regina," Sophia said. "Without being summoned. Why might that be?"

"You needn't make any insinuations," Regina said. "Ivan knocked on my door to tell me you were in some distress. Naturally I was concerned."

"Naturally." Sophia glared at her son. He glanced away.

Color was returning to Sophia's face, and her hands had stopped shaking. Battling with her mother-in-law appeared to require all her focus. "I wouldn't put it past you to sneak up behind me intending to give me a fright, but you're not exactly light on your feet, are you, Regina?"

Regina said nothing.

"Why did you say 'her'?" Ivan asked. "You called the person who hit you 'her.' "

"It was Jenny Hill," his mother replied. "I was unsure at first but now that I've thought it over, I'm positive."

Regina sniffed. "Not that again. You have got to get over blaming Jenny for everything that goes wrong in your life. Accept some responsibility for your own actions."

"I don't have to account to you," Sophia replied. "Not now, not ever. But, if I must, let me assure you I didn't hit myself on the back of the head. As for Jenny Hill, she's been a living ghost, constantly haunting my marriage. Always there, never mentioned but never forgotten by my husband or by you. The one he should have married. The woman he loved; the woman who would have provided him with the business sense you think I don't have." The color began rising in her cheeks, her eyes blazed. "Her husband died, and she and her daughter moved away, and I thought I was rid of her. At last. Although nothing got any better, did it? Not with Ralph. Not with you. The other specter in my marriage. I couldn't believe it when Greg—"

"Please, Mom," Ivan said. "Don't do this. Not now."

"If not now, when? I should have said my piece years ago."

"You have never stopped saying your piece, Sophia," Regina said. "This is all so tedious."

"Why don't I refresh the ice on your head?" I asked, trying to sound as cheerful as I could.

We were still gathered on the veranda when Amy Redmond drove up. Simon and I told her our story, and then Sophia related hers. She emphasized that the attacker must have run off when first Éclair and then Simon and I arrived. She also said that, now her head was clearing, she was sure Jenny Hill had struck her.

"How sure?" Redmond asked.

"I'm not entirely positive, Detective. But I did get a quick glance at the person. At first, I thought it might be my daughter, McKenzie, when I began to turn to greet her. Jenny's the same height and, although she's considerably stouter than McKenzie, she was wearing dark, loose clothes." Sophia snuck a sideways glance at her mother-in-law, substantially shorter than the two women mentioned.

"I'll pay a call on Mrs. Hill," Redmond said.

"You do that," Sophia said.

"Waste of time," Regina said. "Sophia is confused and her brain is trying to make sense of her injury. A common psychological problem."

Before Sophia could retort, the front door opened and Marie's head poked out. Her hair was tousled with sleep, her eyes bleary, and she wore a cotton nightgown that fell to her toes. "Everything okay out here?"

"This is a private conversation," Regina snapped.

Marie recoiled as though she'd been struck. "Well, pardon me for caring. Our bedroom window's open, because I like the night air. I thought I recognized Detective Redmond's voice." She glared at Regina. "Plus, if I may say so, you people are not exactly keeping your voices down."

"Thank you for your concern," Redmond said. "We're good here. Have you and your group been in all night?"

"We went to dinner in town. Got back shortly after nine. Nine thirty maybe? I didn't check the time, but it was almost fully dark. I suggested a game, but some of the others said it had been a long day and they wanted to turn in, so we did. What happened?"

"Did you hear anyone moving around in the house in the last half hour or so? Or out in the garden?"

"People are always coming and going in this house. It is a hotel, after all. The stairs and floorboards in the hallway creak. I heard nothing specific. Not until a short while ago when I heard all this commotion."

"Thank you," Redmond said.

Marie glanced at the watching faces. "I'll go back to my room then."

"You do that," Regina said.

Marie threw the older woman a poisonous look and slipped away.

"When we next gather for Greg's wedding," Regina said, "we'll book an Airbnb, and have the entire house to ourselves."

"That sounds like fun. Not." Ivan picked up the bowl of ice. "Come on, Mom, let's get you inside. I'll call Mac and tell her to get back here. We can take turns checking on you tonight."

"Where is your sister anyway?" Sophia asked.

"Jack has a gig in town, and she went with him."

"Oh, yes," Regina said. "Jack. Him and his useless band. Speaking of useless, where's Greg?"

"Greg," Sophia snapped, "has decided to follow his own path in life. And good for him. Being an artist is not a useless endeavor."

"It is," Regina replied, "if it brings in no income."

I got the feeling this was an old argument. And probably one they shouldn't have been constantly having in front of other members of their family. Never mind total strangers.

"Greg went for dinner and then a movie with Hannah and Jenny," Ivan said.

"He's being surprisingly loyal," Sophia said. "I wonder if that will change when Jenny's in prison."

"Before you go, Detective," Simon said. "If Lily and I might have a word?"

We walked with her to her car. Éclair heard rustling in the bushes and started to head off to investigate, but I called her to me and she came reluctantly.

"Wouldn't want to have Thanksgiving dinner at their house," Redmond said.

"Everyone's saying that," I said. "You don't give any credence to Sophia accusing Jenny, I hope. Sophia initially told us she didn't see her alleged attacker. She later changed her story to say it was likely Jenny."

"I won't give any credence to anything without proof," Redmond said. "But I do have to talk to Jenny Hill about her whereabouts tonight."

"One thing I should mention," Simon said. "Sophia says we interrupted the attack and the attacker ran off. That's not right. We didn't get there all that quickly. I heard a shout, what was likely Sophia calling out as she fell, but we didn't move for several minutes. Not until she called for help, and even then the dog reached her first. If someone meant her serious harm, I don't think they would have given her a chance to cry for help."

"Good point," Redmond said. "What then might have been the motive? If this was a deliberate attack and not just confusion in the dark?"

"Give her a fright?" I said. "She says it wasn't her mother-in-law, but it's pretty obvious they can't stand each other."

Redmond grinned. "You noticed that, did you?"

"Don't have to be any sort of detective," Simon said.

"Maybe Regina did sneak up behind her," I said. "Give her a whack to remind her of her place. And Sophia decided to deal with it later, in her own way."

"That's pure speculation, Lily."

"True, but speculation based on my careful observation of human nature."

Redmond sort of choked, but she didn't reply.

"One more thing, while you're here," I said. "I've been wondering about that Raggedy Ann doll and what it has to do with all this. Did you get any DNA or fingerprints off it? Other than Greg's or Simon's?"

"Not off the doll as it's too highly textured. But we found some on the box it was in. Pretty clear ones, too."

"Did they match with anyone who'd been at the shower, other than those we know touched it after it had been unwrapped?"

"Yes."

"Good. Who?"

"To find that out, Lily, you will have to use your powers of careful observation of the human condition. I'll let you know if I need anything further from you tonight."

"Good one," Simon said as we watched the red lights of her car disappear down the driveway.

I gave his arm a hearty swat.

Before we turned to head back to the cottage, headlights appeared at the top of the driveway.

"Looks like Matt," Simon said.

The sleek red two-seater BMW convertible pulled to a halt and my neighbor jumped out. "Was that Amy Redmond, leaving here? Late for her to be calling, so I thought I'd better check on you guys. Everything okay?"

"Minor incident concerning a guest," I said. "Bernie not with you?"

"Something about having to rush home to respond to the call of her muse."

"Oh, dear," I said. "That usually means she's heading off in an entirely new direction in the book."

"Yeah, I know. I keep telling her to focus, but every idea she has is guaranteed, according to her, to be the big breakthrough. What sort of minor incident?"

Simon explained.

Matt frowned. "Has it occurred to either of you that this might be aimed at you and Rose, Lily?"

"Us? Nonsense. I wasn't hurt. It was over before I got there. Rose didn't even come out of her room."

"I don't mean you two personally, but rather in a business sense." Simon started to speak, but Matt said, "Hear me out. Stuff happens around here. Strange stuff."

"All that stuff, as you call it, has been brought to a successful conclusion," I said. "Charges were laid, the miscreants sentenced. The book thrown at them. Cases closed."

"Yes, but is it possible those incidents put an idea in someone's head?"

"Like who?" Simon said. "And what sort of idea?"

On the veranda Ivan helped his mother inside. Regina followed saying something along the lines of how Ivan was wasting his time here and needed to present the strong, reliable face of the company to the business world. Sophia snapped at her to shut up.

"This is a mighty nice piece of property, Lily." Matt kept his voice low. "Acres of ground, great views, grand house, well-maintained. Not far from town but far enough to be considered private, even exclusive. You've had developers nosing around before."

"And look what happened to him," Simon said.

"You can't be saying a developer, or potential buyer, attacked Sophia to cause trouble for us?" I said. "Preposterous."

"I'm throwing the idea out there, Lily. That's all. You and Rose have weathered earlier problems here extremely well. If anything, you're doing better because of all the publicity."

"I wouldn't put it like that. You make it sound as though we're the ones causing these so-called problems."

"Not what I intended. All I'm saying is, pay attention if any rumors start swirling around about Victoria-on-Sea being an unsafe place to stay. Remember the recent fire?"

"The garden shed burned down."

"Destroyed me best seedlings," Simon growled.

"No one was ever in any danger," I reminded them. "Other than the seedlings. The police caught the person who did it."

"We know that, Lily," Matt said. "But such is the stuff rumors are made of. As is a guest being attacked at night while strolling in your garden." Matt looked at Simon. "Make sure she takes care."

"I will, mate."

"Hey, you two." I waved my arms over my head. "I'm still here! I'm listening. I can look after myself, and I'm perfectly safe on my own property. Someone attacked Sophia tonight specifically because she is Sophia Reynolds. We're a hotel. People bring their problems and their squabbles with them, and I can't do anything about that. I'll admit, I can't always look after Rose, though. No one can look after Rose. Not even herself."

Simon put his arm around me and pulled me close. As

though she understood what I'd said, Éclair rubbed her nose against my leg.

"I'm asking you to pay attention, that's all," Matt said.

"I can do that," I grumbled.

"I don't like what you're suggesting," Simon said. "But I'll admit it does have some validity. I've always wanted to add close protection officer to my résumé. Now's my chance."

# Chapter 21

**T**hink I got something. Sending you a picture. Tell me what you see

I blinked, trying to clear cobwebs from my head, and read the text again. Bernie had sent it overnight, but I'd put my phone on do-not-disturb with only Rose or my mother allowed to override the notification.

In the bathroom, the shower stopped running and a few moments later Simon came into the bedroom, rubbing a towel through his hair. "Problem?"

"I don't know." I studied the picture Bernie'd sent. It was a photo of a photo on a Facebook page. I handed Simon the phone, and he sat on the bed next to me to accept it.

He used his fingers to expand the picture and scrolled through the details. "Looks like Ralph and Sophia Reynolds. They're at a party of some sort. I see a Christmas tree in the background, and one woman's wearing a necklace made to look like a string of Christmas lights. People are in suits and ties and party dresses, meaning it's a fancy affair. They're about the same age as they are now. That

Ralph was, I mean. So a fairly recent picture. Hard to make out many of the other people. I don't recognize the name of the person who posted it, and I don't think I've ever run into her. Alicia Kennedy. Do you know her?"

"No."

"What time did Bernie send that?" He threw the towel to one side. His hair was wet from the shower and he smelled of shampoo and good soap.

"Four a.m."

"She told Matt she had to get home to work on her book and instead she did some poking into the Reynolds family? And you expect me to believe you two are not investigating?"

I gave him my most innocent smile. "Caught red-handed."

"Can't say I'm gobsmacked."

"I suspect Bernie didn't make up an excuse to give to Matt. She might well have gotten several hundred words written before turning her attention to another matter. On the other hand, she might have rushed home full of enthusiasm, and then forgot all about that enthusiasm and headed down a rabbit hole in pursuit of the Reynoldses."

He ruffled my hair and stood up. "Okay. What do you want me to do?"

"Do? About what?"

"Have you thought any more about what Matt had to say last night?"

"No, and I don't intend to. The idea's ridiculous. Matt writes about crime. He's finding criminal conspiracies everywhere he looks."

"You're probably right, but . . . never mind. As for the other matter, you and Bernie investigating the Reynolds murder, I can help. I could charm the charmless McKenzie. She seems up to it."

"You stay away from McKenzie. Samantha was hinting

pretty strongly that McKenzie sabotaged Hannah's shower, but I don't see her as a murder suspect."

"Why not? Completely self-absorbed is my take on her."

"Too self-absorbed, I think, to make any attempt to remain undiscovered. I wish Amy Redmond would tell us whose prints they found on the box the doll came in."

"That the present-giver made no attempt to hide their prints, means she, and I'll agree McKenzie's a mighty good suspect, didn't expect the gift to be printed. Which it wouldn't have been if not for Ralph's death happening so soon after the shower and you pointing out the incident of the doll to the police."

"For fingerprint evidence to mean anything, the cops have to be able to match it with something they have on file. I'd love to know what caused McKenzie to be printed at some point in the past. I'll get Bernie looking into that."

"Because you're not investigating."

"Right. If McKenzie did play the so-called joke with the doll, and she didn't expect the police to have any interest in it, doesn't that go some way to getting her off the hook for killing her father?"

"If she'd planned it all ahead of time, sure. But otherwise, no."

"I still don't see McKenzie doing it. If she killed her own father, my take on her, for what it's worth, is she'd be eager to let everyone know she was justified in doing it. At a guess, I'd say she was going to tell Hannah all about her little joke in her own time. Spring it on her at the wedding, during the speeches maybe. Anything to get the spotlight turned back on her. But events got away from her. Meaning her father's death. Even McKenzie realized the reveal of her tasteless little joke wouldn't be as hilarious as she originally thought it would be."

"Do what you have to do, Lily. But please, try not to put yourself in danger this time."

"All our so-called investigating is being done online," I said. "Nothing dangerous in that."

"Until it is." He pulled his shirt over his head. "We're assuming the attack, if it even was an attack, on Sophia was intended to be relatively harmless."

"What do you mean, if it was an attack? We both saw the injury."

"People can do things to themselves. Such as administer a whack on the back of the head. Redmond didn't say anything about looking for what might have been used, so I'll have a poke around later. But, as I said, if Sophia didn't do it to herself, the assumption the attack was intended not to cause much harm, might not be correct. I'm going up to the shed to get into me gardening clothes and plan the day. See you at the kitchen?"

"Where else, sadly, would I be?"

He gave me a quick kiss, and headed out. He'd put Éclair into the yard before going for his shower, and she dashed inside and leapt onto the bed. She licked my face with gusto.

"There are," I said, giving her a big hug, "worse ways to start a day."

First thing I did on arriving in the B & B kitchen was to put the coffee on. The second thing was to text Bernie: **Got the picture. Ralph and Sophia at a holiday party. So? What am I missing?**

She didn't reply, and I studied the photo again. I then went to Facebook and searched for Alicia Kennedy. Not an uncommon name, and I got a lot of hits. I took a guess she lived near Boston, if she'd been at the same party as Ralph, and that narrowed the search down considerably. I soon found her. Alicia Kennedy, Facebook helpfully told me, was married with two children, lived in a suburb of

Boston, and had two white rescue cats unimaginatively named Snowball and Snowflake. What was of interest to me was that she worked at Reynolds Tools, and the picture had been taken last December at the company holiday party. It was captioned, *Nice to see big boss Ralph Reynolds, now retired, dropping in with wife Sophie.* She'd gotten Sophia's name wrong, but never mind that.

The couple were posing together, but not smiling and not touching. If anything, Sophia looked downright angry. I remembered what I knew about the state of the marriage and particularly what McKenzie said about her dad always having affairs. He must have dragged the unwilling Sophia to the company party as a way of putting on a good corporate front.

The party seemed to be at a restaurant or event hall. Black-and-white-clad waitstaff passed flutes of sparkling wine, glasses of red and white wine or beer, and a selection of elaborate canapés. A party like that would cost a bundle. Likely it cost more than the company could afford.

Ivan was a faint figure in the background, smiling broadly, chatting to a couple of men around his age. I was about to look more closely at the rest of the sea of faces in the photo when Edna came in, accompanied by Detective Amy Redmond, the latter looking positively perky in a pink linen jacket and black jeans. Her hair was nicely arranged and her light makeup freshly applied.

"Don't you ever sleep?" I said to her.

"Considering you were up last night at the same time as me, I could ask the same of you."

"Yes, but you went off to interview suspects. I went to bed."

"Police work never ends. Nor, I've been told, does feeding people. I managed to snatch some sleep and have a shower. I didn't come in by the front door this morning, as

I decided to take a few minutes to gather my thoughts while overlooking the bay. This truly is a special place, Lily. Even by Cape Cod standards."

"Whereupon I arrived," Edna said, "and interrupted said gathering of thoughts."

"Is that coffee I smell?" Redmond asked hopefully.

"Help yourself," I said. "Mugs are right there. Cream in the fridge."

"Thanks, Lily."

"What brings you here so early?" I asked. I started laying out the baking ingredients while Edna took melons, oranges, and apples out of the fridge. "Can you peel and slice two extra apples, Edna?" I asked. "I want to use them in today's muffins."

"Do I have to request you leave the room, Mrs. Harkness?" Redmond said as she took the first welcome sip of her coffee.

"If you ask me not to repeat what you have to say, I will not. I've spent a lot of years married to a newspaperman, and I can divide my world into distinct parts."

"Good to hear. Okay, Lily, I thought you'd want to know that Jenny Hill's in the clear, so far, for last night."

"Last night?" Edna said.

"I'll fill you in later," I said. "I'm glad to hear it."

"At eleven o'clock last night Jenny, along with her daughter and prospective son-in-law, were at a late-night coffee and dessert place in Provincetown. Greg and Hannah are not exactly impartial witnesses, so I'd take any alibi they give her with a grain of salt. But . . ."

"But . . . ?"

"Jenny Hill is, of all things, a devotee of obscure French art house cinema. She, along with Greg and Hannah, went to the showing of a movie in Provincetown last night. Most boring two hours of his life, Greg told me, but that's beside the point. Jenny got to chatting with another couple as they left the theater. This couple have the same taste as she does, and extensive knowledge of that art form. They all went to the coffee place to discuss the movie. Jenny and the female half of the couple exchanged numbers in case they had a chance to catch another such film. I called the woman involved, and she confirms she and her husband were with Jenny, Greg, and Hannah at the time in question. She says the movie finished at ten thirty, and they lingered over coffee and cake for about an hour. I'll call the theater when they open to confirm that time, the coffeehouse to see if anyone remembers them, and I'll have an officer pay a call on the movie-loving couple later to take a statement. I need to get all the times straight and confirmed, but I'm reasonably confident this couple has no reason to lie for Jenny, and that Jenny, if she was making up an alibi, would find something better than a small coffee shop shortly before closing, when they're likely to remember who came in."

"I'm glad," I said. "That's one thing out of the way, but as for who did attack Sophia, if not Jenny, got any ideas?"

She shook her head. "Not yet. I have an officer checking the spot where the incident occurred, in case something significant was dropped. I'll let you know if we find anything, but I believe a rock was used, and there are a lot of rocks around here, and plenty of places to get rid of a specific one."

Edna sliced fruit. "That's not good. Cops going through the shrubbery."

"What happened isn't a secret," I said. "The other guests heard us talking about it."

"You don't want word getting around this place isn't safe at night, Lily."

"Tell me about it," I said. "Matt said much the same

last night. As it's highly unlikely to have been a random attack, surely the incident has to be directly related to the death of Sophia's husband."

"I am acting on that assumption," Redmond said. "I'm inclined to interpret events as you and Simon outlined them to me. It was not a serious attack, and it was not intended to do any real harm. Why then? To put a fright into Sophia? For what aim? A warning? Warning of what? Is she keeping something from me, and did that person figure they'd better give her a gentle reminder to keep her mouth shut? All I can do is ask her. And I will."

As she talked, I combined ingredients for a batch of apple and cinnamon muffins. Edna tossed chopped fruit into the big glass bowl. Redmond finished her coffee and put the mug into the sink. "Which is the other reason I'm here. To have a talk with Sophia. She might have remembered something new. I told her I'd be here at seven. Can I, once again, use your drawing room?"

"You may." I slipped the tray of muffins into the oven. "These'll be ready in about twenty minutes. If you're still here, you're welcome to one."

"Trying to bribe an officer of the law, Lily?"

"Is it working?"

She grinned. "Yes."

"Before you go, I have a question for you. Maybe more of an observation, but . . . Have you remembered that Dave Farland was in this house the night Ralph died?"

"I haven't forgotten, no. Why?"

"He said something last night that got me thinking. I told you Ralph offered Greg money to not marry Hannah. He told Greg that much money would go a long way toward his mural-painting business."

"You reported hearing that conversation, yes."

"Dave and Greg are partners as well as friends. I mean, partners in that mural-painting business. Dave said something last night about it being hard to make a living when starting out as an artist."

"It's hard to make a living after decades of being an artist. For all but a very small number. But never mind that. What are you thinking?"

"Is it possible Greg told Dave he'd turned his dad down? A hundred thousand is a lot of money. Did Dave then go to Ralph to ask for the money?"

"Dave's sharing a room with Ivan," she said. "Both of them claim to have been asleep at the time we believe Ralph Reynolds died. Easy enough to get up in the night under the pretext of needing the bathroom, check your roommate is snoozing happily, and slip into the hallway. But—aside from the fact that we believe the killer spent some time in Ralph's room, enough time to pour each of them a drink, add the digoxin to the bottle, encourage Ralph to have several more drinks—Ralph's death wouldn't get Dave any money."

"Maybe he expected Greg to inherit."

"Possible. No guarantee of that happening and, if anything, it's unlikely. Ralph's wife is still alive. She's the most likely to inherit. She is, in fact, the only beneficiary mentioned in his will. For what that's worth."

"Reading between the lines, you're saying he didn't have much to leave her."

"No comment."

"Dave might not have been thinking things through properly."

Redmond said nothing, but Edna did. "From what I hear about the way that man died, his killer thought it all through quite carefully. It takes a heck of a cold-hearted person to sit in a bedroom chatting to a man, calmly watching him drink the poison you slipped him."

"You think the killing was premeditated?" Redmond asked.

"Not necessarily planned in advance, but this person might have realized it could eventually come to that. They brought the digoxin with them."

"Plenty of people take that medication," the detective said. "Or they live with or are good friends with someone who does. They might have access to it in other ways. Jenny Hill, for example, is a pharmacist. I'm not forgetting that."

We heard voices from the dining room, and Edna picked up the coffeepot. "It was a highly personal killing. In my opinion, anyway. Either that or the exact opposite—a hired killer who had no relationship with the victim so they didn't mind watching him die."

"A contracted hit," Redmond said, "is not something we're considering. Not at this time."

Edna left with her coffeepot.

"Have you given any thought to suicide?" I asked. "That Ralph gave himself the excess medication on purpose and used the whiskey to help it go down?"

"I consider that unlikely. Consider the missing glass, which you pointed out, although I have noticed people bring their room glasses down to the veranda if they're sitting out with a drink. Ralph has no history of depression and he left no note. People usually do, when they take their own life. Significantly, we found no prints on the bottle or Ralph's glass, other than his."

"Wouldn't that indicate he was the only one who touched them?"

"No prints left by your housekeepers on the glass? Nothing left by random liquor store employees on the bottle? They were wiped clean before Ralph helped himself to his last drink. As were the bedside table and the arms of the chair in that room.

"As long as we're talking," she continued. "I'll tell you

something confidential, Lily. Dave Farland has a police record."

I sucked in a breath. She held up a hand. "Don't get too excited. The charges are minor, so I don't think it's a problem telling you about it. Several counts of vandalism in New York City and Boston. He's a mural artist, he says. Another word for that is graffiti, and if the property owner hasn't agreed to display the art, it's a crime. No charges are more recent than two years ago. Around that time, he and Greg Reynolds started looking for work doing large-scale murals. By work, I mean paying gigs, approved of and contracted with the owners of the property. The sides of public buildings like libraries, entire walls inside fashionable restaurants, exteriors of private homes. I've seen some of their designs, and I have to say they're good. But contracts have been slow in coming. The death of Ralph Reynolds wouldn't have helped with that, not in any way. It's seven now, and I need to meet with Sophia."

"Okay, okay. Before you go, what do you know about Samantha, the bridesmaid? Do you have anything on her?"

"You're relentless, Lily, I'll give you that. Samantha Dowling is a kindergarten teacher, which is where she met Hannah who teaches third grade at the same school. Not a lot of call for contract killers in that line of work. Or so they tell me."

I didn't hear from Bernie until I was in the tearoom kitchen, getting bowls and measuring spoons and cups and ingredients out and assembled for another day.

She didn't call ahead, but came through the back door. "Hey."

"Hey, yourself. What brings you here?"

"You do, Lily."

"Okay. Why?"

"You got the text I sent you. The one with the picture of the Christmas party."

"I had a glance at it earlier, but I've been too busy to look at it again. Detective Redmond came by to tell me Jenny Hill has a solid alibi for last night. A new guest sent his eggs back twice, first saying they were overdone, and then they were underdone. His wife complained that we didn't offer dairy-free yoghurt. We would, if you'd been polite enough to request it, was my reply. Although that was only in my head. Two of the bridge women had the nerve to stroll into the dining room at two minutes to nine asking for the full English breakfast. And then—"

"Hold the thought of the bridge women. Why did Jenny Hill need an alibi for last night?"

"Hey! I know something you don't. That doesn't happen often."

"It never happens, and let's make sure it doesn't happen again. As for now, spill. Any coffee in that pot?"

"No, but you can make some if you want. Sophia Reynolds was attacked while walking in the garden last night around eleven."

Bernie came to a complete halt, hand frozen as it extended toward the coffee tin. "Wow. Do you know by who? By whom? Is she okay?"

"She's fine, and I don't know who did it. Simon and I found her after the attacker had fled. What's interesting, and perhaps significant, is it wasn't a serious attack. Either the person had an abrupt change of heart and ran off without finishing the deed, or they didn't intend her any harm other than a good fright and a minor lump on the head."

"Lumps on the noggin can still be dangerous." Bernie rubbed at her own head. "As my mom told me when we were in the ER after I fell off those swings in the Central Park playground."

"Yes, when you were nineteen and swinging upside down from the upper bar of the swing set with your feet hooked over it."

"Good times. Good times. You want a coffee?"

"No, thanks. Have a peek in the freezer, will you, and see if any containers are labeled OS."

"What's OS stand for?"

"Orange scones."

She buried her head in the depths of the freezer and rummaged around. "Nope. Some CS though. And PS. What's that?"

"Currant scones and plain scones, of course. I'd better get a batch of orange ones made in case we have requests for the royal tea today. Take out a container of CS, please. The oldest date first."

Bernie did so. "If Jenny needed an alibi, does that mean the cops think she did it?"

"Sophia said she thought it was Jenny, although she wasn't positive. Naturally Redmond had to check it out. I think Amy Redmond's starting to trust me, even if only a little bit. She came into the kitchen this morning to tell me what she'd learned."

"Considering all we know about the Reynolds family, I wouldn't be surprised if Regina had done it, if only because she's nasty that way."

"As Sophia pointed out, Regina is not exactly quick and agile and able to slip silently away into the dark. Plus Regina, so Sophia said, is considerably shorter than the alleged attacker. Okay, now you're up to date on last night's happenings. Before we go on, I learned some interesting things about Dave Farland." I filled her in briefly on Dave's arrest record.

Bernie threw up her hands. "I don't know why you need me."

"I don't need you, as I am not investigating. I'm listening to the detective and you're the one doing the investigating. Did you know about Dave's past?"

"Yeah. I checked up on him. Not a lot to find. He attempted to express his artistic side through unauthorized means on the undersides of bridges, et cetera. He got slapped on the wrist a couple of times, and then he clearly decided it would be wise to find more legal means of artistic expression. He hooked up with Greg Reynolds in a mural-painting business. They got a couple of contracts. For one, they painted the wall next to the parking lot of a small-town library. Fabulous scene of rows of children reading books. I loved it and next time I'm up that way I'm going to make a detour to see it. But, as we know, small-town libraries don't have much in their budgets for extras such as art, so work's been slow coming in. They're financially pinched, but I don't see Dave killing Ralph in hopes of Greg inheriting. For one thing, Greg's mother's still alive, and even if the Reynolds family was seriously wealthy, which they are not, for all Dave knows if Greg scored big-time financially he might decide he doesn't need a business partner anymore."

"Okay, we can put a line through Dave. What about Samantha? You were going to look into her, too."

"Kindergarten teacher. Parents still alive. Two sisters and one brother, none of whom have anything sketchy about them. Nice middle-class family, and I could find no evidence to the contrary. She's engaged herself; wedding will be in early September."

"Really? Does her fiancé have anything to do with the Reynolds family?"

"No, and he didn't come for Hannah's wedding. He's in England for the summer, doing research for his PhD in British history. Something about family life during the Industrial Revolution."

"We seem to be hitting a lot of dead ends. Did you learn anything else significant?"

Bernie rolled her eyes. "Lily, have you forgotten the picture?"

"The picture? Oh, right. The picture you think is so important you sent it to me in the middle of the night. Why were you working on the case in the middle of the night anyway? Matt said you ditched him because the muse was calling."

"And so she was." Bernie wiggled her fingers as though summoning said muse. "I got a couple of good writing hours in, and then decided to have a last-minute troll through the affairs of the Reynolds family before going to bed."

"Before you let me in on your big reveal, have you found anything that might indicate McKenzie has been fingerprinted at some time?"

"Obviously you're thinking about the Raggedy Ann doll, and the answer is yes. Or yes, probably. A friend of hers had some valuable items stolen about a year ago. McKenzie had been at the friend's house recently. Her prints were likely taken for elimination purposes, as the cops call it. She must have been eliminated, as she was never charged. The prints should have been destroyed. That might not have happened. May I continue?"

"You may."

"When searching on the Internet, you can spend hours upon hours looking at a heck of a lot of unnecessary dross. And then, amongst all that dross, suddenly, a true jewel appears out of apparently nowhere." She beamed at me. "And such happened last night. Have a look at that picture again."

I took out my phone and did so.

"What do you see?"

"According to the person who posted this, it's Reynolds

Tools's annual holiday party for employees and various people in the same office building or who they regularly do business with. I see Ralph and Sophia, clearly not enjoying each other's company, but they never pretended to be a happily married couple. They're about the same age they are now, so the party was likely held last year, if not the year before. Ivan's there, along with waitstaff and a bunch of employees and spouses, clients, and other such. I see a lot of money being spent, which we know the company couldn't afford."

"Focus in. Look to the left of Sophia. The woman in the blue dress. She's partly obscured by that big guy, which is likely why you didn't see her the first time. She has a glass of wine in her hand and a sour look on her face. She's watching Sophia."

I looked. I expanded the image, focusing on the woman Bernie pointed out. And I saw it. "Oh, my gosh."

"Exactly. We have a hit."

# Chapter 22

"Might be a coincidence," I said.

"Sure, if this person had stepped up and said, 'Hey. Ralph and Sophia, fancy meeting you here. What a coincidence.' Instead of pretending not to know them."

"Okay. You've got a point. It could still be a coincidence though, and seeing the Reynoldses were here for a family wedding, she didn't want to interfere. We should be able to find out easily enough."

"That's what I like to hear. What have you got in mind?"

"First, I have in mind to get these scones made. Mary-beth and Cheryl will be here in a few minute, and they can keep an eye on the oven while I run up to the house. I want to have a look at the reservations book."

Bernie gave me the Warrior Princess grin. "That's my girl."

The reservations book, of course, wasn't a real book, but an online record. I have nothing to do with the running of the B & B other than making the breakfasts, so Bernie and I had to pay a call on Rose.

We found her up and dressed and working on her computer. A cup of tea, slice of half-eaten toast and marmalade, and Robert the Bruce were on the desktop beside her.

"Excellent timing," she said when Bernie and I came in. "I need your advice."

"I don't have a lot of time," I said. "I have to get back to the tearoom, but—"

"I'm wondering if I'm paying Edna too much."

That stopped me in my tracks. "Are you nuts?"

"Look at this." She indicated the computer screen. "North Augusta Bakery is advertising for waitstaff, and they're offering half what Edna gets."

"First of all, the reason North Augusta Bakery is looking for help in the middle of the season is that no one wants to work there. Second of all, Edna puts in three hours a day; not many people want those sort of hours, and to start at six thirty. Third, you do realize Edna is doing us a favor? She doesn't need the money; she likes having a job and then having the rest of her day free to pursue her other interests. Fourth—"

"Bernadette," Rose said. "You probably need a source of income, having foolishly given up your job on a whim."

"Oh yeah," Bernie said. "I'm going to come and work for Lily. And you. For half wages."

"Lily, love, surely you don't need to be in the kitchen all the time. Perhaps we can economize by offering a continental breakfast. That impresses some people because they think continental sounds fancy. You would then be free to wait tables."

I choked.

"Why are you talking about economizing, Rose?" Bernie asked. "Are you having cash-flow problems? I can have a look at your books, if you like, see if anything—other than Edna's wages—stands out as being problematic."

"If Edna quits, I quit," I said. "Besides, you can't charge

the rates you do and then turn around and offer the sort of breakfast people can get at the Fly-by-Night Motel."

Rose swung her chair around to face us. Robert the Bruce stood up and stretched, and then he strolled across the keyboard. The page of job advertisements disappeared, and he jumped off the desk. "We're not having cash-flow problems, or any other sort of financial difficulties," my grandmother said. "I went down to the dining room earlier and happened to overhear Regina Reynolds chastising her grandson, the elder one, not the groom-to-be, for failing to pay sufficient attention to business. She wants him to fire his personal assistant on the grounds that she costs too much. Ivan replied that the woman had been the PA to his father for almost thirty years, and she's paid commensurate with her experience and standing, and Regina said sentiment has no place in business. So, I thought . . . perhaps I should be more of a hardheaded businesswoman. Like Regina."

Bernie shook her head. "Need I remind you that just about everyone in Regina's family hates everyone else, and the rot quite likely begins with Regina herself. Hardheaded can be another word for not-nice."

Rose smiled at Bernie. "Such a level head you have, Bernadette. You're quite right. I won't take Regina Reynolds as an example. Now, what brings you two here this morning?"

"We have a question about reservations," I said.

"We're almost completely booked for the rest of the summer, a not-unexpected slow time in October and early November, but looking promising throughout the holiday season, I'm happy to say. So perhaps economizing won't be necessary after all."

"Glad to hear it," I said. "Because if you get rid of Edna, I quit, and that means you'll be serving supermarket-packaged muffins yourself. I'm not interested in future reservations, but in past. Those four women who are here on a bridge vacation. Can you check when they booked?"

"Why do you want to know?"

"I can't say. Yet."

Rose swung back to the computer. She fixed her glasses on her face and typed rapidly. "Two rooms, garden view, each with twin beds, were reserved on April twenty-second."

"Who made the booking?"

"Karen O'Keefe."

Bernie and I exchanged grins and high-fived.

Rose cocked her head in question. Robbie returned to his spot on the desk and also gave us questioning looks.

"Out of interest," Bernie asked, "when did the Reynolds family make their booking?"

More typing. "On April twentieth, Sophia reserved five rooms and put down a deposit. Two days before this Karen. Do you think that's significant?"

"We think it might be highly significant."

"I left my laptop at home," Bernie said. "So I'll go there now and get to work. Hopefully I can find something incriminating. We're going to need a lot more than just a couple of dates to bring this to the attention of the police."

Rose's eyes narrowed. Robbie hissed and stared at me through slits. I looked from one to the other. They did resemble each other to an uncanny degree sometimes. "What's going on?" my grandmother asked.

"Bernie found a photo of Ralph and Sophia at a company party. Karen, one of the bridge group, appears to have been a guest at that party. In the photo she's watching Ralph and Sophia and not looking all that happy. Which proves absolutely nothing. She might have been suffering from an upset tummy or had too much to drink, but it has our Spidey senses tingling. If Karen knew Ralph and Sophia well enough to go to their company holiday party, why wouldn't she say hi on running into them here?

I've just remembered something, Regina recognized her. She said hi."

"Why didn't you mention it earlier?" Bernie asked.

"Because I didn't think anything of it. She said hi in passing, as in simple politeness to someone she doesn't know. But Regina isn't exactly the sort of warm and friendly person who greets random strangers. Karen, in turn, called Regina Mrs. Reynolds. Which, now that I am thinking about it, is very formal for two people on vacation passing in the hallway. Meaning Karen did know the family, some of them anyway. After Ralph died, why wouldn't she mention she knew them from before? From what I've observed, Sophia doesn't appear to know her. They could be pretending. And if they are pretending, all the more reason to want to know why."

"You aren't here all the time, love," Rose pointed out. "Do you know for sure she didn't greet Ralph and Sophia?"

"Well, no," I admitted. "That's why we need to keep digging before we go to Detective Redmond. We can't take vague theories to her."

"When do the bridge women check out?" Bernie asked.

"Tomorrow."

"Gives us some time, then."

"Let me know what help you need," Rose said. "While you're here, love, I was comparing the cost of the blueberries you buy from the local farm to ones sold at the supermarket and you're paying too much."

"Feel free," I said, "to do the shopping yourself. And while you're at it, you can scratch out the line on the website that says baked goods served at our B & B are made with fresh ingredients sourced from local farmers."

Bernie and I left Rose's suite. "Regina," I said, "has a lot to answer for. And I do not mean regarding her own family. What do we do now?"

"Let me do some further digging into this Karen person.

Fortunately, I now have a last name. In the meantime, you do what you do best—bake. I'll come up to the tearoom later and tell you what I learned, if anything, and we can call Amy. Hand everything we know, and what we suspect, over to her."

We walked down the hallway together, and stepped outside. In one of those coincidences that make life interesting, two members of the bridge group were enjoying their coffee on the veranda. Sheila was reading a book on bidding, and Marie scrolled through her phone.

"Good morning," Bernie said cheerfully. "Lovely day."

They looked up from their reading and gave us matching smiles. "It sure is."

"I hope you're enjoying your vacation."

"It's been perfect, thank you. This is such a fabulous place."

"Where are you from, if you don't mind my asking?" Bernie looked at me and jerked her head toward the women.

"What?" I mouthed.

"Boston area," Sheila said. Her eyes wandered back to the page.

Another jerk of the head from Bernie.

"Did you know Pat McClintock's mother moved into an assisted living place?" Marie said.

"No, I didn't," Sheila replied. "That's got to have been a hard decision for Pat."

"Why did you decide on coming to North Augusta?" Bernie asked. "Have you been here before?"

"Never. But it sounded nice when it was suggested."

"Who suggested you come here?"

Shelia lifted her head and looked at Bernie. "Why are you asking that?"

"It's part of a customer satisfaction survey we're doing," I said. "Helps with our marketing if we know what brings people here. And what gets them coming back. I hope you'll be back."

Marie put her phone down. "Okay, I'd be happy to help. I'd love to come here again. The town's lovely and your B & B is the perfect place for a retreat. But, to be honest, I won't be coming again. It's just too expensive for me."

"Noted," I said.

"Me too," Sheila said. "An indulgence once in a while is great, but my husband would have a fit if I ever paid for what five nights at this place costs."

Marie laughed. "You never know. Maybe we'll get lucky and be offered a free vacation again."

"Free?" Bernie said. "Did you win a contest or something?"

"Our friend paid for us all."

"Which friend?" Bernie asked ever-so-innocently.

Now they were comfortably chatting, Sheila and Marie put their book and phone aside. "Karen. We've been talking for ages about having a real bridge vacation. Stay at a nice place, eat restaurant meals, go on day excursions, and play all the bridge we can stand."

"And that's a heck of a lot," Sheila said.

"No whiny kids. No even whinier husbands. No cleaning. No cooking. Heaven. We dithered for ages, right, Sheila? Never could manage to find the time away from our jobs and families, or a place we all wanted to go to. Laurie found that place with a pool which looked fine at first, but it turned out to be a motel on the highway, and I said I wasn't too keen on going someplace like that. Not to pay good money to sit in a dark, badly decorated motel room to play."

"Then, in a stroke of great luck, Karen discovered this place. She said she's always wanted to come to the Outer

Cape, but never had the chance. I said sorry, it's far too expensive for me, but Karen offered to treat us. She came into a small inheritance recently and wanted to use the money for something special, rather than just fritter it away. Wasn't that nice?"

"Very nice," I said.

"Very nice," Bernie repeated. "When was that?"

"Couple of months ago. It would have been cheaper to come in the spring, and I told her that, but Karen wanted to come in the summer, when the gardens would be at their best, she said. Have to say, I didn't know she was such a garden enthusiast. Does she talk gardening with you, Marie?"

"No. I haven't seen her paying any particular attention to the gardens here. Although they're fabulous. The rose garden in particular. I was talking to the gardener the other day, asking him how he manages in such rocky, sandy soil, and with the salty wind blowing off the bay. He's such a cutie and that accent! Makes me wish I was twenty years younger. Anyway he told me—"

"Good friends are you?" Bernie said before the other woman could launch into a recitation of Simon's gardening practices.

"I haven't met him before," Marie said.

"I mean the bridge group. The four of you."

"Marie and I've known each other for years," Sheila said. "Decades even, but we aren't true friends with Laurie or Karen, other than as bridge players. We play twice a week as part of the bridge club in our town, and that's about all. When Karen proposed this trip, I thought it was her way of trying to get closer to us. She's been distracted most of the time, though."

"Distracted how?" Bernie asked.

Sheila shrugged. "As I said, I don't know her all that

well, so I can't really say. She's been off her game since we got here."

"And how," Marie said. "She's one of the best players in our club. This week, she's been on another planet."

"Don't forget she was sick that one night," Shelia pointed out. "Maybe whatever bug she has is lingering more than she's telling us."

"Maybe. Anyway, as for me, I'm not looking forward to going home. It's going to be hard to go back to having nothing but a bowl of soggy cereal for breakfast. Never mind brown bag lunches, and eating my own cooking at dinner. And then cleaning up after." Her phone buzzed with an incoming text and she glanced at it. "Laurie. She and Karen want to know if we're ready to play."

"Any time," Sheila said.

"You should come to Lily's tearoom before you leave," Bernie said. "That'll really spoil you for daily life."

Both women groaned. We wished them a good day and began to go our separate ways, Bernie to her car, and me to the tearoom.

Ivan and Greg Reynolds came onto the veranda. They nodded politely to Shelia and Marie and skipped nimbly down the steps. Bernie gave me a waggle of the eyebrows and jerked her head in the direction of the brothers.

"What?" I mouthed.

Another jerk.

I shrugged. She shook her head. "Morning, guys!" she called.

"Good morning," they replied.

Ivan clicked the fob in his hand and his car flashed its lights in greeting. The car was a late-model Cadillac Escalade, gleaming black. Bernie had parked her rusty old thing next to it; I wouldn't have been surprised if the Escalade had tried to edge farther away. Ivan headed for the driver's seat and Greg rounded the car for the passenger door.

Bernie intercepted him. "I'm Bernie Murphy, Lily's good friend. If I didn't say so before, my condolences on your loss."

"Thank you," Greg said.

"I hope your wedding can be rescheduled without too much trouble."

"I hope so too, but we'll have to see," Greg said.

"I don't want to appear insensitive," Bernie said insensitively, "but I have to ask. When are you checking out?"

"What?"

"Out of here, I mean." She lifted her arms to take in the lovely old house that was Victoria-on-Sea. "I help Rose with financial matters and obviously as this is the high season we—"

"My mother told your grandmother—" Ivan said.

"Lily's grandmother. Not mine."

"Whatever. We told her we'll be checking out tomorrow. As planned."

"Thanks. She forgets, sometimes, to fill me in. You know how it is, when they get to be that age."

"I most definitely do not know how it is," Ivan said more to himself than Bernie. I assumed he was thinking of Regina, his own grandmother.

"Will you be taking your father's remains home?" Bernie asked Greg.

He grimaced. "Not yet, I'm sorry to say. The cops are still holding on to . . . him. My mother wants to get home, and my grandmother says she . . . I mean Ivan . . . can't neglect the company any longer. The family's packing up, but I'll find someplace else to stay. Jenny's . . . she might be needed to stay a bit longer. To help the police."

"Come on," Ivan said. "We're running late as it is."

"We won't keep you any longer," Bernie said. "One more thing, though. This might sound like a silly question, but do your parents play bridge?"

"Bridge? That is a silly question." Ivan got into the car. He tapped the horn, telling his brother to hurry up.

"No," Greg said. "Not that I'm aware of, although I suppose they could have taken it up. Dad golfed and Mom plays tennis, but I don't know about bridge or any other card games. Grandma isn't interested in much other than the stock market and the business news."

Bernie didn't make any attempt to get into her own car. Instead we watched the Reynolds brothers drive away.

"What was that about?" I asked her.

"We now know it's unlikely Ralph and/or Sophia are bridge acquaintances of Karen and her lot. Same for Regina."

"Do we care?"

"It's all part of putting together the various pieces of the puzzle, Lily. You say Regina appeared to recognize Karen, but in a distant and dismissive way. I doubt they were friends or even had mutual interests. If Karen had some small involvement with Reynolds Tools, enough to be invited to their holiday party, Regina likely recognized her from that connection, but it wasn't important enough to her to so much as stop and exchange greetings. Or even tell the police. As for Sophia, if she played bridge, I'd wonder if she'd invited those women here for her own possibly nefarious reasons. Such now seems unlikely."

"It's also unlikely they all participate in dressage competitions. You can't ask them about everything in their lives."

"Dressage, or any other type of equestrianism, Lily, has not been mentioned in any of my online searches. I'm thinking it was easier when I was working for the law firm. I found the dirt. They sent someone out to follow it up. Such is why I have not set my novel in contemporary times. Far too easy to get distracted by all this online stuff."

I smiled at her and didn't point out that Bernie could get distracted by a squirrel. "Speaking of such, I do have a business of my own to run. Let's check in in a few hours."

# Chapter 23

Later that afternoon, Bernie FaceTimed me. "Time's running short as everyone's leaving town tomorrow. I'm bringing Rose in on this call as I have an idea."

"An idea," Cheryl said. "Can't wait to hear it. Not."

"Didn't you happen to mention that your bridge club has changed their weekly meeting to Monday?" Bernie said when Rose had joined the call. I could see more of Robbie's curious face on the screen than Rose's but at least I could hear her.

"Yes, and to the evening rather than the afternoon, overriding my strongly expressed objections. Most inconvenient. I've decided not to go tonight. The only decent player in my new foursome is on vacation. The only decent player other than me, if I'm being honest. I'm thinking of giving the club up. It's becoming boring, and since they switched to playing in the evening, I'm not enjoying it as much."

"What a stroke of luck," Bernie said. "I suggest you go tonight, Rose. Why not invite someone to be your partner? How about Karen?"

"I will do that, but only if you tell me why this sudden interest in my bridge activities."

"I'd also like to know why," Cheryl said as she prepared a pot of English Breakfast. "Always scheming, you two. You three."

Bernie explained our rather hastily thought-up plan.

Or, I should say, her hastily thought-up plan. I had my doubts.

After our talk with Shelia and Marie on the veranda, Bernie and I briefly conferred before she left. "I'll continue looking into Karen's background," Bernie said, "but I think we have enough to act upon."

"Why is it up to us to act upon anything? And, assuming it is up to us, what sort of action are we taking?"

"I have a plan."

"I'm sure you do."

We both now believed Karen O'Keefe was responsible for the death of Ralph Reynolds. Proving it was another matter entirely. Even getting the police to listen to us was another matter entirely. Bernie had come up with a "plan" that involved Rose.

"We have a plan," I said to Amy Redmond. I'd called her earlier, but reached her voice mail. It was after three when she dropped by to ask what I wanted. I suggested we talk outside, to give me a fresh air break. As an extra inducement (okay, a bribe) I offered the good detective a maple pecan square, still warm from the oven.

She took a bite and her eyes widened. "I like this, Lily. This might be the best thing you've made for me yet. And that's saying a great deal. Sweet but not too sweet, and chewy but not too chewy."

"Thanks. Always nice to be appreciated."

"As for your plan. I don't want to hear it."

"Unfortunately," I replied, "you have to. Or Bernie will

act on her own. She and Rose will act on their own, I should say."

"If I must." She sighed. "Go ahead."

We were standing at the back door of Tea by the Sea, in the cool shade of the big old oak tree. Bernie was still at her place searching for further evidence on her computer, and she'd assigned me to tell Redmond what we were up to. When I complained that it wasn't my hastily thought-out plan, Bernie reminded me that only yesterday, I said the detective was beginning to trust me.

I'd cursed my big mouth.

"You really think this woman, if she did kill Ralph, and that's highly questionable, is going to confess all to Rose over a hand of bridge?" Redmond licked the last crumbs of the square's shortbread base off her fingers.

"Rose does have a way of getting people to talk to her. Look what happened in the Smithfield murder."

"I'll admit," Redmond said, "there is something to be said about the sweet little-old-lady act that puts people off guard. Even better if she has that cat on her lap. Totally fits the stereotype."

"Trusting to stereotypes can be dangerous."

"As I've learned since meeting you bunch. On the grounds that it can't do any harm, and it's no more ridiculous than some of Bernie's other schemes, I'll go along with it."

"Great. One more thing."

"Only one?"

"You found McKenzie Reynolds's prints on the box containing the Raggedy Ann doll, didn't you? I've a rough idea of where everyone was when Hannah opened that gift and during the aftermath, and McKenzie didn't come any-where near it. Meaning, if she touched the box at any time, it had to be before it was gift wrapped. You don't have to admit it. You can just . . . wink or something."

"As playing a prank, no matter how mean it might be, is

not a criminal offense, I'm happy to wink away." She did so. "We spoke to her about the incident, and she readily admitted it. Said it was a joke. A lark. She claims she expected Hannah would get the joke and she, McKenzie, was mortified when she failed to do so. We're confident the incident has nothing to do with the death of Ralph Reynolds. Particularly if your guess—"

"My carefully thought-out deduction based on my in-depth knowledge of the human condition."

"If Bernie's guess proves to be right."

"That stupid incident might not have had anything to do with Ralph's death, but it set the tone for the entire weekend."

"See you at seven, as planned," Detective Redmond said.

Simon came into the kitchen as Redmond was driving away. "What did she want this time?"

"Nothing."

He raised one eyebrow.

"I mean nothing new," I said.

Cheryl hummed to herself.

"What do you know, Cheryl?" Simon asked her.

"I know nothing. And, if I did, it would be more than my job's worth to tell you."

"The bus tour's pulling up," Marybeth said. "The patio tables are all set. Are we ready in here?"

I groaned. "Tell me again how many people are in the bus?"

"Twelve. Plus the driver."

"We can manage with what I've got on hand. But it'll leave me hard-pressed for tomorrow and . . . I can't stay late tonight to bake."

"Why not?" Simon asked.

"Because . . . uh . . . I'm doing something with Bernie."

"You and Bernie and Detective Redmond. I can only guess." He went to the sink and turned on the tap. "Okay. Keep your secrets. What do you need doing?"

I came up behind him and wrapped my arms around his waist. "Thanks."

"Other duties as assigned. This job is proving to be more interesting and varied than I expected. Close protection officer/assistant chef/gardener. I wonder if there's any openings at Buckingham Palace."

"Why?" Marybeth asked.

"They need people with a range of skills." He finished washing his hands. I stepped away, and he turned and kissed the top of my head. "Scones?"

"Thanks. I can run a tearoom if we're short of many things, but not scones. Or tea."

Simon's mother owned a catering business. He grew up helping her, knew his way around a kitchen, and had pitched in several times to help me when I needed it. He didn't have to be told what to do and started preparing currant scones, leaving me free to make a variety of mini-cupcakes to put away for tomorrow. We worked in companionable silence while Cheryl and Marybeth bustled in and out of the kitchen, brewing teas and arranging the food stands.

My kitchen is small, it is in fact positively tiny, but the four of us worked well together, and we didn't often get in each other's way.

By five thirty, the freezer was stocked with scones, the cake and cookie tins were full, and pistachio macaron shells were cooling prior to being filled.

Marybeth came in with an armload of dishes. "Another full and satisfied group. They've left. A couple of people are still on the patio dragging out the last of their tea, and that's it for another day."

"Did they tip?" I asked. People in tour groups often don't, thinking it's taken care of in their tour fees.

"Yes, and very well." Cheryl slipped past her daughter, heading for the closet. I was pleased. My employees worked hard and always kept up a warm, cheerful, friendly front no matter how demanding the customer might be.

Cheryl came out with the vacuum cleaner and dragged it into the dining room.

"I'd stay awhile and give you a hand, Lily," Marybeth said, "but the kids—"

I smiled at her. "No problem. Simon to the rescue."

"As always," he said. "We have about an hour until you have to leave for your mysterious appointment, so what's next?"

"The easy stuff," I said. "The chicken I took out of the freezer earlier should be thawed by now, so you can poach it in Darjeeling, please. Recipe's in my binder. Can you boil a dozen eggs? I'll make the sandwich fillings in the morning. I've just enough time to whip up a batch of shortbread before we have to finish here."

At six thirty my phone rang, the tone telling me it was Rose. "We're about ready to leave, love. Do you want me to pick you up?"

"Heavens, no. I can't be seen. This is an undercover operation, remember?"

Simon groaned.

I suddenly realized my cleverly constructed plan had an enormous hole in it. I don't own a car. I never needed one in Manhattan, and since coming to the Cape, Rose and I share her geriatric Ford Focus. Rose needed the car to drive her and Karen to the bridge club gathering. Bernie and I had arranged to meet at the community center. Marybeth and Cheryl had left for the night. I could call Amy Redmond for a lift, but she might have other things on at the moment.

Which meant I'd have to take a cab. At six thirty, the cabs would be busy taking people into town for dinner. They might not be able to get me there on time.

"Problem?" Simon had a decided twinkle in his blue eyes.

I smiled sweetly at him. "I might have encountered a small glitch. I need a lift into town."

"Just so happens, I keep my spare helmet in the garden shed."

"Maybe we could call Matt and ask to borrow his car?"

"Matt's gone to North Dakota and won't be back until tomorrow. Interviews to conduct for the new book."

I thought. I didn't know which bothered me more: Simon knowing what Bernie and I were up to, or the prospect of riding on his motorcycle.

The oven timer tinged to tell me the shortbread was ready. Time to decide.

"Okay," I said. "You can take me. We're going to a bridge game."

His face fell so much I almost broke out laughing. "Bridge? All this secrecy around a card game?"

"Yup."

His eyes narrowed. "You don't play bridge, Lily."

"I'm always eager to learn new things." I took the beautifully golden cookies out of the oven. "These need about five minutes to cool and then we can be on our way. You go and get the bike. And"—gulp—"the extra helmet."

"Good thing you're wearing long trousers today."

I glanced down at my jeans-covered legs. "Why?"

"In case you come off. Bare skin on tarmac or gravel is not a good thing. I have a jacket you can wear." He slipped out the back.

I reconsidered my options. We were only going into town. Fortunately, the community center was on this side of North Augusta. It was daylight. It was a Monday evening so tourist traffic should be light. If I survived the journey, I could beg a ride home in a car.

I took a deep breath. "You can do this, Lily," I said.

# Chapter 24

It wasn't as bad as I feared. Simon put the spare helmet on my head and tested the straps before handing me a jean jacket, full of holes and numerous poorly applied patches. I eyed the jacket with suspicion. "Are these tread marks I see?"

"No, that's a rip from being snagged on a rose thorn. This is the jacket I wear if it's cold, and I'm working in the potting shed or planting."

Suitably dressed, trying to control my panic, I awkwardly swung my leg over the back of the enormous machine and tried to settle into the seat. Simon showed me where to put my feet, snapped the visor of his own helmet over his face, and jumped nimbly on. I held on to him for dear life, and the motorcycle roared into action.

By the time we reached the top of the driveway, I was ready to get off. But after that, once he hit the open road and sped up, it wasn't so bad. The weather was good, the sky clear, and he didn't go too fast. Houses lining the ocean to our left passed in less than a total blur. Once I opened my eyes at any rate. Simon might have approached a fence lining the road too closely, and I feared for my right knee, but contact was avoided. Simon's body was warm and strong under my grip. I wondered if I was holding on too tight. I wouldn't want to cut off his breathing so he passed out and we crashed as he was coming around a cliffside corner. I let go, fractionally. The bike hit a bump, I yelped, and held on even harder than before. I was starting to think maybe a longer trip wouldn't be so bad after all when we pulled up to the North Augusta Community Center. To my intense disappointment Bernie, Rose, and Amy Redmond were not around to notice how brave I'd been.

Simon pulled off his helmet and twisted in his seat. "Still alive back there?"

"It wasn't so bad."

He held out his hand and I clambered off.

"Keep the helmet with you," he said. "I'll park over there and join you."

"You're coming in?"

"Can't have you hitching a ride home."

"I—"

Too late to argue. He wheeled the motorcycle to a parking space, leaving me dressed in a far-too-big, ratty old jean jacket and carrying a motorcycle helmet. I took a quick peek at my phone. Five to seven. People were entering or leaving the center with yoga mats tucked under their arms or accompanied by kids wearing or carrying sports gear. Bridge players, most of them in their fifties and up, dressed in street clothes, were arriving.

I waited for Simon to join me. He was here now, and I couldn't have him blundering around trying to find me.

He ran up the steps, also carrying his helmet. "Where to?"

When we planned this expedition, Rose explained the layout of the community center and the room where the bridge club met. "We're going to meeting room A," I said. "Must be that way."

We walked past the reception desk and down the hall. A large room was to our left, and I saw women and men in sleek fitness gear laying out their yoga mats and doing warm-up stretches.

We passed meeting room B on our right. It was arranged with several small tables, each surrounded by four chairs. I took a sideways peek and spotted Rose sitting comfortably at a table against the far wall. Karen O'Keefe sat opposite her and two other women were preparing to sit down. Rose was dressed in a loose-fitting, high-necked yellow blouse.

Simon and I slipped into meeting room A, conveniently located on the other side of the wall from Rose's table in the much larger room B.

Bernie and Amy Redmond looked up as we came in. A table for six filled the small room, and the only window looked out over the parking lot. A small electronic device sat in the center of the table.

"What's he doing here?" Bernie asked.

"Don't ask," I said.

"I'm here in my role of chauffeur and close protection officer," he said. "Don't blame Lily. I didn't give her a lot of choice."

"You can't see anything from here," I said. "I can't hear anything, either, other than a mixed-up, indistinct babble of voices. Shall I assume Rose is wired?"

"It worked the last time," Bernie said.

"Wire?" Simon said.

"Keep your voices down," Redmond said as she switched on the machine. We heard throats clearing, greetings being exchanged, chairs scraping the floor.

"Isn't this nice?" Rose's staticky voice emerged from the machine on the table. "Ladies, this is Karen, visiting us from . . . someplace in Massachusetts."

Everyone said a version of hello. And the game began.

If you think playing bridge is boring, try listening to a game without seeing what's going on. Cards were dealt, the women went around the table either bidding or passing, play began, the round finished, the score was recorded.

Repeat.

Repeat.

These were serious bridge players. General chitchat was not permitted or tolerated. I got the vague idea Rose and Karen were winning, but not by much.

At eight o'clock, someone, who they referred to as the director, announced, "Break time. Be back in ten minutes, everyone."

"What! What!" Simon, snoozing in his uncomfortable chair, jerked awake.

"Some close protection officer you are," Bernie said.

"I'm ready to swing into action at a moment's notice. And action is what's seriously missing from this scene."

"I'm beginning to think this was a waste of time," Redmond said.

"You're an excellent player," Rose's voice came through the speaker. "Thank you for joining me tonight."

"As are you," Karen said. "Although I've noticed you're overly fond of spades."

"I always bid high when I have a good spade hand," Rose said.

"Which is fine, until your opponents notice your strategy."

"A risk, I'll admit. Speaking of risks, love, I appreciate that you and your friends stayed on at Victoria-on-Sea after that unfortunate man was murdered. Such a dreadful business. Many people might have left under the circumstances."

"One of my friends suggested going home, but I pointed out to her that we'd lose what we'd paid, right?"

"Such is in the registration agreement, yes."

"Besides, it's not as though a serial killer offed him, is it? We were in no danger."

"How can you know that? Not that I think a serial killer is operating in the area, but . . ."

"It was a personal thing, right? My money's on his mother. Is she ever a dragon. I couldn't help but overhear a lot of what went on. Not that I was trying to listen, of course, none of my business, but your house, outside the bedrooms, is a public area, right?"

"People do talk sometimes as though they're in their own home," Rose said.

"If not the mother, then the wife. It was obvious, before he died I mean, they didn't love each other. It had to be a personal killing. Someone he invited into his room to have a drink with slipped him something, right?"

Amy Redmond broke into an enormous grin. She lifted her right thumb in the air. "Got her. I have to say, I had my doubts about this, but she slipped up. That piece of info is not public knowledge. We only said he was found dead in his room."

"Can we leave now?" Simon asked.

"I need more than that. As she said, the house is leaky. She can claim to have overheard the Reynolds family or even a couple of officers talking about the situation. Although, if any of my officers chatted in a public place about the details of the case, I'll have their heads."

"Ready for another round?" came a voice at Rose's table.

"Please, no," Simon groaned.

And the game began once again. We overheard a bit of drama when someone at the next table demanded, in a very loud voice, that the director be called. Accusations of irregular play, if not out-and-out cheating, were made and denied. Finally the director gave the alleged miscreant a warning and departed.

"Two spades," Rose said.

"Are you sure?" Karen asked.

"No talking!" said one of the players.

"I am sure," Rose said.

The game resumed.

And on it went.

Even Bernie started dozing. I felt my own eyes closing.

At last, someone called, "Last hand, ladies and gentlemen."

"Is it still summer?" Simon asked.

Sounds of people getting to their feet. Good nights were exchanged. Someone suggested a quick stop at a bar.

"It was nice meeting you, Karen," a woman said.

"Next week, Rose?" another woman said.

"Most definitely," Rose replied. "Always such an enjoyable evening."

Amy Redmond moved to stand up and gather her equipment, but she lifted her hands when Rose said, "You don't mind sitting for a few minutes, do you, love? A challenging game always takes quite a bit out of me."

"A few minutes won't matter," Karen replied. "We passed a café when we came in. Why don't we grab a cup of coffee?"

Redmond shook her head. "Not a good idea. I don't know that this has the range, and the food service area is fully in the open."

As if Rose got the message she said, "Not for me. I can't drink caffeinated beverages so late in the day. The decaffeinated stuff they make here isn't fit to be called tea. Or coffee, I've been told." She groaned lightly. "A nice stretch and a bit of a relax, and I'll be ready to go. You and your friends are leaving tomorrow?"

"Yes."

"As is the Reynolds family. You said you'd never met them before. Didn't I see you chatting to the man who died? What was his name again?"

"Ralph."

"Oh yes. Ralph."

"You must be mistaken," Karen said. "I never spoke to him."

"I am rarely mistaken about what happens on my own property."

Karen coughed. "I mean, other than that night when we encountered each other out walking at the back of the house. We chatted briefly, and he told me he was here for his son's wedding."

"So he was. With his wife and the rest of his family."

"That's what he said. Before we went our separate ways. Are you ready to go?"

"You weren't invited to the wedding."

"Me? Why would I have been?"

"Because you work at the sandwich restaurant on the ground floor of the building in which his company is located. Do you not?"

"I do, but that's not—how do you know that?"

"I know a great many things, love." All of which Bernie learned during this afternoon's deep dive into Karen O'Keefe's Internet profile. It's amazing the things you can learn these days, from the comfort of your own kitchen table.

Redmond glanced at Bernie in something approaching approval. Bernie grinned.

"You and Ralph Reynolds met over submarine sand-wiches and soft drinks," Rose's voice said. "I'm sure he told you his marriage wasn't a good one. That, I can assure you, was the absolute truth. It wasn't, and it had never been so. His mother had something to do with that."

"What do you want from me?" Karen asked.

"I want nothing from you. I like to show people how clever I am, that's all. I am what you Americans call a snoop, always have been. I like knowing things about people. You needn't check the corners of the room. I can assure you I'm quite alone. My granddaughter thinks I'm an addled old fool. I have been known to play up to her prejudices on occasion. For my own amusement. She's waiting for me to keel over soon and inherit the house. That is not going to happen. Neither the keeling nor the inheriting. Although she doesn't know that. Not while she's still useful to me, at any rate. What happened with your Ralph made me realize I need to be on my guard. My granddaughter might one day decide she's tired of waiting for me to pass away through natural causes. What did you put in Ralph's drink anyway?"

"What makes you think it was me? As you said, he and his wife hated each other."

"Divorce is a common occurrence these days. She had no reason to kill him. After decades of marriage and three children, she would be able to count on getting a good divorce settlement. Except the settlement wouldn't have amounted to much, considering he had little money of his own. His mother had no reason to kill him, either. She kept firm control of the purse strings, after all. I'm assuming you didn't know that."

"I knew it. You seem to know a lot about his family's affairs."

"Walls are thin, even in old houses." Mentally, I winced. I hoped that comment wouldn't get Bernie or Redmond wondering how thin the walls at Victoria-on-Sea truly were. Particularly in our drawing room. "A pleasant state of affairs for an elderly lady who has difficulty sleeping, but has nothing wrong with her hearing. Or her natural curiosity."

"I didn't care about the money. I . . ." Karen's voice broke.

Redmond grinned. The dam was breaking and the flood was sure to follow.

"I only wanted us to be together," Karen continued. "But we had to have something to live on and at our age we couldn't start over with nothing. We needed something to get us started in our new lives. We couldn't stay in the town we lived in, not with his mother being so vindictive and his wife sure to be out for revenge, no matter that she hated him. Ralph had his salary from the company, and then a miserly pension after he stepped down. After she pushed him out, rather. His mother would never have continued to support him if he disgraced the family by leaving his marriage. In favor of a divorced, childless, fast-food clerk in her fifties, of all things." Karen began to cry. Deep, wracking, sobs, full of self-pity.

"He changed his mind about leaving his wife," Rose said, her voice perfectly calm, sounding as though she were discussing the breakfast menu at the B & B. "You followed him to his son's wedding, expecting him to make the official announcement to his family that weekend. Weren't you worried Sophia or Regina would recognize you and wonder what you were doing here? Or even Ivan."

I couldn't see Karen's face but I could hear the anger in her voice as she spat out the words. "Sophia never came to the office; that Ivan would never look a sandwich-maker in the face. His mother's a sharp-eyed old thing, though, and I think she recognized me when she saw me at the B & B, but she doesn't have enough interest in anyone or anything outside of her own circle to so much as stop to wonder what I was doing there."

"I spent many years of my life as a servant," Rose said. "Much the same. I doubt my employers would have noticed me if they saw me lying in the street calling for help, or care if they did happen to recognize me. Never mind that now. You convinced your friends to come on this supposed bridge vacation with you, and then he couldn't go through with it after all. And so . . . that made you angry. I'm sorry, dear, but that's a common story. My own husband conducted affairs for years. Always stringing them along. Always dumping them in the end. Eventually, I decided to take it upon myself to break the pattern once and for all. If you get my meaning."

"I believe I do," Karen said.

"Wow, I never realized what a good liar your grandmother is," Simon said.

"It's coming as a shock to me, too," I said.

"Love the way she causally implied she murdered your grandfather," Bernie said. "I'd believe her, if I didn't know firsthand how devoted they were to each other."

"Shush," Redmond snapped.

"No," Karen said. "He didn't change his mind. He never meant to leave with me, and I finally realized it. All the time we'd been together, I'd been giving him what money I could. He told me he was putting funds aside as well. I thought we were building a nest egg to use to start our lives together. You must think I'm mighty stupid, Rose."

"Naïve, foolish perhaps, but no, not stupid. You're not the first woman to be lied to, and who wanted to believe the lies."

"I did love him, but . . . when I realized not only did he have no intention of leaving his family for me, he intended to use my hard-earned savings for his own ends . . ."

Silence filled the room.

"I've said too much. You won't tell anyone about this conversation, will you, Rose?"

"I promise, I will not repeat a word."

"My friends and I should have left the next day, the day

after he died. Laurie wanted to, but I was worried questions would be asked as to why we left abruptly. Maybe I wanted to stay to see how the family behaved. Remind myself what an awful bunch they are. And that he was, in the end, no better. I'd like to go now, please."

"I have enough." Amy Redmond pushed the button on the machine. "Time to end this. The finer points can come later in an official interview."

I got to my feet and scooped up my helmet, feeling quite satisfied with the results of our evening.

"Another successful case." Bernie leapt to her own feet with a shout and such enthusiasm her chair fell over and crashed to the floor. She yelped and then froze, eyes wide in shock, hands to her mouth.

"What's that?" we heard Karen say. "Is someone listening in there?"

"Mice in the walls, I suspect," Rose said calmly. "Such a poorly constructed building. Political corruption, they say. I'm feeling ever so much better. Time we were off."

"You tricked me," Karen yelled.

Redmond, Bernie, and Simon headed for the door. They collided with each other in a bundle of bodies. But I'd been closest and I made it into the hallway first.

I burst into the game room. Karen was standing, looming over Rose, her fists raised. Fear crossed Rose's face and she cowered in her chair, one hand scrabbling for her cane.

"Hey!" I shouted. "Get away from her."

Karen swung around. Beneath the large frames of her glasses, her eyes bulged, and her face was a bright, furious red. Veins stood out in her neck. "You!" she screamed at me. "Stay back. All of you. I don't know what you think you heard, but I'm not going to jail because of a crazy old woman's need to gossip." She turned again and lunged at Rose. I ran across the room, my only thought of protecting my grandmother.

"Lily!" Simon yelled.

"I've got this, Lily," Amy Redmond said. "Get out of the way."

Karen O'Keefe grabbed Rose's cane and wrenched it out of my grandmother's hand. She raised the cane high.

With a mighty yell, I swung my own arm before she could get the weapon into position. I hit the side of her head with the motorcycle helmet. It made an almighty crunch. Karen dropped to the floor. And there she lay, moaning.

# Chapter 25

"Another line to add to my résumé. Supplier of defensive weaponry," Simon said.

We were in the kitchen of Victoria-on-Sea, and I was getting the breakfasts started.

We hadn't been needed for much last night, not after the felling of Karen O'Keefe. Redmond arrested her on the spot and called for backup. She'd be around, the detective told us, to get our statements this morning.

Bernie, full of restless energy, had been on the doorstep of Victoria-on-Sea when Simon and I arrived to open the kitchen, and Rose, equally full of restless energy, had put in an appearance only minutes later. As for me, I'd slept the long, lovely sleep of the innocent.

Edna burst into the kitchen at the same time as Rose. "The police have made an arrest in the murder of Ralph Reynolds."

"Is that so," Rose said.

"You don't seem at all surprised, any of you," Edna said. "I'm therefore guessing it will not come as a surprise to tell you the alleged killer was a guest at this very establishment."

"Shocking what people get up to these days. Lily, is my tea ready?"

"Give me a minute, Rose."

"Why don't I get your tea," Edna said, "as everything seems to be under control here. Bernie's making the fruit salad. Simon's mixing muffin batter, and the sausages and bacon are already on. Sausages *and* bacon. And it's not even Sunday. Éclair's under the table and Robbie on top of it. All appears to be right with the world."

"So it is," I said. "We're going to need a good deal of coffee this morning. Detectives Williams and Redmond will be here shortly to speak to Karen's friends and the Reynolds family, fill them in on what's happening. It's not going to be easy for them to hear why Ralph died."

"What did happen?" Edna asked. "Why did he die?"

Rose, Bernie, and Simon looked at me. "Okay," I said. "I can tell you what we know, because all of this is hearsay and guesswork. The police still have to build a solid case they can take to court. One of the bridge players, Karen, the one with the black glasses, was having an affair with Ralph. She expected him to leave Sophia for her."

Edna snorted.

"Yeah. Same old story. She came here, this week, thinking he'd be making the big announcement to his family after Greg's wedding. No doubt she expected to be formally introduced to his children and likely had some idea of spitting in Sophia's face. Literally or figuratively. That she had to come under the pretext of being with her bridge group indicates to me she must have known, even if only deep down, he wasn't likely to welcome her popping into his family time. Otherwise, it would have been enough for her to come to the Cape by herself, and stay at another place until Ralph sent for her. Cheaper, too, as she paid for two rooms here, not one. But come she did, and under the pretext of a bridge get-together. I didn't see her and Ralph together at any time, so he might not have even known she was here. She and her friends didn't check in until Thursday afternoon. That night, following the shower, I overheard Ralph and Greg arguing at the cliff edge. Ralph offered Greg a hundred thousand dollars not to marry Hannah."

"Wow!" Bernie said. "You never told me that. What did Greg have to say?"

"He turned his father down flat and walked away angry. What other people said was right: Ralph did threaten the happiness of Jenny's daughter. But it wasn't Jenny who killed him."

"Why did Karen care who Greg married?" Edna asked.

"She didn't. Not in the least. After Greg left his dad, I saw that someone else had been listening to the conversation. A shadow in the deeper shadows. No one I could identify."

"Karen," Bernie said.

"Yes. She knew Ralph didn't have much money in his own name. He and Karen had been saving for a long time, so she thought, in order to have sufficient funds to get them started on their new life once they were officially together. Then she heard Ralph offer Greg what she realized was her own life savings. At last Karen's carefully constructed house of cards fell apart. She realized Ralph not only didn't intend to marry her, he had no hesitation in using the money she'd handed to him for his own personal ends."

"So she killed him," Edna said.

"Yes. I confess I feel sorry for her. He strung her along for what must have been years. She had her hopes for the future pinned on him, not to mention allowing him to manage her savings. And then . . . she finally understood he intended to betray her."

"She didn't have to kill him," Edna said.

"No, and there my sympathy for her ends. Anyway, to continue, the police assumed all along he'd been killed by someone he had no worries about inviting into his room for a drink. I guess, and it is only a guess, she tapped on his door and said, 'Surprise!' He invited her in, offered her a drink, probably pleased at the chance of a little fun and games with his lover in a room directly across the hall from his unloved wife and hated mother. I have the feeling Ralph Reynolds wasn't too terribly bright."

"Men never are," Bernie said. "Not when it comes to what Lily so modestly calls fun and games."

"I take offense at that," Simon said with a deep growl and a serious frown. "I like to think I'm not so single-minded as to welcome a killer into my room." Then he grinned at me. "Except perhaps when it comes to Lily."

I blushed. Rose choked. Bernie snorted with laughter, and Edna simply smiled. Éclair thumped her tail on the floor, and Robbie hissed at her.

"Once Karen was in his room, drinks served, and he was lying back on the bed, maybe with his eyes closed, maybe even drifting off, it was easy enough for her to dump something in the bottle. She probably poured herself a small drink also, and had enough of her wits about her to wipe her prints off the bottle and Ralph's glass and to take her own glass with her. Easy enough to get rid of it. I'm going to assume it's currently at the bottom of the ocean."

"Why didn't she leave after he died, do you think?" Edna asked. "Surely she'd want to get as far away as possible."

"She said she was worried it would cast suspicion on her. I think she simply wanted to know what was going on." I thought of Karen, listening around corners, peeking into rooms. Curious, I'd believed, because she was interested in how the police worked.

"Perhaps, in her own way, she was in mourning," Rose said. "And she wanted to be near him."

"That might be," Simon said. "Human emotions can be conflicting things."

I took the muffins out of the oven. "Better do another batch," I said, "if Detective Williams will be here this morning."

"Yes, ma'am," Simon said.

"I hear voices in the dining room," Edna said. "Time to get to work. One question, first. Was it Karen who attacked Sophia the other night? And if so, why? No harm was done."

"I don't know," I admitted. "Karen knew Sophia didn't love Ralph, and vice versa. I don't know why she'd want to frighten her." I took off my apron. "I'll pop into the dining room this morning. Make sure everything's okay."

Laurie, Sheila, and Marie had taken their seats in the sun-filled room. They sat quietly, staring into their coffee cups.

"Hi," I said. "Everything okay?"

"Not really," Laurie said. "We got a call from the police last night. Do you know about that?"

"I'm aware of what happened, yes."

"Karen's been arrested. For killing that man. I can't believe it. Surely, they've made a mistake. She didn't even know the guy."

I said nothing.

"I thought she was acting odd this week," Sheila said. "But we didn't know her well, not outside of bridge, so I suppose I didn't know what was odd and what was just being normally weird."

"You're due to leave today," I said. "Our reservations book is full, but I can speak to my grandmother and see if she can make some adjustments if . . ."

"No, thank you," Marie said. "We won't be staying.

We talked it over after the cops called. We decided I'll stay an extra day or two, to try to see Karen and ask if there's anything I can do. Sheila and Laurie have jobs and families to get back to, but I own my own business so I can take the time. Your house is truly lovely, but it's expensive, and a place to enjoy oneself. I won't be staying on for pleasure. I've found a room in a motel on the highway and made a booking."

I had nothing to say to that, so I simply wished them a good day and left them. Edna took my place. "Good morning, ladies. We have an egg-white frittata on offer today as well as the usual full breakfast. Today's muffins are apple and cinnamon."

No one from the Reynolds family came down, and breakfast service was finished by eight thirty. Bernie had a sudden inspiration for her book and rushed home to jot the idea down. Simon helped Edna wash up what few dishes there were before returning to his plants. Rose, accompanied by Robert the Bruce, settled herself at the reception desk to await the arrival of the police.

Éclair and I went home.

# Chapter 26

❦

I did not go back to the house to talk to the police. Rose later told me they spoke to Sophia and Regina in turn, and then to McKenzie, Greg, and Ivan. Sophia and Regina went upstairs together, not exactly leaning on each other for support but not hurling accusations and insults at the other, either. Shortly thereafter, the family checked out and departed. Regina, Sophia, Ivan, and McKenzie were going home. As were Dave, Jenny Hill, and Samantha. Greg would stay in North Augusta and wait until his father's body was released. He'd taken Jenny's place in the hotel she was staying at with Hannah.

I was alone in the tearoom kitchen at nine o'clock that night, getting food ready for tomorrow. I'd given Cheryl and Marybeth a rundown of events when they arrived, and then spent most of the day barely noticing what I was baking. The entire situation was all so terribly sad. Dysfunctional families, broken lives, nasty people, bad feelings, liars, and vengeful lovers.

I had one short break, when Simon came into the kitchen in midafternoon. He carried a rough bouquet of short-stemmed roses, purple lobelia, and leaves of green hosta, and handed it to me.

"How nice," I said. "Marybeth, can you find a place for this on a table in one of the alcoves."

"It's not a table setting," Simon said. "It's for you, Lily. Come with me."

"I can't leave, Simon. We have a full house."

"Ten minutes. Marybeth?"

"We've got this," she said.

Simon took one of my hands, and I carried the flowers in the other. All we did for ten minutes was walk together down the winding garden paths, admiring the plants, listening to the sea, feeling the hot sun on our heads and arms. And that was all I needed.

"Lots of things I considered doing in my life," Simon said as we headed back to the tearoom. "Tech company billionaire. Prime minister. Nuclear scientist. Astronaut. Rock star."

"Close protection officer."

"Instead, I chose to be a gardener so I could bring people moments like this. I know you're bothered by what went on here, Lily. As am I. The nastiness, the sheer unnecessary meanness of some people. Life seems not worth living sometimes. And then—there are roses." He lifted my bouquet and pressed it to my face. I took a deep breath and the crazy, messed-up world spun back into its proper orbit. And I was happy.

I rarely try making anything I haven't done before when the tearoom's at our busiest, but tonight I made an exception. Maybe I needed to focus my mind on something different. I found a recipe for a Battenberg cake I'd been wanting to try. Battenberg is a complicated cake to make, as it consists of two different cakes held together with jam and topped with marzipan, but the pink-and-cream checkerboard pattern is attractive and it looks beautiful as part of the sweets offering at tea. I took out my equipment and ingredients and got to work.

I was slipping the cake batters into the hot oven when a car turned into the driveway and a few minutes later a light tap sounded on the kitchen door.

I pulled off my oven mitts and opened the door. Amy Redmond stood there. "I figured I'd find you here, Lily."

"Come in. Would you like a cup of tea? I have some chicken salad fillings in the fridge, and I could quickly put together a sandwich for you."

"No, thanks. I won't stay long. I thought you'd want to know what's happening. You can tell Simon and Bernie."

"Don't forget Rose."

"Fear not, I never forget Rose. Karen called a lawyer, as is of course her right, and she's clammed up. Not saying a word."

"Is that recording we made admissible in court?"

"Recording?" She raised one eyebrow. "What recording?"

"But—"

"It's illegal in the state of Massachusetts for one party to record another without the agreement of all parties. I didn't record anything. I simply connected to the device Rose had on her in order to amplify the conversation. Much like a hearing aid."

"Oh. Okay."

"Rose will testify in court about what Karen told her. Karen's lawyer will naturally attempt to argue that Karen was making up a story for an old lady's amusement. However, I'm not concerned. The truth is out there, and I have plenty of material to build on it. For starters, when she and her friends were initially questioned after the death, Karen flat out told us she had never before met Ralph Reynolds or any members of his family. We have the picture Bernie found on Facebook as proof she was lying.

We'll find more proof she was lying, and about more important things. Her bank records, for example, show she was sending money regularly to a joint account she held with Ralph Reynolds. She was extraordinarily naïve. Willful blindness, perhaps, until she couldn't remain blind any longer. Contrary to what he told Karen about them both putting away their savings, hers was the only money going into that account."

"Thanks for letting me know. I'm pretty satisfied we know why Karen killed Ralph, and why she so foolishly hung around after. But one thing has been bothering me. Who attacked Sophia? That can't have been a coincidence."

"It wasn't. Karen denies killing Ralph. Being interviewed by the police is a tricky business, Lily. You have to think fast, and keep all sorts of balls in the air. Karen dropped one. She doesn't admit to attacking Sophia, but she did say she was glad that incident proved Jenny Hill hadn't killed Ralph."

"I don't get it."

"I believe when Karen killed Ralph she didn't worry about what might happen if someone else was blamed for it. If that someone was either Sophia or Regina, she didn't much care. But when Jenny came under suspicion, Karen had a change of heart. She didn't want to see an innocent woman go to jail. If she knew Jenny was having a night out with Hannah and—"

"Yes! She did know. I can testify to that. Karen was there, on the veranda, when Greg told us he was going for dinner with Hannah and Jenny and then to a movie Jenny particularly wanted to see. Karen knew Jenny would have an alibi. Rather convoluted thinking."

"Which is why Sophia came to no harm. It might help Karen's case if she admits to it. She was guilt-stricken at the idea of Jenny taking the fall, and she took concrete steps to avoid that happening. Some juries like that sort of thing."

"I'm not going to say I now like Karen, but it was a kind thing to do."

"Good night, Lily. You take care. One more thing. You haven't given your official statement yet. Be at the police station tomorrow morning."

"I have to work."

"Ten o'clock should suit. Be there."

# Chapter 27

And that, I thought, was the end of that. Rose would have to testify at Karen's trial, and perhaps Bernie, Simon, and me also. Otherwise, I hoped never to see anyone in the Reynolds family ever again.

Several days later Cheryl came into the tearoom kitchen and said, "Couple of women are asking if you have a moment, Lily."

"A moment. I never have a moment. If they're going to complain, tell them I've gone out. Tell them I quit."

"Not a complaint. You know them."

Grumbling, I washed my hands, took off my apron and hairnet, and shook out my hair. I walked through the restaurant and out to the patio. At four o'clock on a sunny Saturday every table in the place was taken. Two women sat at a small table tucked into a corner next to the low drystone wall, moss and tiny flowers spilling out of the cracks. Hannah Hill stood up and waved when she saw me. She'd been served the cream tea for two.

I was, as Simon would put it, gobsmacked to see who she was dining with.

"Lily," McKenzie Reynolds said when I reached the table. "Thank you, this was all super nice."

"Do you have a minute to join us?" Hannah asked. "I'm sure you're busy but . . ."

"Happy to." I spotted a spare chair and asked if I could have it. The occupants of the table smiled and told me it was free. I pulled it over to Hannah and McKenzie and waved to Cheryl. "I'd love a pot of Creamy Earl Grey, please, and some of whatever sandwiches we have going."

"Sure. Be right back."

I sat down. I looked at Hannah. I looked at McKenzie.

"Greg's father's going home tomorrow," Hannah said. "Greg's in town to arrange the details. We wanted to stay here, but you didn't have any rooms free."

"Busy time of year for us," I said.

"I came to be with Greg," McKenzie said. "And, I will admit, because Jack's band was so popular at that place in town, they were asked to perform some more."

"How's your mother doing?" I asked.

"Okay. Mom's a survivor. Grandma's not been around much. Seems there've been some problems in the company, and she's trying to whip Ivan into shape to handle them."

"Is he going to be able to do that?"

"I genuinely believe he's going to try his best. It might be too late, and his best might not be good enough. But that is not your problem." She cleared her throat and glanced away.

Cheryl slipped a teapot and matching cup and a plate of sandwiches in front of me. I poured the tea, breathing in the deep rich scent of the touch of vanilla and caramel added to the classic tea blend, added a splash of milk and a few grains of sugar, and I waited.

Eventually, McKenzie took a deep breath and turned back to face me. "I've come to apologize. You and your staff went to so much trouble to create the perfect wedding shower for Hannah and I . . . ruined it."

I didn't say I knew. I glanced at Hannah. She was smiling at McKenzie.

"Mac," Hannah said, "broke down and confessed to Greg and me after that woman was arrested for killing their father."

"I'd say it was intended to be a joke, but that's not true," McKenzie said. "Greg told me about the Raggedy Ann doll Hannah's father had given her not long before he died. He was thinking about using the story in his speech at the wedding, as a way of remembering Hannah's absent dad. I . . . okay, this is hard for me to say, although I already told Greg and Hannah. I'm jealous of Hannah. She has such a close, loving relationship with her mom. She has Greg, who's a great guy. I have . . . well, you've met my parents and my grandmother."

"And . . ." Hannah prompted.

"Yeah, okay. Spit it out, girl," McKenzie said to herself. "I didn't like . . . don't like not being in the spotlight."

"You don't need to tell me this," I said.

"But I do," McKenzie said. "It's like those twelve-step programs, right? You're supposed to apologize to everyone you've hurt. I know you don't care personally about our family dramas, but this place is your business and you work hard here. Truth be told, I'm kinda jealous of you, too. Having this lovely place. Not to mention—" She nodded to the garden, where Simon was wielding the hedge trimmer, the sun shining off his blond hair. "That totally delectable guy. Don't worry. I won't sabotage anything. And, yeah. I'm sorry for crawling all over him the other night. Jack and I . . . well not much is happening there. I think we'll be finished soon. I don't think he much cares one way or another about that."

"Thank you for your honesty."

"What happened with my dad's tough to deal with. The lies, the deceit. He and Mom should have divorced years ago. You know what they say—the only thing worse than being from a broken family is living in one. Grandma never helped the situation any. And then for Dad to . . . cheat that woman. If what the police are saying is true. Gave me a lot to think about, is all I'm saying."

"How's your mom doing? I sensed a great deal of anger there."

"No kidding. I wasn't around when Greg and Hannah started dating, but Ivan told me Mom was upset about it. He didn't know why. Being Ivan, he was too lazy to try to find out why. I figured right from the get-go Dad was still carrying a torch for Jenny. Although he covered it up in his usual way, by a combination of denial and anger. Anger toward Jenny, most of all. And, through Jenny, at Hannah. Jenny must have been thinking she'd had a lucky escape when she met Max Hill and dumped my dad. Anyway, back to Mom. A friend suggested she see a therapist, supposedly to deal with Dad's betrayal of her and then his death. I'm hoping a good therapist will dig a lot deeper and help her sort out some of her issues. And she does have a good therapist. My grandma's paying for it. Believe it or not, they're going to have some sessions together."

I nibbled on my herbed egg sandwich. Pretty good, if I do say so myself.

McKenzie took a deep breath before continuing. "My stupid stunt didn't contribute to my dad's death, but then the cops started asking me questions about it, and for a while I wondered if it had. If my own stupidity had caused my father's death. Turns out I get off on that score, but I decided to come clean with Hannah and Greg. The least I could do was clear up that tiny cloud hanging over them."

Hannah put her hand in the center of the table, and McKenzie laid hers on top of it.

"And now," Hannah said, "on to cheerier topics. Sophia's insurance company is giving her a good portion of the money she put down for the wedding reception. We've rescheduled the wedding for two months from now. It's going to be held at the small church my parents were married in. Our reception is going to be low-key, simple, and exactly what Greg and I want."

"I'm glad to hear that," I said. And I was. Perhaps some good could come out of the tragic events.

I left the tearoom at a good time that evening, and Simon and I joined Rose on the veranda. Guests came and went, bidding us a good evening. A honeymooning couple, well into their fifties, wandered through the gardens, hand in hand. A car pulled into the lot and a teenage boy leapt out. He ran up the steps, all arms and legs and fury, his face like a thundercloud, and slammed the door behind him. His parents got out of the car, also looking as though storms were moving in. The father caught Rose's eye and shrugged in embarrassment. Robbie snoozed on Rose's lap, and Éclair had settled at my feet.

"Something interesting came in the mail today, love," my grandmother said.

"What was that?"

"A letter, all the way from England."

"Buckingham Palace?" Simon asked. "Looking to hire a close protection officer slash gardener?"

"No. An invitation." She dug into the cavernous pockets of her wide skirt and showed us a card. Thick creamy card stock with elaborate gold trim, the printed invitation perfectly centered in flowing gold script. "I've been invited to a birthday party."

"In England?" Simon said. "That's nice. Have you been back since you moved to America?"

"Several times. I couldn't attend my grandmother's funeral as I was pregnant with one of the boys, but I did go to my dear father's and later my mother's. And again for a couple of family weddings. This invitation, however, is not from a relative."

I could tell by the way she was dragging it out, whatever this was, it meant something special to Rose. I waited for her to enjoy the drama and then get on with it.

"I have been invited to the hundredth birthday celebration of Elizabeth, the Dowager Countess of Frockmorton. The party is to be held at Thornecroft Castle." Rose beamed. "A note included with the invitation says her ladyship is hoping to reconnect with many of the favored staff and tradespeople from over her long years."

"Are you going to go?" Simon asked.

"I'd like to. The party's in late October, when the season here is winding down, before it picks up again for the holiday rush. I should be able to close the B & B for a week. Naturally, a lady of my advanced years would find it difficult to travel so far on her own." She smiled at me.

"You want me to go to England with you?" I asked.

"As I said, I've been back to England several times over the years, but not to Thornecroft Castle. I'd like to see it again. And I'd like you to see it with me, love."

I looked at Simon. He gave me a broad wink. "Just so happens, the winter job I have is in Yorkshire. Not that far from Thornecroft Castle."

"Wouldn't mind a holiday," I said. "I've never been to England."

Rose clapped her hands, startling Robbie. "Imagine, me going to Lady Frockmorton's party! As a guest, not to work in the kitchen."

"Speaking of kitchen maids," I said, reluctantly pushing myself to my feet. "I've just remembered that I'm almost out of eggs in the B & B kitchen. I won't have enough if every one of the guests wants eggs tomorrow. That means a run to the store before I can finally rest my weary kitchen maid legs."

"I'll give you a lift on the bike," Simon said.

I eyed him carefully. "I suppose it would be okay going to the store. But what about coming back? I don't want scrambled eggs yet."

"I'll be careful on the turns and the bumps."

"Live dangerously, love," Rose said. "That's my motto, and it's never led me astray. Someday perhaps. But not yet."

# Recipes

# Banana Bread with Walnuts

Overripe bananas. What to do with them? If there's one thing likely to be in every cook's repertoire, whether home cook, amateur baker, or professional pastry chef, it's banana bread. Because, after all, no one wants to throw out those fast-expiring bananas. For her own enjoyment, Lily likes nuts in her banana bread, but when baking for the breakfasts at Victoria-on-Sea, she leaves them out, just to be safe. This version has nuts included.

Note: Lily makes gluten-free banana bread for the guests when requested, but this recipe is NOT gluten-free.

### Ingredients:
1¼ cups unbleached all-purpose flour
1 teaspoon baking soda
½ teaspoon fine salt
2 large eggs, at room temperature
½ teaspoon vanilla extract
½ cup unsalted butter, at room temperature
1 cup sugar
3 very ripe bananas, peeled, and mashed with a fork
½ cup toasted walnut pieces

### Instructions:
Lightly brush a 9 by 5 by 3-inch loaf pan with butter. Preheat the oven to 350°F.

Sift the flour, baking soda, and salt into a medium bowl, set aside. Whisk the eggs and vanilla together in a small bowl.

Cream the butter and sugar until light and fluffy. Gradually pour the egg mixture into the butter while mixing until incorporated. Add the mashed bananas.

With a rubber spatula, mix in the flour mixture until just incorporated. Fold in the nuts and transfer the batter to the prepared pan.

Bake for 55 minutes or until a toothpick inserted into the center of the bread comes out clean. Cool the bread in the pan on a wire rack for 5 minutes. Turn the bread out of the pan and let cool completely on the rack.

# Egg Salad Sandwiches with Herby Mayonnaise

A highly popular teatime option, these colorful sandwiches are in regular rotation at Tea by the Sea.

*Makes six full size sandwiches or twenty-four tea sandwiches*

## Ingredients:
6 hard-boiled eggs, shells removed
½ cup mayonnaise
¼ cup grated Parmesan cheese
1 green onion, finely chopped
12 slices white bread, crusts removed, lightly buttered
Salt and pepper
⅔ cup finely chopped and packed mixed fresh herbs, such as basil, dill, chives, Italian parsley

## Instructions:
In a large bowl, crush the eggs with a fork. Add the mayonnaise and combine. Stir in the Parmesan cheese and green onion. Season with salt and pepper.

Spread the egg mixture on half of the previously buttered bread slices.

Sprinkle with chopped herbs.

Cover with the remaining slices of bread.

Cut each sandwich into 4 wedges.

# Maple Pecan Squares

A delicious addition to the sweets course, these squares are always a hit at Tea by the Sea.

*Makes 36 squares*

### Ingredients:
Shortbread base:
1 cup all-purpose flour
⅓ cup light brown sugar, packed
¼ cup coarsely chopped pecans
½ tsp salt
¼ tsp baking powder
¼ tsp ground cinnamon
⅓ cup unsalted butter, at room temperature

### Topping:
¼ cup unsalted butter, melted
½ cup light brown sugar, packed
⅓ cup pure maple syrup
2 tsp vanilla extract
¼ tsp fine salt
1 large egg
1¾ cups coarsely chopped pecans

### Instructions:
Preheat oven to 350°F.

Grease and line a 9-inch square pan with parchment paper so that it hangs over the sides.

For base, pulse flour, brown sugar, pecans, salt, baking powder, and cinnamon in a food processor to combine. Add butter and pulse until mixture is crumbly. Press mixture into prepared pan and bake for 20 minutes, until it just browns around the edges. Cool.

For topping, whisk melted butter, brown sugar, maple syrup, vanilla, salt, and egg until smooth. Stir in chopped pecans and pour over shortbread base. Bake for 22 to 25 minutes, until bubbling around the edges. Cool completely before slicing.

# *Acknowledgments*

Discovering new places to enjoy afternoon tea continues to be a delight, as does learning more all the time about tea and the wonderful treats that go with it.

Special thanks to my good friend Cheryl Freedman, who read an early version of this manuscript with her keen editor's and mystery lover's eye and provided valuable comments. Also to my agent, Kim Lionetti of Bookends, and the team at Kensington for allowing me to indulge my passion for writing and for afternoon tea.